# SCREAMING AT A WALL
## GREG EVERETT

GRUNDLE INK PUBLICATIONS

Published by Grundle Ink Publications. All rights reserved.
Published 2002. Second Edition 2003.
Printed in the United States of America
10 9 8 7 6 5 4 3 2

Grundle Ink Publications
www.grundleink.com

ISBN: 0-9708152-7-1

**Cover Photograph:** Abbie Caldwell

*This book is a work of fiction. Any resemblance of characters to persons living or dead is strictly coincidental.*

SCREAMING AT A WALL

PREFACE TO THIS EDITION

*This is supposed to be a preface, not an interview.*
Just do it.

*Fine. Why a new edition of the book?*
My work schedule tends to reflect my inexorable feeling that I'm running out of time. The original book was published immediately after it was written. The layout and cover design were almost completed before the actual book was, and I made no revisions to the manuscript before publication. It was essentially a copyedited first draft. A radical overhaul was necessary to protect me from any further humiliation.

*So what's different?*
The originally turgid manuscript has been trimmed down severely. I've also reluctantly removed the fifty pages of front material and replaced it with this innovative new preface.

*You cut almost 50,000 words. How'd you manage that?*
There was an excess of insufficiently relevant detail in the original edition.

On top of that, it was abounding with completely authentic conversations, but authentic conversations between members of the 18-25 demographic tend to consist in print as endless strings of one- to three-word lines. It's all been cut down to the necessary minimum to accommodate even the most limited of attention spans.

*Didn't removing that much text create problems with maintaining a coherent storyline?*
Maybe. A lot of extraneous text was removed without a problem, but there are occasional unavoidable cuts that might lead readers to believe they're missing something. Let me assure them now that if it's not in there, it's not important.

*So why'd you remove the rest of the front material?*
It wasn't important enough to justify either the financial or environmental cost of the extra pages it required. It was basically just a bloated set-up with an excess of profanity and ridicule of mental health professionals. My sense of efficiency has matured greatly since the first edition was released.

*Don't you think readers of this edition will be missing out?*
Their lives may feel a little less complete, but the lack of front material shouldn't be extraordinarily detrimental. So they don't feel left out, I'll quickly summarize the key points:

> 1. This book was an accidental product of insomnia and reckless drug abuse. I apologize.
> 2. You probably shouldn't read it.
> 3. I like potatoes.

*Can you tell us what the book's about?*
Not really.

*You don't know what your own book's about?*
I can give you a synopsis of the storyline, but if you're requesting I provide some kind of thematic analysis, I'll politely decline.

*I don't understand.*
It's about whatever you want it to be about. If you want, it's a profound and

relevant social commentary. Or it's just a stupid book written to impress women that has absolutely no redeeming social or literary value. Readers and critics have come up with all kinds of descriptions and themes for it. They all seem somewhat reasonable to me.

*Some would say the book is grossly self-indulgent. Do you want to defend yourself?*
Not really. Of course it's self-indulgent. I wrote it when I was twenty-one. And I've noticed that generally those who attack the book's self-indulgent nature are simply bitter about the lack of literature indulging them instead.

*What should readers expect from the book?*
As little as possible. My intention was to write a book specifically for people who don't read. I realize that sounds a little stupid, but it made sense to me at the time. The result was that I generally avoided the conventions that characterize most novels, and this can be disorienting and even disappointing for readers whose expectations align with literary tradition.

*I guess that's adequate. Anything else you want to add?*
No. I feel pretty good.

CHAPTER ONE

I tuck my hair behind my ears and look at Bryan. "We'll tell Dick to get it."

"What?"

"He has those keys every morning. Mrs. Anderson gives him her key ring to unlock the gates."

Bryan thinks briefly. "He won't."

"Yeah he will," I assure him.

Bryan thinks again the way Bryan thinks, rubbing the fingers of one hand against the palm of the other compulsively like a crank addict who hasn't slept in three days and is in desperate need of a new project after cleaning the entire kitchen with a toothbrush. "OK."

I smile and we glance around the school. The seventh and eighth graders have been polarized on the small campus according to tacit social instruction, and we're drifting as usual within the ambiguous separation. We're not torn between our older friends and the friends of our immediate peer group; we don't really like any of them.

"There's Slimy," I tell Bryan, nodding to the kid we call Slimy the Worm. Slimy is one of Dick's friends. Slimy is also the unfortunate young man we spend much of our free time depositing in campus trashcans. To address the increasing successfulness of Slimy's escape attempts—due primarily to an increase in spastic wriggling—Bryan and I have modified our approach. Instead of bringing Slimy to the trashcan, we now bring the trashcan to Slimy. Trashcans don't wriggle.

"Slimy, where's Dick?" I ask him.

He backs up slowly from us, visibly noting potential escape routes.

"No trashcans today, man, we just need to find Dick."

Slimy points. "Over there, I think."

Bryan feigns a lunge and Slimy cowers involuntarily behind a pole. Bryan is that kid with the accelerated puberty genes that caused him to grow six inches and a beard during summer vacation, leaving him relatively emotionally underdeveloped and unsure of how to employ his new physical power. I laugh quickly to conceal my sympathy for Slimy. I know the only reason my conscience allows me to drop kids in trashcans is my overriding fear of being dropped into one myself by a genetic anomaly who doesn't happen to be my friend.

Dick sees us approaching and stops talking to the little butt-faced girl he always talks to.

"We have a job for you," Bryan tells him.

His eyes bounce back and forth nervously between the two of us. "What."

"We need the key to the lockers."

Dick thinks for a moment. "Why."

Bryan and I consult each other with a quick glance. We haven't actually discussed that particular issue in depth. It apparently seemed reasonable to assume we'd be overwhelmed by inspiration once we'd acquired mechanical access to every locker in the school.

"Can't tell you," I say wisely.

Dick shifts uncomfortably on his feet. "Mrs. Anderson'll know I took it."

"Maybe," Bryan shrugs.

"Look, Dick, it's simple," I explain. "Take the key tomorrow morning and we won't duct tape you upside down to a pole."

Dick thinks about being duct taped upside down to a pole. "OK."


It's foggy. I can feel my face tingling with the swelling mist as I lean against the wall and scan the deserted campus for Dick. Finally he emerges from the darkness at the end of the outdoor hallway and walks obediently to Bryan and me.

"Key," Bryan says.

Dick hands him the key reluctantly. "We're gonna get busted."

"No we're not," Bryan says. "Now go away."

Dick goes away.

I look at Bryan and Bryan looks at me. We have the key. The Key. Immediate access to the contents of every locker in the entire school: drugs, liquor, cash, loaded firearms, attractive women with neither clothing nor moral reservations about engaging in sexual intercourse with thirteen-year-olds.

Bryan and I walk to the nearest wall of lockers and glance around cautiously to ensure we're not being watched. Individuals like us should be watched at all times. Bryan slides the key in slowly. Our erections grow.

I hear something around the corner. "Wait," I tell Bryan.

"Fuck!"

I turn back to him.

"The key broke off in the lock!"

◻   ◻   ◻

Each day in health class, we're expected to somehow translate our current emotional conditions into numerical values between one and ten and plot these figures on graphs supplied by our abnormally concerned teacher. I'm typically between seven and eight, always a fraction because I'm "different," but today I'm drooping sullenly around three and seven thirteenths with my recent attempt at fame and glory and power shot down by poor manufacturing and metal fatigue.

Mrs. Anderson discovered her key was missing as predicted and confronted Dick, who fingered Bryan and me without a fight. We're not extraordinarily pleased by Dick's lack of intestinal fortitude, but expected nothing less. I'm not concerned. The school's principal long ago abandoned her attempts to discipline me. Initially stern and severe according to convention, she quickly learned with the abundance of time we continued to share in her office that expending any kind of disciplinary effort on me was ultimately futile.

"Ms. Delao tells me you and Bryan are being disruptive in her classroom again," Ms. Wolfe said during one of my recent visits. "She mentioned something about you two screwing around with your desks."

"We weren't screwing around," I assured her sincerely. "We were exploring alternative sitting positions."

Ms. Wolfe stared at me, attempting unsuccessfully to conceal her amusement. "What does that mean?"

I carefully explained the great unutilized potential Bryan and I saw in the one-piece deskchairs common in public schools, and expressed our terrible disappointment with our fellow students' lack of imagination and independence. They just sat there passively like stuffed animals with all six legs on the floor. Refusing to succumb to the dangerous comfort of unchallenged tradition and popular conduct, Bryan and I instead pushed our desks onto their backs and climbed in as one would normally sit in a deskchair, except we and the deskchair as a unit were rotated ninety degrees backward.

Ms. Wolfe finally surrendered and allowed her uncomfortably suppressed laughter to escape. It was funny. "Would you please just sit like everyone else from now on?"

An anonymous student walks into the room and hands Mrs. Kalin an office summons. I stand up before her face even registers her disappointment in me and head out the door. Maybe I should discuss with Ms. Wolfe the wisdom of ordering a supply of summons imprinted with my name. Efficiency is key for our under-funded public schools, and it seems irresponsible to let myself become a financial burden unnecessarily.

I step into the office and greet everyone. The office ladies have of course grown to love me. They're overweight and rosy-cheeked and unnaturally cheerful, and their polyester slacks are a little too tight, revealing the outlines of unusually wide undergarments when they bend over to grab a file from that bottom drawer, and I'm like their son, the one who can't stay out of trouble but is still somehow irresistibly adorable, the one they want to shower in unbridled displays of affection, and they can't wait to run home each day and tell their girlfriends over Tupperwared leftovers just what I've managed to get myself into now.

"Hi Greg!" they say.

"Hi!"

Ms. Wolfe appears in the doorway of her office and waves me in with her customary face of disapproval, but I know better. She loves me too.

"Sit down," she says.

I sit down.

"Mrs. Anderson had her locker key stolen yesterday," she tells me. "You know anything about this?"

"Yes I do. Bryan and I made Dick take it for us."

"Really," she says. "And how'd you do that?"

"I told him if he didn't we were gonna duct tape him upside down to a pole."

Ms. Wolfe considers the threat. "Is that possible?"

"Bryan's a big guy," I shrug. "He could hold him while I tape."

"That's horrible."

I shrug again. She loves it.

"OK, we're getting off topic," she says. "What were you planning on doing with the key?"

"I don't know," I tell her honestly. "We figured that part would work itself out once we had it."

"Were you gonna steal anything?"

"Steal what? I don't even use my own books."

Ms. Wolfe contains her laughter with a reluctant grin and shakes her head. I'm telling you, she loves me. I can see it in her eyes and hear it in her voice. She dreams of me. I know she has dreams about me, dreams that make her slightly uncomfortable in the morning with the realization that I'm both one of her students and quite underage, but she brushes the fleeting thought of impropriety aside and revels in the beauty and glory of the dream, wishing she could one morning wake from one of these dreams to see my face resting gently on the pillow beside her, sleeping so peacefully and gently, so sweet and young and innocent, not like those hairy overweight jack-offs her age, and realize it wasn't a dream at all, but a surreal memory of the most wonderful and intense night she's ever experienced, a night she'll never forget, a night she'll forever cherish, a night of which the memory will bring tears to her eyes, not tears of sorrow, or even joy, but more the sorrow of no longer feeling the joy she once felt in my—

"I trust this won't happen again," she says.

"No ma'am."

Ms. Wolfe laughs and waves me out.

. . .

Bryan grabs a knife from his desk. It's a large knife. It's an illegally catalog-ordered knife with absolutely no practical application aside from killing people. "I can't believe we didn't get in trouble," he says, punching the air with the studded brass knuckles on the knife's handle.

"We should celebrate," I suggest, dropping onto the edge of his broken waterbed and riding the wave.

Bryan and I developed the habit of sniffing glue some months back. Sniffing glue is undoubtedly the most inefficient method of getting high in terms of the Brain Damage to High ratio, but with the recent disappearance of my exceedingly responsible older friend JD, supplier of all things bad and inappropriate, I've temporarily lost my access to more efficient substances. Fortunately, Bryan and I are restrictively health-conscious young men, inspired by the glossy pages of various fitness-oriented men's periodicals. Realizing we were causing irreversible damage to our brains—which we value, acknowledging brains provide a relatively important service—we decided it would be wise to restrict our glue intake to special occasions.

"It's Thursday!"

Eventually we just wore it out. Once the rebellious nature of glue sniffing dissipates with the occasional practice's progression to a routine, the high is distilled to little more than indistinctive dizziness.

Bryan digs through a drawer under his bed and pulls out a large bottle containing a sickening mixture of assorted liquors taken secretly from various unattended liquor cabinets. I think there's even some white wine in it.

I unscrew the cap and take a hit from the bottle, making the face I imagine appropriate for drinking stale urine. Our additions to the bottle have been unrecorded, but I know there's Kahlua and some kind of blue liquor in it. I assume that's why it looks like dirty anti-freeze and tastes like fermenting chocolate.

I choke and hand the bottle to Bryan. "That shit's foul."

Bryan knocks one back and makes the stale urine face. "Yeah, but it fucks you up."

"Right."

Now we must go look for something to break.

. . .

Bryan and I are in a gang. We have a large membership of two. This is all we want. We don't trust anyone but each other. Sometimes we don't even trust each other. How much can you really trust guys like us? We light fires and sniff glue and drink stale urine and break shit for fun. We're wild and unpredictable and undeserving of trust.

The name of our gang is Violent Attitude. It's a little lame, but you'll generally find people who sniff glue aren't extraordinarily creative. We have violent attitudes and total disregard for the establishment. We aren't sure exactly what the establishment is, but we're pretty sure it involves people in positions of power and their bullshit bureaucratic institutions and rules and laws and procedures, and this is bad and deserving of disregard.

I glance around from my seat on the curb. The Emporium in Sunnyvale has been abandoned for months and the parking lot is barren, littered with newspapers and cellophane food packaging. It's the perfect backdrop. The sun has just slipped below the horizon and the sky is pale and cloudless, the breeze cool on my bare arms. I smell burning flesh and turn to Bryan. His eyes are squeezed shut and his jaw is clenched. I guess because of the hot cigarette lighter burning a smiley face into his upper arm.

"Pussy."

"Fuck you," Bryan says and hands me the lighter.

After impressing Bryan with my admirable tolerance for self-inflicted pain, I look down at the swollen grey burn on my arm, my eyes shifting and sweeping slowly over the collection of scars surrounding it, lighter and faded with time. This has become a habit. Probably because I'm short and skinny and have to overcompensate for my pervasive feelings of inadequacy and fear of rejection, the same psychology that allows me to override my sense of compassion and guilt to place individuals in garbage cans for entertainment. I don't know if I want the pain itself, or the feeling that slowly replaces it. I'm a little lightheaded and pulsing impatiently with adrenaline. I feel powerful, I feel in control, I feel endless, I feel unstoppable. Pain is the line few will cross. The screaming line that divides me from them, from their weakness and their complaints, from their socially distorted primitive fears.

Besides, it's healthier than sniffing glue.

It doesn't actually matter who Ted is. He's anyone with more confidence and less of an unconscious need for validation than I have, anyone I believe I can use to further my undeserved social status by exploiting those qualities with mild public humiliation.

"Come on, man, we got you faded like bleach," Kramer tells me. He says things like this. "You can't let him talk shit like that."

But apparently my assessment of Ted was less than accurate. According to Kramer, Ted hasn't simply submitted to my superiority and has been doing a little mouthing off of his own in my absence, making some bold threats. Despite some slight discomfort, I don't really care. I know Ted will never start anything with me unprovoked, and I'm all for maintaining peace for the sake of simplicity. And when it comes down to it, I'm actually a complete pussy. No reason to expose myself unnecessarily.

"Fuck that little bitch," Kramer says. "We'll take care of any of his pussy skater friends who try to jump in."

But Kramer is a persuasive guy. The idea of someone of his impressive physical stature at my back is dangerously reassuring. It helps me forget my own unimpressive physical stature. Shit, I have every skateboard-riding eighth grader and most of the remaining at my back. The situation seems to be rapidly escalating into a school-wide skater war. The building energy continues to distract me from my pussiness and begins to somehow convince me this is actually a good idea. I can't imagine being the sole cause of a small riot is without inherent benefits. I'll be a legend. The droves of newly sexually-maturing girls will stand in silent awe as I pass them in the hallways, clutching their binders to their recently swelling chests, their fear and curiosity inspiring an unfamiliar strain of excitement they can only describe to themselves as an irresistible urge to be naked with me and—

"Look," Kramer says, "I'll set it up. Tomorrow, after school."

"Whatever," I tell him. Fuck it.


Everyone is here. Holy shit, it's like an exodus, like the school finally cracked and the fluid collection of students spilled into the church parking lot down the street. Someone yells from the edge of the parking lot and breaks me out of my blurred daydreams of future legend status and its accompanying casual sex. I turn to face the street and see the steadily approaching pack of thirteen-year-old skaters, Ted front and center.

"Hey, man, if any of those fuckers jump in, we'll all jump in," Kramer reassures me.

The pack reaches the parking lot and we face off silently across the pavement. Ted and I cautiously approach each other and stop a few feet apart. The audience slowly circles in around us.

"I don't wanna fight you, man," Ted says finally.

Unacceptable. We are going to fight. We are going to fight and start a riot and I am going to be a legend. I'm not throwing away my chance for fame because he's more mature and reasonable than I am.

"Then why the fuck did you come?" I demand. Riot.

Ted pauses. "Look, man, I don't want a fight."

I don't really even have a problem with Ted. I just want to kill him. "Why the fuck did you come?" I yell, shoving him across the pavement. Legend.

Ted stumbles back into the waiting arms of his friends. He clearly has more self-control than I do. The skaters push him back up onto his feet and I shove him again. Ted stumbles back but regains his balance. I push him again.

Ted doesn't have that much self-control.

My head snaps back with the impact of Ted's fist and I'm swinging, unattached from myself. I don't even feel his fists striking me anymore. He's a blur, a pulsing mass of yellow. Is he wearing a yellow shirt? I wish I were confident enough to wear bold colors. Suddenly Ted has my sweatshirt hood and I'm being pulled down. Eating a few more quick fists, I push myself back up again and drive my knee into his ribs. We hit the pavement, beyond thought, beyond reason. I've even forgotten about my audience. We're swinging wildly, tearing at each other, unaware of ourselves and our fashion abilities.

"Cops!"

We're not that unaware.

Scrambling to my feet, I regain my blurred vision in time to see Ted and the rest of the pack sprinting out of the lot and down the street. A police cruiser bounces into the driveway and parks abruptly alongside the remaining crowd.

Kramer is on me immediately. "Fuck, man!"

I'm not sure what that means. *Fuck, man, you just kicked that guy's ass?* Or *Fuck, man, that guy just kicked your ass?* I wipe some blood from my mouth and look at it on my hand. I don't feel anything yet.

"Put your hood on," Kramer tells me quietly. "So the pig can't see your face."

I slip my hood on and step onto my skateboard, rolling back and forth casually, watching the cop step out of his car. Short. He's going to be an asshole. I quickly drop my head so he can't see my face.

The cop glances around at all of us. "What's going on?"

Kramer steps in without hesitation. "Sir, we were walking home from school and we saw a fight here, so we stopped to watch."

There are at least forty of us still in the parking lot. We were not all walking home from school together.

"Who was fighting?"

"We don't know, sir. Two guys, I think maybe from that halfway house," Kramer says, pointing across the street. "That's a halfway house, right sir?"

He looks at the house and nods slightly. "Where'd these two guys go?"

"Sir, they ran down the street when you pulled up."

The cop pulls his notebook from his breast pocket and opens it to a clean page. "Can you describe them?"

Now Dave steps in. "Well, like he said, it was two guys, and they were wearing spandex shorts, you know, like biker shorts," he tells the cop. "One had blue shorts and one had pink shorts."

The cop stares at Dave. Dave is pushing it.

"My guess is those are gang colors," Dave adds.

"What's your name?" the cop asks him.

"My name's Dave, sir."

"Well, Dave, you better start telling me the truth."

"Sir, I am telling you the truth," Dave assures him.

Dave is really pushing it.

"Dave, do you have any picture ID?"

Dave fishes through his pocket and holds something out to the cop. "I got a dime," he shrugs.

Dave has gone too far.

The cop grabs Dave and slams him against the side of his patrol car. "You better quit fucking around with me!" he yells. "You ever heard of obstruction of justice?"

Dave just grins at him while the rest of us struggle to contain our laughter.

The cop finally throws Dave off his car in frustration and shoves his notebook back into his pocket. "I'm coming back in five minutes," he tells us, "and if anyone's still here, they're going to jail!"

We all nod slightly. Dave salutes.

The cop slams his door and peels out of the parking lot, disappearing down the street. I push my hood off and run my hands over my face. Mental note: Do not wear hooded garments when expecting to fight. I look at the dried blood on my hand. I think I got my ass kicked. I'm not really sure. But I'm pretty sure I'm still a pussy.

□　□　□

The fight failed to transform me into a legend as expected. But it doesn't really matter now because it's been long forgotten by the thirty-second MTV attention span junior high school students who witnessed it. After all the trouble I've caused at this school directly involving the school without receiving any formal discipline from the school—stealing the locker key, assorted acts of creative vandalism, theft of various office supplies and teaching aids, truancy achieved by jumping the back fence into the concrete river channel, breaking down the door to the student store, vandalizing the student store, stealing from the student store, extortion while working in the student store—I was disciplined for the fight, which didn't even take place at the school. The explanation, I feel, is based less on the nature of the event itself than on the school's recent staff change: the resigning of the principal Ms. Wolfe and the hiring of Mr. Wiener as her replacement.

It seems Mr. Weiner neither understands me nor recognizes my undeniable genius. He also shares his psychological configuration with short cops: it's obvious he was beaten up and hung on doorknobs by his underwear when he was in school, and he's now seeking his emotional vengeance. Apparently he's selected me as the first subject of his disciplinary tactics to show this new school he's one Wiener not to be fiddled around with.

Again in health class I received a summons, and again I made my familiar walk to the office and greeted the cheery office ladies with the tight slacks and large undergarments. My reception by Mr. Wiener was less cordial. He tried intimidation. I know he's not legally permitted to hit me, so I wasn't concerned.

"It's none of your business," I reminded him.

"It is my business."

"How are you even involved if it wasn't on school property? This can't be legal."

"The school's responsible for its students after school until they return home."

"Fine, we all went home and then came back before the fight," I told him. "Now can I go?"

"No."

"Why?"

"Because that doesn't make sense," he said.

Your face doesn't make sense.

"Why not?"

"Why would you go home and come all the way back?" he asked me.

Because fuck you.

"I wanted to drop off my school gear and change into my fighting attire," I explained patiently.

"Don't get smart."

"As a school principal, isn't your fundamental objective to encourage me to get smart?"

"You know what I mean," Mr. Weiner said.

"I do?"

"Yes."

"You don't think it's conceivable that by making such an assumption—effectively an unsubstantiated assessment of my intelligence—you may be preventing an accurate evaluation of my abilities, thereby preventing the possible discovery of one or more debilitating learning disorders, leaving me struggling with my schoolwork and doomed to fail?"

"No."

That's it? No? Ms. Wolfe would've given me a hand-job for that one.

"So why am I in here, anyway?" I asked him.

"I'm trying to determine what happened with you and Ted."

"Would you like me to explain?"

"Please."

"We don't like each other, and being young and immature, we still believe punching each other in the face will resolve our problems."

Mr. Weiner nodded wisely. "But it didn't, did it?"

"I don't know," I shrugged. "Ted and I are on better terms now than we were before."

"Why do you think that is?"

"Who cares why?"

"Apparently I do."

Apparently you need a girlfriend.

"You know what, I'm in here instead of in class learning about sexually transmitted diseases and strategies for improving my emotional health, and nothing's gonna change."

Mr. Wiener slid a pink pad of paper in front of him and scribbled a few words on it, tearing off the top page and handing it to me dramatically. "I'm suspending you for the rest of the day."

I couldn't help it. I laughed.

"You think that's funny?" he demanded.

That's typically what laughter indicates.

I burst from my chair and stood at attention. "Sir, no sir!"

Mr. Wiener didn't look amused. "Give this to your teacher and go home for the rest of the day. You can come back tomorrow."

"Sir, yes sir!"

I saluted, made an about-face, and goose-stepped out of Mr. Wiener's office. I'm not sure I understand the logic behind punishing students by dismissing them from a place they don't want to be. But logic that provides me a day off from school is not something I feel compelled to argue with. Back in my classroom, I grabbed my binder from my desk and proudly presented Mrs. Kalin my little pink note, personally autographed by Mr. Wiener himself.

"What're you gonna do for the rest of the day?" she asked me, genuinely concerned as always.

"Take drugs and threaten young children with broken glass."

"Greg," she scolded playfully.

"OK, I won't threaten any kids."

Mrs. Kalin made the Oh-you're-so-naughty-and-cute-I-want-to-cheat-on-my-husband-with-you smile she always gives me and waved as I exited the room.

. . .

My Spanish teacher is saying something as usual. I'm not listening, also as usual. Staci and I sit at the back table by the door in Spanish because this seems the most appropriate location for people uninterested in learning. We don't pay attention in class. We try to draw on each other with various writing implements because we don't know of any better way to express our sexual attraction.

"So you got suspended?" Staci asks me.

"Yeah," I shrug casually.

Staci seems impressed by this. I don't think she's ever been in trouble. She's a quiet Korean girl with stereotypically strict parents and limited exposure to people like me. I fight and break shit and steal things and get suspended. I think it turns her on. But I have difficulty understanding my attraction to her. I don't know if it's genuine, or simply an extension of my natural curiosity that seems to translate simply into the desire to have sex with every single girl on the planet. I swipe at her arm with my pen and miss.

"Greg, what're you doing back there?"

I look up at my teacher. I think her two front teeth are fake. I wonder if she got into a bar fight. "Nothing."

"That's probably accurate," she sighs. "What'd I just say?"

"Something Spanish," I guess.

Staci giggles. She thinks I'm funny.

"Don't encourage him, Staci."

Staci glances up and nods, but quickly returns to giggling. The teacher finally turns around again to write something on the blackboard and Staci lunges at me with her pen. I jump out of the way and return fire, striking with a long black line down her forearm.

"You dick!" Staci laughs as quietly as she can.

The teacher turns around again and stares at me. She's not amused like the rest of us. "Greg, come sit up here," she says, pointing to a vacant chair directly in front of her.

"I'd rather not."

"It's not an option," she explains.

"OK." I grab my unopened book and binder and wave to Staci as I walk up the aisle.

Staci giggles again. "Send me a postcard!"

□     □     □

I watch the ripples in the pool reflect the setting sun and wait impatiently for something to happen. Jesse and I showed up at this girl's house early because Jesse told her he'd help set up for her party and I happened to be with him. I haven't done anything and I don't plan on doing anything. What needs to be set up? What we need are people and alcohol and drugs and all the dumb shit people do when given alcohol and drugs. I'm only here because Brandi is going to be here. Brandi is the most beautiful girl I know—quite possibly the most beautiful girl in the entire universe—and she's now my girlfriend.

"Hey tough guy," Brad says.

I blink and look up from the pool. People are starting to show up.

"Fuck you, tough guy," I tell Brad.

Brad and I use the word *tough* entirely too much. It's our word. It was somehow decided Brad and I needed a word and *tough* seemed like a reasonable choice.

"If we were an ice-cream flavor, we'd be Toughness Supreme," Brad tells me. He's serious.

"Good one."

And then Brandi appears from the sliding glass doors in the back of the house. She's still beautiful.

"Hey," Brandi says, kissing me on the cheek.

"Hey," I say, getting kissed on the cheek.

Brad looks around. There are a lot of people at the house now who aren't as tough as we are. "You wanna get outta here?" he asks us. "Let's go over to the school or something."

I look at Brandi and she nods. "Yeah," I tell Brad. "Get Derek and Jessica and let's get the fuck outta here."

Brad disappears and I look at Brandi.

"So..." Brandi and I don't talk much. We're fourteen. "It sucks that you're moving."

"Yeah, only a couple weeks," she says. "It sucks I have to leave."

I've been in love—or whatever it is fourteen-year-olds think is love—with this girl for two years, never believing I could be good enough for her.

When I recently learned I was wrong—or at least that Brandi had made some kind of error in judgment—I promptly broke my ex-girlfriend's heart and ruined a friendship—although both temporarily because we're fourteen years old and most things are temporary when you're fourteen years old—to be with her.

Until recently, Brandi's best friend, Kala, was my girlfriend. I'd love to tell you all about Kala, but I don't really know anything more than the size of her breasts relative to my hands. Our relationship was both ephemeral and undeveloped, and was halted abruptly over the phone by Kala, who unknowingly prevented what her phone call had temporarily delayed from being classified as cheating. The girl with whom I wasn't technically cheating quickly exhausted my brief relationship attention span and was soon replaced by Brandi. Kala was apparently displeased.

I endured some kind of distorted group therapy/marriage counseling session in my health classroom after school a couple weeks ago—because Brandi asked me to come and I would probably do anything she asked me to do not involving the severing of digits or the shaving of my head into a swastika and walking through Compton with twenty dollar bills stapled to my shirt—and listened to my unnaturally concerned health teacher discuss the awkward situation my selfish lack of compassion had managed to create with me seated appropriately but uncomfortably in between the two girls. And now Brandi's leaving.

Brad and his girlfriend reappear with Derek and Jessica and we walk down the street to Los Altos High School, wandering out onto the soccer fields. We drop down onto the deep green grass and glance around at each other, making occasional comments about sprinklers and getting wet and toughness. This is what we do: hang out. Hanging out consists of doing absolutely nothing with at least one other person.

We pretend we don't, but we all know why we came here. We're not stupid. I mean not extraordinarily stupid. We've recently escaped eighth grade and our blood is raging with new hormones. At least the guys' blood. The girls seem pretty indifferent, like they might enjoy us and our attention sometimes but wouldn't really notice if we weren't around. They don't need us poking and groping and whatever else we do to satisfy our immature sexual curiosity.

I look at Brandi and Brandi looks at me and we dismiss ourselves from the group. Walking in silence to a large sheet metal storage shed near the baseball diamond because it's an obvious destination and offers no immediate reasons to avoid it, we lie down in the grass without a word and begin what we really came here for. There's nothing spontaneous or romantic about it. It's almost planned, then executed following the guidelines we've somehow come to agree on without ever actually discussing them formally. I know what I'm allowed to do and she knows what I'm going to do because we've practiced this same routine a million times on a million patches of grass on a million weekends.

Brandi is gorgeous. Have I mentioned this yet? She's so incredibly beautiful. My attention span with girls being limited as it is, my attraction to them generally fades quickly and leaves me disappointed and seeking a fresh face. But Brandi is overwhelming. I can't imagine ever thinking she's anything less than the most stunningly beautiful girl I've ever seen within three hundred yards. These full, soft lips, almost fluffy. And her body. Krist, her body! If I were a girl, I would want her body, because then I could say, "Krist, look at my body!"

I unbutton Brandi's shirt and slide my hand slowly over her warm skin as the fabric slips to her sides. Carefully arranging myself to support my weight on an elbow, I reach around to her back and unhook her bra with one hand. This is an advanced technique. It's taken me many months of practicing with other girls to perfect it, but I've got it down. I'm sure— This is ridiculous. How lame are we to— Krist, look at this girl! I cannot believe she lets me do this. Doesn't she see I'm not good enough for her? Doesn't she see she deserves more than I could ever give her? Me and my long hair and my earrings and my scars and my bad attitude, her and her beautiful face and her beautiful body and those soft, full, beautiful lips. I don't understand.

Her skin is hot on my cheek. "I don't want you to move," I tell her.

"I know," she whispers. "I'll miss you."

□    □    □

We belong at the YMCA. Look at us: skinny and weak and unsure of what we're doing. The typical YMCA weight room clientele. Kodi is at least a head taller than I am and even thinner—which seems entirely impossible until you've see it—with this sandy hair that just kind of floats above his head like those big dumb hats they make you wear in little league. His face seems naturally to reveal a chronic degree of confusion regarding his whereabouts and reasons for being in said unknown whereabouts. He and I are about as close to being brothers as is possible without having shared a womb and have found a strange equilibrium by imitating various qualities of each other in ultimately equal portions, which somehow allows us to maintain distinct identities.

After briefly consulting the mirror to gauge the stunning visible progress we know we've made in the last hour, we head out into the sunlight to find Kodi's older brother. Older Brother is waiting for us outside with one of his longhaired stoner friends. I touch my own hair, now short and respectable because I finally realized I look like a girl with long hair and looking like a girl can be embarrassing when you're not a girl. We all pile into the 1979 Chevy Caprice, known among our circle as The Beast for reasons obvious to anyone who's had the privilege of driving one of these fine automobiles, particularly one of the hubcap-deficient models two-toned with black paint and grey primer.

I watch from the back seat as the stoner digs through his duffel bag and extracts a small bong. I smile at my cultured understanding of drug paraphernalia. I know what a bong is. Hippies use them to get in touch with their earthly spirituality or whatever. Since starting a couple years ago with cheap weed and a horrible brass eyebrow-burning excuse for a pipe, I've been smoking every chance I find, but practical complications like funding and access have disappointingly limited my exposure and retarded my progress to real drugs.

I glance at Kodi. He still looks like he doesn't know where he is. I laugh to myself and roll down my window. The clear blue sky is pale with the summer's bright afternoon sun. I hear the scraping of metal on flint and the gurgling of the bong and turn back to the stoner. He raises his head and hands the bong over his shoulder to me. I make a cursory inspection of the device. I'm intelligent and somewhat mechanically inclined. I can figure this out.

"You have to cover the hole."

"What?"

"You have to cover that hole in the back to fill it up," Kodi tells me again.

"I know." I don't know.

"Then you have to let it go to get the hit."

"I know." I don't know that either.

I cover the hole like I know what I'm doing and flick the lighter. The glass chamber quickly fills with white smoke and I slip my thumb from the hole, inhaling deeply and watching the smoke slide from the tube. Holding my breath, I pass the bong to Kodi and finally let the smoke curl from my lips, feeling the feeling one feels when one has just performed an act of staggering social rebellion deserving of widespread recognition and admiration from his peers who have not yet achieved this level of intense life experience.

I sit back against the beaten upholstery and smile with satisfaction. This is progress. This is revolutionary. From sniffing glue and drinking stolen liquor at the Emporium to smoking sparkling bud from a glass bong in the YMCA parking lot. This is it. I'm on my way. The master of my destiny. Nothing can stop—

"Here." Kodi hands me the bong again.

Look at me. Cool and collected. Confident. Virtually glowing with experience. I am the future. I am—

"Hole."

"What?"

"Cover the hole," Kodi says.

"Right."

I cover the hole with my thumb and watch the purple flame twist and bend as it's sucked into the bowl. The bud crackles and hisses, the glass chamber filling slowly with the clean white smoke. I slide my thumb off the hole and pull the hit into my chest, the smoke cool and smooth, bringing it all in, pulling up every last wisp from the chamber, because I need this smoke, I need all of it, I need this cool white smoke.

□　　□　　□

That's it? Kodi unwraps the foil and spreads it out on his kitchen table. This can't be right. A little white scrap of paper with a faded drawing of an eagle or some kind of predatory bird, maybe a falcon or a hawk, or those other things, the ones with the— Whatever. Someone's fucking with us.

Most people put these things on their tongues, but most people are stupid. I pick up one of the little squares—fuck, this is way too small— and put it under my tongue over the dense collection of superficial blood vessels intended to more completely and efficiently absorb brain-damaging chemicals. I look at Kodi. He's put the other tab of acid under his tongue and is now crumpling up the foil.

"How long does it take to kick in?" Kodi wonders.

"I don't know," I shrug.

We sit at the table and space out for a while. I can feel the paper dissolving in my mouth. A guy I used to sit next to in science class told me that if you drew a picture of some kind of fruit on a piece of binder paper and you really believed in yourself, you would taste the fruit when you ate the paper. We spent the rest of the year drawing fruit and eating paper. My fruit tasted like ink.

Kodi is a year older than I am and attends a different high school because of the wildly illogical district lines that obviously benefit someone other than high school students. Our family lives seem to be polar opposites despite the long-term friendship of our parents that created our own. He attends church regularly with his parents—who remain married—while I travel back and forth weekly between my divorced parents' homes shamelessly ridiculing institutional religion. Our general attitudes toward life are fittingly discordant. He seems unconcerned with most things and perfectly content to submit to his parents' wishes. I, on the other hand, am not content with anything but chronic discontent and am continually encouraging Kodi to step just a little further from under his parents' reign, which, along with my history of long hair, earrings, and accordingly inappropriate behavior, has earned me a less than wonderful reputation with them. He somehow manages to convince himself that using drugs as recreation is an acceptable deviation from his family's guidance, but continues to actively avoid any confrontation with his parents regarding even the most pedestrian of daily issues.

Kodi looks at me. "You know what a mole is?"

"The animal or the number?"

"The number."

"Kind of."

"It's this number." Kodi grabs a notepad and a pencil and writes: $6.02257 \times 10^{23}$.

"That's big," I say.

Kodi writes it again without the decimal point and carefully counts out eighteen zeros. It takes the entire length of the notepad.

I'm laughing a little. "That's a lot of zeros."

Kodi is laughing a little too. "Yeah."

We study the notepad thoughtfully.

"I wish I had this many dollars," Kodi says.

"Yeah. You could buy the world and charge everyone rent."

We're laughing again, a little harder than the last time.

"One of my teachers said if you had a mole of M&Ms, they would cover the earth," I tell him.

Kodi thinks for a minute, then draws a big circle on the notepad. "This is the earth," he explains.

We're laughing harder.

Kodi begins carefully drawing small circles around the rim of the big circle. "One, two, three…"

We're now laughing uncontrollably. Kodi is still trying to draw the circles, but his hand is shaking too much from laughing so hard and he can't count because he can't breathe. So we laugh harder. I'm having trouble staying in my chair. I lean over the table and hold on. I'm going to die laughing, right here in my best friend's kitchen, on this undulating white tile with the grey grout, at the base of these floor to ceiling windows, in the streaming sunlight, I'm going to die laughing.

"—"

Kodi is trying to say something.

"—"

It's not working.

"I—"

It's coming.

"I think—"

He has to stop and try to breathe.

"—it's working."

Older Brother walks into the kitchen and stares at us. "Come on, we gotta go."


We're in San Jose. Why are we in San Jose? Right, we're in San Jose because we're cleaning up a yard for someone. Why are we doing this? I give up and look around the yard. Not much to it. Just a cement pad two-cars wide surrounded by a couple feet of dirt on each side. I guess we're supposed to get all the leaves off or something. I look over at Kodi. He's standing motionless by the fence staring down into a trashcan. He seems to be having the same trouble I am.

"Greg."

It's been long time. I think. I'm not sure. I think it's been a pretty long time since he walked over to that trashcan and looked inside. And then he just stayed there.

"Greg," Kodi says again.

"What."

"Come here."

I walk over to the trashcan the way I imagine I'd walk if I forgot I had arms. "What."

"Look in there," Kodi tells me without shifting his stare from the trashcan.

I look in. It's full of dead leaves Older Brother has been sweeping up while the two of us have been attempting to overcome the paralyzing effects of extremely high-speed internal monologue. But these aren't ordinary dead leaves. They're moving. I mean, they're not moving, but they're not still. Kind of trembling. Like my eyes can't focus on them. These leaves are beautiful. But they're horrible. Now I know why Kodi's been standing here for so long. I can't look away. I've never seen leaves like these before. I think they're breathing. I'm going to climb into the trashcan. I'm going to climb into this trashcan and sit in—

"What the fuck're you guys doing?"

Kodi and I turn around slowly to look at Older Brother. I want to say something but I don't remember how to talk.

"What're you guys doing?"

Kodi and I consult each other with a brief glance and shrug.

Older Brother points to the side of the house. "Clean up all that shit under the deck."

We walk around to the side of the house and kneel down to look under the deck.

"Holy shit."

I glance at Kodi. "What."

"Look," he says, pointing to a paper cup in the dirt.

I look. "What the fuck..."

Dry purple liquid is eating away the cup like a slow wave of acid, tearing away tiny pieces of the waxed paper as it deliberately spreads from the rim.

"Touch it."

"No way."

"Come on."

"You touch it."

"No way."

Kodi grabs a stick from the dirt and pokes the cup. "What is that shit?"

"I don't know."

"Is it still eating the cup?"

"I think so."

"But it looks dried, doesn't it?"

"Yeah, kinda."

Summoning every ounce of courage I can summon from wherever it is auxiliary courage is stored, I squint my eyes and outstretch my hand.

I've touched the cup.

I pull back quickly and wait for my hand to start melting, to combust, to do whatever a hand does when it touches weird purple liquid in San Jose.

It doesn't do anything.

I pick up the cup and bring it to my face to inspect this purple liquid. Kodi leans in closer to see. We both have hepatitis now. No, cancer. We have cancer now. I bet we do. This shit is cancerous. We have tumors and we're going to die. I'm going to waste away in a sweaty hospital bed and die all because of this stupid purple shit on a cup under the deck of some house in San Jose, a house I've never even seen before, a house at which I'm doing yard work for no logical or fully explicable reason, because instead of asking why, I just got into The Beast as instructed and sat next to a big trashcan and some rakes and other assorted odd-smelling gardening implements, and a gasoline container I think, which is probably overheating right now, sitting in a closed car in the sun, a car of dark paint color—dark colors of course absorb more of the light spectrum and the associated heat— and will be reaching its ignition temperature at the very moment I open the door of The Beast so that when I plop my skinny ass down on that faded upholstery and slam the heavy door shut the sudden increase in the vehicle's interior pressure will be just enough to ignite the heated gasoline and cause an explosion the size two or so gallons of gasoline makes in these conditions, easily big enough to eject me from The Beast, my shredded remains showering down onto the street along with shards of twisted metal and smoking plastic and other materials used in the manufacturing of automobiles in 1979, and there'll be so much left unsaid, so much left undone, I'm still a virgin for Krist's sake, I mean I've come close a few times, but there've always been external complications, you know how it is when you're fourteen, I mean, you don't really have anywhere to do it, not even a car, not even the tiny backseat of a car, so small it forces you to think of creative and uncomfortable wrestling position variations requiring unnatural bending and stretching and bumping of body parts against car parts, so you just make out for six hours and then have to go home with your balls so swollen you walk like a cowboy, or one of those biker guys with the leather chaps, except you don't look tough and mean, just stupid and turgid and frustrated, I mean fuck, sometimes I think I'll never have sex and spend the remainder of my life sharing wildly exaggerated versions of my incomplete sexual exploits with my friends and coworkers to cover for the fact that I've never even seen a girl completely naked, which I guess is OK because maybe it would be worse to have had a naked girl right in front of me and not have been able to do it with her, I mean goddamn it, man, I was so close, but her parents came home and I had to extract my hand from her pants and sit there politely with this unrequited erection and the—

"Let's go."

CHAPTER TWO

High school is lame. This is the profound conclusion at which I've arrived after much thoughtful consideration. It's a worn out rerun of the last two years with a few extra faces: faces convinced they stand out from the crowd when their straining attempts to stand out are exactly what push them back in. What was rebellious a year ago is now an institution. When you can purchase your individualism like an outfit in the mall with your mother's credit card, it's not individualism. It's fashion.

Drug use was a cause for popular shame a year ago, but the mainstream has suddenly embraced it as a measure of social status and spends inordinate amounts of time sharing their experiences with anyone who'll listen. Except I later find these experienced people quietly coming to me for supplies. And they've never experienced anything: never touched any of it, never seen any of it, wouldn't know cocaine from crushed caffeine pills—which by the way is a great substitute when needing to make a quick buck by selling counterfeit drugs to the aforementioned people, who would drop forty dollars on a balloon full of urine if you promised it would get them high.

They don't need any of it. They don't need the drugs or the alcohol, just like they don't need those pants or those shoes or those shirts or any of the other shit they buy according to MTV's shopping list. I want my independence again, my seemingly natural and casual individualism, my righteous distinction from the masses. I need this. And now they're building stairs, escalators, elevators with leather couches to carry them down gently to this hole, where they won't sit in the dirt because it's too dirty and pull the couches from the elevators to sit with their friends and discuss their importance to this segment of the population, their role in this demographic, their obligation to their peers to remain visibly in style.

When they approach me, I lie. I don't care what they believe. I only supply those whose level of drug experience I'm comfortable with. The rest I don't trust enough to even speak to about anything, let alone sell them that anything. They'll sidle up to me like there's nothing more natural than us being the best of friends when a year prior I was listening to them in the background quietly condemning me and my lifestyle in weak impersonations of their parents' voices. Their intentions seep right through their nervous smiles long before they make their stumbling requests.

Standard opening line: "So, dude, what're you doing tonight?"

Standard response to discourage further interaction: "Don't know."

Obvious bridge to ensuing request: "Getting fucked up?"

Most efficient reply: "Yes."

Attempt to relate in an effort to minimize distrust: "Cool, yeah, we're just getting high and shit..."

[Insert subtle facial expression of irritated exhaustion]

And here it is: "Can you hook us up?"

Let us now pause for a moment of reflection: Isn't this the same jack-off who's spent far too much of his free time talking shit about me using drugs? A year ago I was a delinquent, some stupid fuck-up, but now I'm his friend because he wants what I have. Now the game is televised. It's on MTV with all the pretty faces and the pretty dilemmas with their matching solutions and he wants a piece of it for his wardrobe.

"What do you need?"

"I don't know, a gram..."

"Are you kidding?"

"What do you mean?"

"How many are you planning to feed?"

"I don't know, a few..."

"And you want a gram?"

"Yeah, I know, it's a lot for just a few people, but—"

"A gram is like a fucking ball of lint. It won't get a few kittens stoned."

"So how much do—"

"I'll get you an eighth."

"Yeah, dude, uh…"

"You don't have anything to smoke it with."

"No."

"Why don't I just get you some acid instead? Or some blow, you can get some cash from your mommy, she buys all those clothes for you, right? No wait, how about some meth, that shit's fun!"

"Nah, dude, we just—"

"What're you a fucking pussy? Weed is for lightweights. Come on, let me get you some gack, you can build a castle or something for your girlfriend."

"Dude, I don't know about that shit, could you just hook up some bud?"

"I don't do drugs."

"Dude—"

"Don't call me dude."

"Man—"

"Fuck you."

My fury and logical desire to clean up and quit all the drugs and drinking is countered by my carefully developed apathy and genuine enjoyment of drugs and drinking. I like what I'm doing. I like eating acid and tripping until sunrise. I like secretly snorting lines of blow off of CD cases and bathroom counters until my nose bleeds and my heart trembles. But I need to distinguish myself again. Myself used to be not them. Now them is me and I don't want to see it. I'm fading into the television show. And I don't even have a girl and her rapidly maturing breasts to distract me anymore.

I look around the school's library and think about what a piece of shit it is. I've heard this entire school was built for $100,000. I believe it. The walls are unevenly stained C-grade plywood, the floors cheap industrial tile. The furniture was probably purchased secondhand over the years at state prison garage sales. I guess that's the state institution trickle-down effect. The table I'm sitting at right now is barely standing. The legs are bent and uneven, the plastic wood veneer chipped, the vinyl edge peeling from idle students like me picking at it with our pens.

I guess I'm in here with my world history class. Something about making a newspaper. I don't know. It's a group project; I don't burden myself with extraneous details. I wisely placed myself in a group of intelligent and motivated young men with whom being friends has proved invaluable. They've made it clear to me they have no problem picking up my slack. Not that I'm completely useless. I offer to go find any books they may need, and I find and collect them remarkably efficiently for someone who's never really paid enough attention to understand the Dewey Decimal System. This is my official job. My unofficial job is apparently serving as some kind of mascot, a visible connection to the unfamiliar and unreachable glittering world of high school popularity—not glittering like gold or silver, or even polished steel, more like wet snot—for these social misfits.

These are the guys who sit cross-legged on the cement in front of the library during lunch eating something Mom made for them and reading books they're not required to read. The guys who actually do homework, more than is assigned, who enthusiastically raise their hands in class with correct and excessively complete answers. The guys who are in the physics club, the chess club, the computer club, all the clubs not specifically social or involving interaction with anyone who doesn't play chess and understand computers and advanced physics. The guys who seem to spend extended periods of time each morning determining and executing the most vicariously embarrassing hair configurations imaginable. Not that I'm in any kind of position to comment on hair configurations—my entire head is shaved except for some long bangs I dyed red. I don't even like red.

But I like these guys. They just do what they do. They don't strain themselves for attention. They don't watch MTV and buy clothes in the mall. They don't ask me for drugs and they don't lie to impress me. They're a relief from the obnoxious little imposters who populate this place. They're a relief from myself.

Plus they do a lot of work for me.

I didn't think it was possible, but I'm actually even less concerned with schoolwork than usual today. I'm sitting at this table looking across the library at Laina, one of the girls in the class I think I'm in. She sits with her friend next to me in the back of the room, but we've never talked. The only connection we've made was last week when I leaned my head against the cabinet next to me, which made a much louder noise on contact than I'd expected. Assuming I'd hit my head on the cabinet accidentally, Laina and her little friend decided to laugh at me. I didn't think anything of it. People laugh at me all the time. I'm funny.

But yesterday I was talking to Jesse:

"You know that girl Laina in your history class?" he asked me.

"Yeah."

"You should get her number."

"Why."

"Because."

"Because why."

"Because she wants to give it to you."

"She wants to give it to me?"

"Her number."

"Oh."

So here I am, thinking about Laina instead of world history. She's sitting at a table across the main room of the library with her all-female group doing whatever it is I should probably be doing. This is not mitigating the severity of my predicament. In these circumstances, girls become ruthless and unforgiving and must be avoided at all practical costs. Their presence is not conducive to the obtaining of telephone numbers by the unfortunate gender. They may think I'm the hottest guy in school, the greatest thing in the world next to that non-smearing lipstick, but they won't behave accordingly when I approach their friend. They'll focus their cold, black, judgmental little eyes on me, jeopardizing my concentrated efforts to ignore their evaluations and focus on the task at hand. I'll be so nervous, so afraid of disappointing them, so terrified of shattering their illusions of my perfection, that instead of being the smooth, confident guy who's frequently given telephone numbers by girls that I am, I'll be a complete jack-off whose mouth attempts to insert different words into his sentences than had been anticipated by his brain, producing combination words that are obviously the result of being exceedingly nervous and a little mentally retarded, and they'll all point their twisted little fingers at me and laugh, forcing me to flee the scene and sprint to the nearest room featuring a deadbolt and windowless walls so I can spend some uninterrupted time hitting myself and obsessing over my devastating inadequacies, all the retarded combination words I made, how lame and virginal I'll always be, and how I should probably just involve myself in some kind of fatal accident to prevent any further humiliation.

I look at Laina. She looks Filipino. Maybe half-Filipino. One of her friends looks Filipino and the other two look Mexican. I check my own pigment status: I'm from another planet. One of those funny stoner white guys with the fucked up punker haircuts who are kind of entertaining to talk to in Ceramics for an hour at a time, but not anyone they'd ever play house with. Her friends don't see me as the hottest guy in school, because I'm not the hottest guy in school. If I'm lucky, they might consider me the greatest thing in my pants next to my underwear. I can't go over and talk to her. I'll be dismantled so fast. I'll be humiliated, reduced to ashes and tears of self-pity, smoldering in the dirt, stepped over unnoticed by the cute white platform sneakers of the same ones who destroyed me. The cynical and exploitive yearbook staff will produce a two-page spread dedicated to my social failure, adorned with crudely snapped and inartistically cropped photographs of me hiding my face and my stupid haircut, flushed with shame and humiliation, unable to—

Shit, they're getting up. They're all getting up and leaving. Except Laina. They walked out of the library! Everyone but Laina. Sitting there all by herself. No one else around the table...

Fuck. Now I have no excuse.

I watch her closely, leaning on an elbow and holding her head in her hand, her long brown hair slipping through her fingers. Beautiful. She wants to talk to me? She must use drugs. Whichever ones make partially brain dead fashionally retarded whiteboys like me attractive. Maybe Jesse is fucking with me. Maybe this is some elaborate plan he and that schemer girlfriend of his developed to secure vengeance for something I did to offend one of them. I mean, I don't remember doing anything offensive, but I don't remember a lot of what I've done. I'm sure I could have upset one or both of them at some point—maybe I was fucked up on something and made a comment to one of them that seemed funny at the time, something I didn't really mean, something that maybe touched on some unresolved psychological fixation, shit, I don't know, I don't even know what I do when I'm sober most of the time—and they were conniving enough to stay quiet and keep smiling and talking to me like they would when not offended, carefully plotting their revenge and patiently waiting for the ideal moment to strike. Either they got Laina in on it and instructed her to humiliate me as publicly and severely as possible, or worse, she's not in on it at all because Jesse and Company knows she'll take care of the humiliation on her own. But what if Jesse's not fucking with me? I have to do it. She's gorgeous. I think I'd rather get rejected and humiliated by a girl like her than miss a chance of being accepted and humiliated by a girl like her. I have to do it now, when she's alone.

What's that noise?

I check my shirt—wrinkled and sitting unevenly on my skinny shoulders. I tug my pants into proper position because exceedingly oversized pants you buy at cheap clothing stores and cut to length ride up your ass when you're sitting and you have to pull them down again before you stand up or you look like one of the guys in my group with their navy blue Dockers cranked up to their armpits.

What is that noise?

Make sure my pant legs are seated properly over the tops of my shoes, my shoes are tied and the long laces tucked out of sight, my earrings are hanging right, check my hair—fuck, why am I checking my hair, all I have are some red bangs, for Krist's sake, it's not like my hair can really be out of position or in any way—

What the fuck is that noise?

Is that my heart? In my face?

I try to breathe. It's just a phone number. Seven digits. Maybe ten, she might live in 408 or something. But still. I check my hair again and push back in my prison chair. The misfits all look up at me from the work I should be doing.

"I'll be right back," I tell them casually. "I gotta go talk to someone." That's right, fellas, I do this all the time. I mean, it's not like I chose the lifestyle, you know, the ladies chose it for me.

Krist I hope she doesn't look up before I get over there. If she sees me coming it's going to be so awkward, like what is she supposed to do, watch me the whole time? I'll have sex with her, but eye contact is a big step. Besides, sometimes I think I walk kind of funny, like my hips are fucked up or something, I don't want—

Here's the table. Laina looks up at me.

"Hey." Did my voice crack?

"Hi," she smiles.

I sit down next to her. "You're all alone," I say.

That was fucking brilliant. I need an agent.

"Yeah..."

"What'd your group ditch you?"

That's good, shithead. Keep it up.

"Kind of," she says. "They went to smoke."

OK. I've made it through the introduction relatively painlessly, although I've come off as completely tactless and a little developmentally disabled, but now what? Do I move into the body of the conversation, or do I just skip it and proceed directly to the sales pitch? I mean, I should probably talk to her a little before I just ask her for her number, you know, loosen her up, demonstrate what an outstanding example of masculine perfection—

Shit, her friends are coming back in.

"So could I call you sometime?"

Laina looks up at me shyly and I realize she's struggling to formulate a polite way to turn me down.

"Yeah," she finally smiles.

Nevermind. I'm a fucking stud.

□   □   □

The first bell rings. This means I have four minutes to get to my photo class on time.

"You're gonna be late," Laina tells me.

"Yeah."

Laina looks at me and laughs. But while she laughs, I know she's swearing at me under her breath. I have what she wants: the inexplicable ability to maintain reasonably good grades without exerting myself in the least. Unlike me, Laina works hard. She's part of some kind of tutorial program at the high school, willing to put in greater than expected effort, but never quite able to achieve the grades and the comfort with school she deserves. I think she finds herself trapped between school and her less motivated friends, unable to satisfy both simultaneously, and left constantly stumbling along the middle.

"Aren't you cold?" Laina asks me. I wear T-shirts when it's cold.

"Not really," I shrug. "I like it."

"You're a freak," she laughs.

"You are."

"Shut up."

"You shut up."

The final bell rings. This means I'm late.

"You're late," Laina says. "You're gonna get dropped."

"I'll reinstate myself."

"How?"

"You just tell one of those office ladies you need to get back into the class and you're on the role sheet again the next day."

"You have sex with Mrs. Fierre to convince her, huh?"

"Totally."

"Gross."

"You're gross."

"You are."

This is us. Laina and me. This is how we are. We're confident enough in each other's maturity—at least our presumed maturity—that we can act like seven-year-olds. Laina is my girlfriend now. I guess. I don't know what exactly determines this, if it's a time limit like common-law marriage or what, but I know she's my girlfriend. Laina is completely unlike any girl I know. She's unconcerned with girlish details like makeup and hair, for which she deserves only limited credit, being naturally beautiful enough to not require she be concerned with such facial accessories. The abnormally powerful attraction to Asian girls I developed as a result of—or at least following—my long term but never sexually productive flirtation with the beautiful and Korean Staci has either been satisfied by Laina's Filipino blood or simply eclipsed by her general beauty and seeming female perfection. She's somehow able to let me forget my distractingly obvious inadequacies and be comfortable enough with her to drop the bullshit routine and be what I'm guessing might actually be the closest to myself I've ever been.

Laina grabs my hand and we sit on the cement planter box we always sit on. She leans her head on my shoulder and I pull a few strands of her hair from her face and tuck them behind her ear. Her hair is beautiful. Long, straight, dark, almost as smooth as my skills with the ladies.

"Are you gonna go to photo?" Laina asks me.

"Are you gonna go to photo?"

"I'm not in the class."

"So?"

"So I'm not going."

"Then no."


I walk through the automatic doors and smile at the smooth blue floor tile. Through recent impulsive experimentation, I've discovered it to be the ideal surface for sliding on one's shoes, should those shoes be those old canvas Vans, the very shoes I wear every day despite the holes my socks spill out of and Kala's frequent slights: "Hey Greg, the eighties called. They want their shoes back." Fuck the eighties, I'm keeping the shoes.

Kala and I have finally emerged from the extended silence that followed my indiscretion with Brandi and are actually on speaking terms again, although our conversations tend to be limited in depth and quality, consisting primarily of signifying remarks about my shoes. I guess she doesn't feel the need to hate me anymore with Brandi no longer rolling around in the grass with me.

I run and slide across the blue floor toward the back of the bike shop. This is my second week of employment here. The manager has been trying unsuccessfully because of my age to hire me for a few months, during which I spent much time in the shop unintentionally establishing the friendly relationship with him that now blurs my new guy status and allows me to slide recklessly across the floor without consequence.

My ride stops abruptly on a scuffmark and I trip through the service door into the work area. The shop's ever-curious manager Jeff has disassembled a newly released suspension fork—model Judy XL—and is leaning over one of its legs, compressing and releasing the shock sensually against his workbench.

"Oh, Judy!" Jeff squeals, pumping the stanchion tube in and out of the leg.

I stare at him and he stops.

"What."

"You're a freak."

"It's so smooth!"

"Gross."

"Get your skinny ass to work."

I flip Jeff off just for being a manager and wind my way through scattered boxes and bikes to my workbench, tucked all the way in the back among the fields of assembled back stock bikes sprouting from the ceiling. I'm separated from the rest of the work area by the clutter, but I can still see Jeff having sex with a suspension fork. I like it back here. I have my own radio and pestering customers have no access to me. I grab my shop apron from the bike stand and slip it over my head.

"What do we need?" I yell at Jeff.

"Sixteen-inch Avalanche!"

This is my job. Jeff tells me what bikes we need for the sales floor and I build them. If I've mistakenly done something to temporarily damage my spiritual status, Jeff sends me out front to help customers. I don't like customers. They ask stupid questions and don't understand simple answers. I entertain myself by speaking to them in artificial accents and making faces and obscene hand gestures each time they look away.

Heading deeper into the back of the shop, past the large garage into which we throw with disregard and often subsequently damage the bikes customers bring trustingly to us to repair, I run upstairs into one of the storage rooms and walk down the first row of stacked boxes looking for a sixteen-inch Avalanche. Ignoring the basic laws of physics, we stack the boxes three-high, supplying those on the top row with just enough potential energy to kill us if they fall.

I find my assigned bike and start tugging on the cardboard. Behind me, another fifty-pound box ejects violently from the stack and slams onto the plywood floor at my feet. K bursts into laugher from behind the row while I check my pants for internal damage. Here we believe almost killing your friend with a heavy box is funny.

"Hey bitch," K says, walking around the corner.

"Fuck you."

K and I are buddies even though he throws bikes at me. He was transferred up here from our other shop at the same time I was hired, and he's now the head repair mechanic. We bonded quickly in typical male fashion through mild violence and ridicule of others. K is the kind of guy you see and immediately want on your team: a gnarly twenty-one-year-old punk with a long goatee, a lot of metal in his ears, a nasty smoker's cough, and a '76 Camaro with a dent in the front fender from the guy's head he slammed into it.

"I gotta go build this hoopty," I tell him, pushing the box out the door and running down the stairs with it sliding dangerously behind me.

□   □   □

Monday morning. Only a couple more weeks of school before summer. I look around the quad at everyone hurrying to their classes. They look like ants. Except bigger. And with clothes. And other things. I realized late last night that I never called Laina this weekend. I'm pretty sure I was supposed to. Boyfriends presumably call their girlfriends on the weekend. I don't know why I didn't call. I guess I forgot. Maybe that means something. Or maybe I'm just a little stupid and preoccupied with work and drugs. I see her in front of the gym and catch up.

"Hey."

She stops and looks away. "Hey."

"What's wrong?"

"Nothing."

"I know you're mad."

"I'm not mad," she says.

"Then why won't you look at me?"

Laina turns and looks at me. She does things like this.

"That's not what I mean."

"I'm fine," she says.

"Well, look, I'm sorry I didn't call this weekend," I tell her. "I don't know, I was just out of it."

"Mm."

"Why won't you just tell me you're pissed off?"

"I'm not. I gotta go to class." Laina slips into the hallway and disappears in the swarm.

Fuck. I look around as the campus slowly empties of bodies. She'll get over it.

Manny looks up at our ceramics teacher, the same recovering hippie who taught our photo class last semester and suggested we turn in pictures of our sisters in bikinis.

"What's this?"

"Uh… It's a flower vase," Manny says.

Mr. Tyson looks over Manny's project thoughtfully. It's a tall cylinder with the sides dented in artistically, kind of like a flower vase, except there's a hole near the lower end.

"What's this?"

"Uh... A hole," Manny says.

Mr. Tyson knows exactly what it is. It's a bong. Flower vases do not have holes in them.

He looks at the pot leaves etched into the sides. "What're these?"

"Uh... Maple leaves."

"OK," Mr. Tyson says. "Good flower vase."

Manny looks at me and laughs.

I walk to the window by our table and look out into the quad. Laina doesn't have a class this period. Every day I slip out of ceramics and hang out with her under the redwood trees for a while since this is more appealing to me than making shit with clay. But class is almost over and Laina still hasn't shown up.

"She's not out there today?"

"She's pissed," I tell Manny. "I didn't call her this weekend."

"Why not?"

"I don't know, it's not like I didn't wanna talk to her, I just forgot to call, and then it was today."

"And she didn't call you?"

"No, she never calls me," I tell him. "Unless I leave a message on her machine."

"What's her problem with the phone?"

"No idea," I shrug. "But she's pissed now."

"That's bullshit," Manny says. "She could've called you."

"Yeah, I guess."

"What do you mean you guess? She can use a phone just as well as you can. How the fuck can she get pissed at you for not calling her when she won't call you?"

I walk to the window again and check for Laina. Nothing.

◻    ◻    ◻

The manager quit the bike shop last week and I've relocated to the workbench across from K's to reduce the amount of yelling across the shop formerly required for us to converse, which has also conveniently reduced the number of obscenities and assorted inappropriate things customers overhear through the service window due to the volume of our voices. Our new manager's favorite line to us is, "Less talk, more work." Our new manager sucks.

"So you never called her," K guesses, turning the pedals of the bike in his stand.

"Uh-uh."

K shakes his head at me as he watches the bike's rear wheel spin. "That's kinda fucked."

"How is that fucked?" I protest. "She has a phone. She has fingers and at least one functioning ear. I tried to apologize that day and she blew me off. If she wanted to talk to me, she could've called me."

"Yeah, but dude, you knew she wouldn't call."

"I guess," I shrug. "But fuck that."

Laina and I skillfully managed to make it through the rest of the school year without saying a word to each other. Fuck her. She could have called. She should have called. Girlfriends call their boyfriends on the weekends.

I tighten the bolts on my bike's stem and move to the front wheel to work on the brakes. Brent rolls around the corner on his bike and stops next to my bench, a good stopping point to break up the exhausting distance between the back of the store and the front of the store.

"Where the hell're you going?" I ask him. "Slacker."

"I gotta drop some shit off at school."

K laughs. "I don't know if I'd call it school."

"You can call it whatever you want," Brent shrugs, "but my diploma won't look any different than yours, and I only have to go in once a week."

I compare Brent's schedule to my own. "I wanna do that," I realize out loud.

"Hey," our new manager says. "Less talk, more work."

CHAPTER THREE

I slide my bedroom window open and the cool morning air creeps in slowly as I pull a small glass pipe from the tin box at my feet and methodically pack it. The minimum age for the adult education program in which Brent inspired me to enroll is sixteen. But even at the tender age of fifteen, I know quitters never win. I enlisted my stunning charm and persuaded the one-woman administration to accept me despite my age, because I am independent and motivated and responsible and worthy of an adult education diploma program.

I take the bus across the train tracks behind downtown Mountain View every Tuesday afternoon to meet with my two teachers for the amount of time required to hand pieces of paper to them, take new pieces of paper from them, and speak a few sentence fragments about said exchanged papers. A requirement requires me to take a lab science, so I attend real high school every morning for chemistry.

The first morning of class, my chemistry teacher pulled me into his little office to investigate the unfamiliar note alongside my name on his role sheet.

"So what's your deal?" he asked me.

"My deal?"

"Yeah, this Adult Ed thing."

"Oh. It's just independent studies. I do all my work each week and go turn it in."

"So technically you're not even a student at Mountain View."

"Not anymore. They say I'm a 'guest'."

"How come you chose to do that?"

"I'm not a big fan of school."

"What do you do all day then?"

Drugs.

"Work and ride."

"Ride?"

"Bikes. Trials."

"Oh, cool!"

Mr. Deever thinks I'm cool.

"Well anyway, I just wanted to let you know where I stand with you," he said. "You don't have to come to class. You'll be graded on the work you do like everyone else, but attendance is up to you."

I haven't missed a day of his class.

I take one last hit from the pipe and blow the ash out of the bowl. The walk from my house to the classroom takes about five minutes. Sometimes I try to count the number of steps it takes, because at 7:00 in the morning this seems extraordinarily interesting to me, but I end up arriving in class and realizing I forgot about counting somewhere along the line. Apparently my drug regimen has not improved my concentration.

Stepping into the room, I sit in my customary prison deskchair in the back behind Kala.

She turns around. "Hey."

"Hey back."

Kala stares at me. "Are you stoned?"

I shrug.

"Greg…" she scolds. Kala is the most maternal of the company I keep. Unfortunately, her attempts at caring for me are negated by her own steadily increasing self-destructive habits. It's like having one of those fat doctors who smell like cigarettes tell you you're not taking care of yourself.

Mr. Deever walks from his office to the front of the room with his customary can of SlimFast. He's not really fat, but he drinks SlimFast anyway and likes to make fun of himself for drinking SlimFast because SlimFast is pretty funny and we laugh. I turn and look out the window. Bryan dropped out of school this year because Bryan does things like drop out of school. I think he's in some program at one of the local junior colleges that isn't as unendurably lame as high school but actually requires regular physical attendance of classes. He's not as independent and motivated and responsible as I am. Kodi works at the bike shop now, and I'm rapidly reducing my number of non-bike-shop friends for convenience and the minimizing of unnecessary expenditures of time and energy that could be put to better use riding bicycles or using drugs—not particularly complementary activities, but somehow similarly appealing to me.

I don't really see anyone else since I'm only at school for fifty minutes a day, during the earliest period of the day, so premature it's actually called Zero Period and should not be attended by anyone who requires sleep. The only person outside the shop I still talk to regularly is Kala. We've actually become good friends who are able to call each other obscene words in greeting without consequence now that the Brandi incident and my obvious assholeness is long over. She's my only remaining connection to the high school scene.


It's 8:00 in the morning and my school day is over. But I'm not free. Today is Thursday, and Thursday morning means community service at the Los Altos Library before I go to work.

I grab my bike and head out into the streets. I fucking hate pigs. I want to pistol-whip them all with their own guns and have sex with their wives—who will enjoy sex with me much more than with their pig husbands—and their daughters—who will be virgins until I have sex with them and will subsequently become recklessly promiscuous.

Until recently, Kodi and I rode at Oak School every day, jumping onto picnic tables and other assorted equipment, then jumping off, then doing other things to get up onto other things and doing other things to get back off. This is what bicycle trials involves: riding a bike through obstacle courses that shouldn't be ridden through on a bike because they rarely allow more than a few rotations of the tires at a time and require doing things that bikes were obviously not intended to do. Kodi and I need a place to ride because riding is what we do when not doing too many drugs to ride, and to stay competitive, we need to ride and progress and learn to do more things that will win competitions and impress people and ultimately encourage attractive women to have sex with us.

Teachers would step out of their classrooms and watch us because we're more entertaining than their students' homework. They loved us because we are loveable and should be loved. They clapped for us and told us how great we were, and we thanked them and did great things for them to see because they might have cute daughters. But apparently someone wasn't in the fan club. I found out from my sources—I have sources—my name had been given to the Los Altos Police Department and they were looking for me—which is kind of cool, to have the cops looking for you—so I rode down to the police station to see what their problem was.

"My name's Greg Everett," I told the fat pig receptionist behind the glass. "I heard you guys were looking for me." I was a wanted man and she was impressed.

"Just have a seat," she said, not impressed.

Fine. I sat down and waited.

A few minutes later, a short cop walked out and silently motioned for me to follow him. Pigs do things like this because they're tough and confident and they have guns and they're allowed to shoot people who don't follow them when instructed. Walking behind him, I realized I was about to get fucked because people like me put people like him in trashcans until they get badges and guns, and then people like him shoot people like me until we're dead.

The cop led me to one of the little holding rooms, which was carpeted and furnished with comfortable chairs because there aren't any real criminals in Los Altos who don't need to be treated well to prevent punitive lawsuits. He flipped through some papers in his little cop folder like he knew what he was doing and stared at me.

"We received a complaint from a staff member at Oak School about some vandalism," he said finally.

"Vandalism?"

"He says you ride your bike there on tables and benches and that you've damaged a lot of property."

"What property have I damaged?"

"His main complaint concerns the picnic tables on the side of the school. He says you've destroyed the surface of them."

"The only damage I've done is put some holes in the wood from the spikes in my pedals and on my skid plate."

"So you're aware the tables are damaged."

"They were damaged when I was eating off them five years ago in elementary school."

"But you're aware your riding on them has furthered the damage."

"I guess."

"Well, what I'm gonna do right now is read you your rights—"

"You're arresting me?"

"Yes."

"For what?"

"Vandalism."

I thought fleetingly about urinating on him, but decided he'd be able to shoot me before I could get unzipped and into position. So here I am. Pedaling my ass all the way to downtown Los Altos because some jerk-off called the cops to come take care of his problem like some whiny little five-year-old calling his mommy to get his toy back from the big kid. And because I happened to be paired up with a short pig who's never experienced any criminal activity more intense than thirteen-year-olds burning rubber cement on playgrounds and needed to act tough with me because women won't have sex with him.

I roll my bike into the back room of the library and find my cart. My primary duty is shelving returned books. When I first began my service, I placed the books where they belonged because it seemed like the appropriate thing to do. I found this less fun than I believed community service should be. I now slide the books in where I think they look nice. Today I'm feeling particularly insubordinate, so I'm shelving violent and sexually oriented and otherwise non-child-appropriate books in the children's section. I do not channel my anger constructively. I am not servicing my community. It is members of my community who put me here. My community can get fucked. Finally I grow tired of shelving and hide on a yellow beanbag chair in the children's room until my time is up.


K watches me as I ride into the bike shop and drop my backpack on my workbench. "You're late," he tells me. He knows I was at the library and thinks this is funny.

"Fuck you."

"I need you to box a bike for me," he says, handing me a service order.

Customers bring us their bikes to have them packed in boxes for shipping. This provides much entertainment for young criminals like us. I look at the name on the invoice and then at the bike waiting for me in my stand. I know who this is.

"Hey, you remember this lady?"

K thinks about it and his face lights up. "Yeah."

We do not like this woman. We do not appreciate being yelled at and insulted during the rare times we actually provide genuine customer service, and we do not easily forget.

I begin disassembling the bike while my mind rifles through the list of "complimentary services" we provide while fixing bikes for people we don't like. Cutting out pictures of pornography and putting them in between the tire and innertube won't work because this lady won't fix her own flat tires and find them. Loosening the brake cables is probably a bad idea because I don't think I want to kill her. Unscrewing the pedals so they fall out when she's riding won't work because I have to take the pedals off to box the bike anyway. Loosening the derailleur cables so she's stuck in the lowest gear won't work because I know she'll take the bike to another shop to have it reassembled, and they'll fix that if they're even remotely competent.

"Hey dickface, you gonna eat that?" I ask K, pointing at the egg roll that came with his Chinese food.

"You want it?"

"Yeah."

K hands me the egg roll and watches with a smile as I push it into the seat tube of the bike frame.

"That's gonna smell good in a few days."

"It'll match her breath."

We use lithium grease to lubricate seat tubes and prevent the seat posts from seizing. Lithium grease is white. Mayonnaise is also white. K knows this. He retrieves a jar of mayonnaise from the refrigerator in back and scoops several spoonfuls into the seat tube with the egg roll.

I slide the partially disassembled bike into the box next to my bench and think for a minute. I'm out of creative ideas, so I just throw in some tomato slices from a half-eaten sandwich on Kodi's bench and call it complete. Smiling with satisfaction, I tape up the box nice and tight and slide it back into the repair yard, where it'll wait to be picked up by its soon-to-be-very-unfond-of-bike-shop-employees owner. I park it neatly and head back into the work area.

K pulls a pack of cigarettes from his breast pocket. "Smoke break!"

I don't smoke, but I take smoke breaks. Workplace legislation requires employees be given one fifteen-minute break for every four hours worked. We take one twenty-minute break for every hour worked because the quality of our labor is much greater than the average worker's and we demand appropriate compensation.

K lights his cigarette as we walk out into the parking lot and flips his Zippo shut like someone who flips Zippos shut way too often. "So whatever happened to that girl?" he asks.

"Who, Laina?"

"Yeah."

"Haven't seen her since last year," I tell him. "Apparently she and Kala are buddies now."

"You still think about her?"

I think about her all the time.

"Hell no."

He nods. "So what're you doing for your birthday?"

"Nothing," I shrug. "What is there to do?"

"I don't know," he says. "Get your driver's license?"

□     □     □

I shift into second and floor the gas. The car kind of goes faster. It's a silver four-cylinder 1986 Volvo station wagon with dark blue vinyl interior, but it's mine. The state government actually granted me legal authorization to drive a motor vehicle on public roadways. Clearly the DMV does not conduct background checks. I turn up the radio and try to look as cool as one can look driving a silver 1986 Volvo station wagon with blue vinyl interior.

My driving test was a waste of time:

"Pull out and turn left."

I pulled out and turned left.

"Change lanes."

I changed lanes.

"Turn down this street."

I turned.

"Make a three-point turn here."

I made a—what the fuck, why is there a duck in the middle of the road—three point turn.

"OK, head back to the parking lot."

That was it. They gave me a license. A sixteen-year-old misfit who drinks whiskey and smokes marijuana and snorts cocaine and drops LSD and eats mushrooms and pops ecstasy, who unremorsefully vandalizes elementary schools, who shelves adult books in the children's section at the library, who puts egg rolls and mayonnaise into people's bikes for a living. I'm allowed to drive a car.

I pull to a stop at the intersection of Cuesta and Grant and watch the cars passing me from their left turn, hoping as usual for a glimpse of some anonymous beautiful woman I'll never have sex with. Like that one. Wait, that's Staci! I used to draw on her arm in Spanish!

Staci sees me and waves frantically. Then she's gone.


My mother is gone for the weekend. I assume she told me where she was going, but I heard *I'm going to be gone this weekend* and my receiving equipment shut down temporarily to provide my brain the resources required to think of everything I could do in her absence. Of course there's the default teenage demonstration of irresponsibility party, but I'm not stupid. I've seen the theft and the broken glass and the cigarette burns and the spilled beer and the orange puke.

I could use drugs at home.

No wait, I already do that.

I could bring girls home and do it with them. It would be like having my own place. No one around to interrupt our romantic evening and prevent its culminating in sexual intercourse. Now all I need is a girl.

My mind sorts quickly through the list of girls I know: she wouldn't have sex with me; she hates me; she just wants to be my friend; she'd have sex with me, but she's kind of gross; she'd have sex with me, but she'd want a relationship or something lame like that; she won't talk to me anymore; she'd have sex with me, but not only after one night, she's one of those silly old-fashioned girls who actually wants to wait to get to know me before she lets me stick my—

The phone is ringing.

"Yeah."

"Is this Greg?"

"Yeah."

"This is Staci."

Staci! I didn't think of Staci.

"Hey, what're you doing?"

"Nothing, did you see me driving by earlier?"

"Yeah!"

"I was thinking maybe we should get together sometime," she says. "I haven't seen you in like a year!"

Would she have sex with me in one night?

"Yeah, what about tonight?"

"OK, yeah!" she says. "I kinda have to sneak out, though, so I can't get out until like 11:00. Is that OK?"

We're totally having sex.

"Yeah, you want me to just pick you up?"

"You remember where I live?"

"Of course."

"Good," she says. "Meet me across the street at 11:00."


OK. Check the hair in the rear view: good as it's going to get. It's short and respectable now. I may still be short, but I'm not respectable, and this should seemingly be reflected in my chosen hairstyle. But I realized that by creating the illusion of respectability, I could more easily maintain the trust—namely of teachers and parents and other authority figures— necessary to get away with all the things I shouldn't be getting away with. I figure the extent to which I'm willing to compromise my appearance to prevent unwanted attention and maintain my bad habits is the true measure of my commitment to those habits instead of the lifestyle fashions of which they've somehow become accessories. OK, check the pits. Doing all right. Try to straighten out the wrinkled shirt. Still wrinkled. Double-check the condom supply in the door compartment. OK.

I look out the window into the dark and see Staci hurrying across the street. She opens the door and slides onto the bitchin blue vinyl seat.

"Hey," she smiles. She's gorgeous.

"Hey back."

I fire up the Silver Bullet and pull out into the street. I have no idea what to do.

"Where're we going?" Staci asks me.

"I don't know," I shrug. "Where do you wanna go?"

"I don't know."

I can't just suggest we go to my place. That would be too forward. I don't want to seem desperate or rude or presumptuous or in any way discourage her from sleeping with me. One must be indirect and vague and slightly dishonest. This is how it's done. I watch television.

"Your hair's all short now," Staci says, touching my short hair.

"Yeah. I hate it."

"It looks good."

"I don't know," I shrug. "I feel lame actually *styling* my hair." It's a stupid conversation, but at least it's noise. And she's making compliments, which means she wants to have sex with me.

"You wanna just go to the park or something?" I ask her.

"OK."

OK. We have a destination. I can stop driving around aimlessly. I head to Cuesta Park and we bounce into the empty parking lot. Pulling up into a space, I shut down but leave the stereo on because it's playing a disco tape and everyone knows disco is conducive to casual sex.

"So you don't go to Mountain View anymore, huh?"

"No," Staci says. "My parents said I wasn't doing well enough, so they sent me to a private school."

"That's bullshit."

"Yeah. I guess I'm doing better, though," she shrugs. "What about you, aren't you doing some independent studies thing?"

"Yeah, how'd you know?"

"Lisa told me. She still—"

"Fuck."

I'm saying *fuck* because a very bright pair of headlights has pulled up behind the Bullet. This is how the fuzz park to prevent the escape of powerful and evasive vehicles like silver four-cylinder 1986 Volvo station wagons. I roll down my window and wait for what I'm sure will be a short cop. This car has a small oil leak. He'll probably arrest me for vandalism.

The flashlight appears and glares in at me. When it slowly descends and my eyes readjust, I'm staring at a female cop. This could go either way. My experience with female cops is that they generally fall into one of two categories. The first consists of very cool women because all women have an inherent amount of coolness of which I'm very much in awe, and they can get so much cooler in positions like this. The second, however, is distinguished by psychology similar to short cops'—women who've become bitter and jaded from all the misogynistic jack-off men who treat women like shit and are now out for vengeance. Members of the second category are still better than short male cops because they're women, and I like any woman better than any man, even if she wants to misdirect all her castrating anger at me to get back at all the assholes who've done her and her righteous sisters wrong.

"What're you doing out here?" she asks me.

Trying to not be a virgin.

"Talking."

She looks carefully into the car for anything that would give her probable cause for a search. But all my drugs are tucked safely up under the dashboard in a convenient little hole I discovered last week while looking for a convenient little hole to tuck drugs into. Also discouraging this cop from hassling me is my new respectable haircut. I look like a fine, upstanding young citizen. It can sometimes be difficult to believe, but cops are people, and all people by nature are prejudiced in some way to some degree, whether consciously or not. I'm young, white, clean-cut, and driving a silver 1986 Volvo station wagon with blue vinyl interior. I'm going to be given the benefit of the doubt.

"Can I see your license, registration, and insurance?"

I hand her the paperwork and she walks back to her patrol car to look me up in her little cop computer. Staci looks nervous. Apparently she's not as innocent as she was when I met her and is now running with some Korean gangsters I'm smart enough to be a little afraid of. I wonder if she has warrants or something.

The cop shows up again and hands me my gear. "You guys know it's past curfew?"

"There's a curfew?" I didn't know there was a curfew.

"Yeah. You need to go home."

"OK."

The cop walks to her cruiser and pulls back enough to allow me to escape the parking space.

"So you wanna just go to my house?" I ask Staci.

"Yeah."

That cop doesn't know it, but she just gave me the excuse I needed to take Staci to my house where we can do it. I roll around the parking blocks and head for the driveway. The cop is right behind me. I pull out of the driveway and head for Grant Road. The cop stays behind me.

"What's she gonna do, follow me all the way home?"

Staci shrugs. "It's Los Altos. She doesn't have anything else to do."

"Should we fuck with her?"

"Yeah," Staci grins.

I slow down to twenty-five in a thirty-five zone. Then I speed up to thirty-five. Then I slow down to twenty-five. From where we are, I can get home making only three turns. Instead I turn left onto a narrow street that runs along the edge of the area's only remaining farm. The cop follows. The street meanders through a poorly laid-out housing development and I turn onto another small street. The cop follows.

About a dozen unnecessary turns later, we finally emerge onto the street that runs along the front of Mountain View High School. I drive seventeen miles an hour because it's a school zone. In front of the football field, I turn as slowly as I can onto my street. The cop floors it and swerves violently around us.

"She's so pissed!"

"Yeah," Staci laughs.

I roll up into my driveway and Staci follows me inside and upstairs. She sits down on the edge of my bed, and I close the door and sit on the weight bench against the wall because I don't want to make her uncomfortable.

Staci starts looking through the stack of CDs next to the bed. "God, I don't recognize any of these guys."

"That's because you have bad taste."

Staci turns on the radio.

"See, look what station you chose," I tell her.

"This is the best station!"

"For the hearing impaired!"

"You suck."

"For the right price."

"You're sick."

"Totally."

This is my chance. I transfer to the bed, pretending to actually be concerned with the choice of music when really it's just an excuse to get closer to Staci, who's back to thumbing through the CD cases.

"Oh, I know these guys." Staci looks at the song list on the CD and frowns. "The only song I know isn't on here."

"Sorry."

"I guess the radio's OK," she says.

I slide back on the bed and open the window to spit my gum out.

"You remember eighth grade?" Staci asks me.

"Spanish."

"I had so much fun in that class."

"I got into so much trouble in that class. That lady hated my guts."

Krist, she smells good. Look at that hair. Like a sheet of black silk. I want to touch her hair so bad, just reach out and—

"You remember the grad dance?"

"Yeah," I nod, not touching her hair.

"I never got to dance with you."

"Yeah, I was pissed."

"You were?" Staci laughs a little. "God, I was so in love with you in eighth grade."

"Really?"

"Yeah," she blushes.

"Why didn't you ever say anything?"

"What was I gonna say?"

"I don't know, you could've just started making out with me in Spanish or something."

"Shut up," she laughs. "Besides, you always had girlfriends."

And now it's quiet.

Staci drops her eyes a little and looks up at me again. "Could I... kiss you?" she whispers.

Figuring this isn't a question that really warrants a verbal response, I lean forward and kiss her instead.

Staci pulls away slowly and looks at me. "I've wanted to do that for so long," she says softly.

"So have I."

[Don't make that face. I'm not lying to her. Just because I approached this situation in a juvenile and sarcastically womanizing manner doesn't mean Staci doesn't mean anything to me. It means I'm a little underdeveloped and I have to substitute something physical like sex for everything I really want.]

Staci's smile grows. "Really?"

She kisses me again and pulls me down on top of her. I break from her lips and move slowly around to her ear, and Krist, even her ears are perfect! And she's not wearing earrings. She must have planned this. We are going to do it. She knows it, too. I slide my hand slowly inside her sweatshirt. Her stomach is hot. I cautiously move my hand to the clasp of her bra—I don't want to push her too far—but she doesn't stop me. Fuck, look at this girl, she's incredible! How was she ever in love with me? I should be on my knees begging her to even look—

Staci pulls away gently and looks into my eyes. "You have soft lips," she whispers.

I'm not sure how to respond to that one. I have limited experience fielding compliments about the texture of my facial anatomy. Instead of words—because words can be so stumbling and pedestrian and unintimate, and because I have none—I roll onto my back.

Staci doesn't wait for an invitation. She rolls on top of me and moves her lips slowly to my ear. "I wanna fuck you."

□   □   □

K shakes his head at me and laughs. "You set the alarm for A.M. instead of P.M., didn't you?"

I nod. "Woke up at 4:00 A.M. and fucking freaked out."

I am stupid. After dropping Staci off at dawn, I agreed to pick her up again that night. I had a competition in Monterey the morning after, and knowing sleep was not on that night's activity list, I wisely caught up on a little rest before I was due to meet Staci. My alarm-setting skills, however, prevented this strategy from being completely successful.

"Did you call her?" K asks me.

"At 4:00 A.M.? I couldn't," I shrug. "And I had to leave for Monterey at 6:00. I tried calling her all day from payphones, but she never answered."

"So…"

"So I don't know," I shrug again. "She probably thinks I stood her up and hates my guts."

I throw a bike up into my stand and look over the work order. I've started helping K with repairs now that spring has brought a surge of new business to the shop. He gives me anything he doesn't "have time to do," and I spend my remaining workday building new bikes as usual, constantly breaking previous speed and volume records, which sometimes results in less than satisfactory assembly quality. But that's why we check out purchased bikes before they leave the shop.

"I hate that little bitch," K says, redirecting our discussion to our friend Paul.

"You didn't miss much," I shrug. "I was fucking up so bad."

Paul declared last week he would absolutely not be appearing for work on Sunday even if he weren't granted the day off for the races as requested. That left the ever-loyal employee K stuck covering for him and unable to accompany me to Monterey.

"He's still a fucker," K says.

Paul was hired a few months ago. We do not like Paul. He's a year older than I am, an exemplary moral Christian brat who should be hit in the face at least once a day. In an effort to reinforce our verbal abuse of him, K and I sneak into the repair yard and fuck with his bike whenever possible: loosen his derailleur cables so he has to ride home in the lowest gear, extract the valve cores so his tires are completely flat, remove important components and hide them, anything we can think of that won't actually kill him.

K looks out the service window into the front of the shop. There's a customer waiting at the counter. I guess customers see counters as logical places to wait for help.

"Paul!" K yells. "Front!"

Paul steps around the corner in his typically indolent fashion and stops at our benches. "It's not my turn."

K looks at him. "Excuse you?"

"It's not my turn," Paul repeats.

"Your turn? This isn't kindergarten."

"I went out last time."

K stares at Paul. Finally he surrenders and shuffles out onto the sales floor even though it's not his turn.

"What a little fucker," K says, shaking his head.

"Seriously," I nod, because he seriously is a little fucker.

Paul reappears after ringing up the customer and walks to K's bench. "What's your problem?"

"What?"

"What's your problem?"

K doesn't even look up from the wheel he's truing. "You're my fucking problem."

Paul is silent. "You wanna take it outside?"

I freeze and wait for K to kill him.

K finally looks up from the wheel. "What'd you just say?"

Paul steadies himself unsteadily. "You wanna take it outside?"

K stares at him for a moment and explodes into laughter. There's nothing more humiliating than having your best threat laughed at like a joke. Paul's not sure what to do. Dropping his eyes, he skulks back to his bench without another word. I resume breathing and laugh.

"So what happened, anyway?" K asks me.

"What?"

"At the race."

"Don't know," I shrug. "Couldn't concentrate. My balance was fucked."

"That Staci girl is fucking you up," he says.

"I know. And she won't call me back." I shrug. "I bought her flowers yesterday and went down to her school to try and find her, but I couldn't."

"What'd you do with the flowers?"

"I disposed of them in the most convenient manner."

"What the fuck does that mean?"

"I threw em out the window."

I cut the corroded brake cables and pull off all the housing to replace it. It's been three days since I've seen Staci and I still can't get ahold of her. I know she's gotten my pages, but she won't call me because I'm an asshole.

"You know what, man?" K says. "Fuck her."

"Yeah…" I agree reluctantly.

"Fuck her."

□ □ □

I stare at the notebook on the bed in front of me. I should be working on some history assignment that will affect my grade, which will affect my

GPA, which will affect my graduation status, which will affect my options for higher education, which will have a permanent impact on my future. I'm talking to Kala on the phone instead. I'll worry about my future when it gets here.

"So how's Laina?"

Kala is silent. "Fine... Why..."

"Just wondering." What I actually mean is that I can't get Laina out of my head and I miss her and I want to talk about her because I can't talk to her. But I can't tell Kala that.

"I miss her." OK, I guess I can tell Kala that.

"What?"

"I miss her. I think about her all the time."

"Greg..."

"I know, I fucked up and she hates me."

"She doesn't hate you," Kala says, "she's just hurt."

"I should call her."

"And say what?"

"I don't know. Try to apologize."

"Mm."

"You don't think it's a good idea?"

"Well, what do you want to happen?"

"I don't know."

"Do you wanna get back together with her?"

"No. Well, yeah. I don't know." I look back down at the paper in front of me. I've drawn out Laina's name and I'm carefully shading the block letters. I wonder if I have a learning disorder.

"Oh, guess what?" Kala asks excitedly, wisely changing the subject. "Remember Val?"

"Yeah..."

"Well I've been talking to her a lot this year."

"So?"

"So remember how she was so in love with you in junior high?"

"I guess..."

"Well she still is."

She must have some kind of chemical imbalance.

"She's really cool, Greg, you should call her."

"Yeah. Maybe."

. . .

I called Val like Kala suggested. I guess I've exhausted my other options and need a warm female body to occupy the current void in my romantic fantasies. I'm not completely comfortable with a girl who thinks she's in love with me. But I'm here with her anyway, walking up a steep dead-end road to a bare hill above downtown Los Altos one of my old girlfriends use to call Cuffs for reasons I've never been able to figure out. I spread a blanket out over the dry grass and we sit together, gazing out over the flickering sea of lights wrapping around the black curve of the bay. I don't even know what I'm doing here with Val. I'm thinking about Laina. I called her the other night despite Kala's discouragement:

"Laina?"

"Yeah."

"It's Greg."

Silence.

"Look, I know this is out of the blue, but I just wanted to tell you I'm sorry."

"OK."

"I know it doesn't change anything, and I don't expect you to really care, but I'm sorry."

"OK."

That was it. She said three words. Only two after she knew it was me. Only one word, really. And not even a real word. I guess I expected her to break down in tears and tell me how much she misses me and how much she wants to try again or something. I'm a little delusional at times.

Val kisses me and pulls me down on top of her. I guess it's time for this. I miss Laina. I miss Staci. But I'm here with Val. I should be thinking about Val. I shouldn't be here with Val. She doesn't mean anything to me. I've tried to tell myself she does, but I know I'm lying. I'm just using her feelings to fill in the empty spaces where mine should be.

Val pulls away slightly and looks up at me. "What're you thinking right now?"

Val likes this question. I don't.

"I don't know."

"You don't know?"

"Too many things to understand," I shrug. I've found this is always a safe answer. Its vagueness allows for endless interpretations. Right now Val believes I'm thinking of some romantic fantasy involving her. I don't want to talk. I don't want to think. I want to have sex with her and never see her again. I don't want anything. I don't want this. I want to fall in love with her.

I kiss Val again, trying to ignore the distracting noise in my head. I get her bra off. I wish I could talk to Staci and explain everything. I don't want her to hate me. Maybe I should just let it go. I work my hand down Val's stomach and trace the edge of her pants, slipping my fingers in slowly. Maybe I shouldn't have called Laina like that. I don't know what I expected her to say. I feel the coarse upper edge of hair and Val gently stops my hand.

"It's too cold," she whispers.

"Sorry." I lie back and look up into the sky. Most of the stars are drowned out by the ambient light from the cities below. Val's hand runs up and down my chest as she nestles her face into my neck.

"What're you thinking right now?" I ask her. It's my turn.

Val is quiet. "It's... It's not for now."

"It's not for now?"

"Uh-uh," she says shyly. "Some other time."

I shrug.

Val giggles quietly and kisses my neck. "If I get my mom to go outta town this weekend, would you come stay with me?"

Let's see: I can't even make myself think about her when my hand is in her pants, I don't like talking to her that much, I'm really not at all interested in getting involved with her, and what I really want is to get back together with Laina.

"Sure."

□    □    □

I look up at Val's apartment from the Bullet. I shouldn't be here. But I am. I said I'd be here, and here I am. I shake my head slightly and head up the stairs to Val's place. I could just leave and not call her. She'd get over it. No, I can't. I don't want to hurt her. I just don't want to see her. I knock on the door and turn to face the street, wondering if I could run away before she answers.

The door swings open and Val smiles at me the way Val smiles when she's nervous. "Hey. Come on in."

I come on in and follow Val to her bedroom. She closes and locks the door behind her.

"Just in case my mom comes home," she explains.

I sit down on Val's couch and look around the room. It looks a little like mine, but more MTV pop culture than drug abuse.

Val sits down next to me. "Have you seen *The Shining*?"

"Uh-uh."

Val is shocked. I guess I'm supposed to have seen *The Shining*. "You wanna watch it?"

"OK." Now I will have seen *The Shining*.

Val pushes the video in and walks back to the couch, climbing up onto the back and straddling me to massage my shoulders. Maybe if I close my eyes and concentrate, I can pretend Val is really Laina. But they don't feel the same. They don't smell the same. Laina's hair is softer and smoother and her lips are fuller, her—

Val gets tired of massaging and slips down onto the couch with me. I spend the rest of the movie thinking about whether or not I really want to have sex with her. Within thirty seconds I've compiled a list of every negative trait she possesses. Each time I stumble across something positive, I immediately compare her to Laina or Staci and the quality quickly fades in contrast.

The movie ends and Val looks at me with the well-the-movie's-over-so-I-guess-we-should-have-sex-now smile. She gets up and turns off the TV, grabbing my hand and pulling me from the couch to her bed. I do not want to be here. I lie back and Val is on me, all over me. I guess it's a little late to get out of it now. She starts making her way down my neck with her lips, inching her knees lower. Val's fingers find my belt and fumble with the buckle—OK, it's a belt buckle. I reach down and undo it for her. I might as well help. Val figures out how the zipper on my jeans works and I lift my hips enough for her to tug the drawers down. I can feel the heat from her mouth.

Val pauses and glances up at me. "Remember the other night when you asked me what I was thinking and I said it wasn't for now?"

Less talk, more work.

Val grins. "This is what I was thinking."

. . .

I wake up to a magazine picture of some corny boy-model MTV VJ on the wall in front of my face and feel a hand on my waist. Where the fuck—

Val's.

I look over at her. She's still asleep. Shit. I'm even on the wrong side of the bed, up against the wall, so I can't just slip out and take off. Where are my pants? On the floor. Shirt? Over there. OK. I know where all my gear is so I can make a quick escape. I check the clock behind Val's head. I don't have to be at work for another hour, and I'm only about five minutes away, but—

Val stirs and slowly opens her eyes. "Hey," she whispers. "How long've you been awake?"

"A few minutes," I shrug. "I gotta go."

Val looks at the clock. "Already?"

"Yeah, I gotta be at work early."

She protests by wrapping her arm around my waist.

"I gotta go," I tell her again, sitting up.

Val pouts silently while I crawl over her and pull on my jeans. Propping herself up on one elbow, she watches me dress. I slip on my shoes, find my wallet—how the fuck did my wallet get under the couch—and stand up again. I guess I should at least kiss her goodbye. I wonder if a handshake would be sufficient. *Nice working with you. Push it up there, buddy.* I guess that probably won't cut it.

"OK," I say, glancing uncomfortably around the room like I'm worried I'm forgetting something even though I didn't bring anything to forget. "I'll see you later."

I kiss her quickly and head for the door.

"OK," she says quietly. "Call me."

"Yeah."

I'm a liar.

□   □   □

I look down the street as Bryan turns the corner. "I've been here before!"

Bryan glances at me like I'm retarded. "What?"

"I've been to this house before!" I tell him. "With Kodi, there was a

SCREAMING AT A WALL | 69

party here!"

Bryan's not impressed. I think it's great.

We park in the driveway and I follow Bryan inside. He knows the guy who lives here. I imagine I've met him because I've been here before, but my increasingly deficient memory doesn't provide assistance for such trivia. Kala is standing in the kitchen and smiles when she sees me. Seeing me makes people smile.

"Hey!" she says.

"Hey back."

The guy comes around the corner and Bryan shakes his hand.

"Greg, this is Avery," Bryan says.

I shake the guy named Avery's hand. "What's up."

He looks at me. "Have I met you before?"

"Maybe. I think I was here a while ago at some party. Do you have an empty oil barrel in your backyard?"

"Yeah!"

"Yeah, that was me and my friend rolling around in it!"

"Oh shit, I remember you!" he laughs. "You guys were so fucking trashed!"

The three of us follow him upstairs to his room. We dust a few bowls and I think about the envelope of coke in my sock. I need to hit the bathroom and pull a few lines, but I'm rapidly exhausting my supply of excuses for frequent and lengthy bathroom trips, so I go downstairs to get some water instead. Bryan and Kala follow.

I finish my water and set the glass in the sink.

"Does anyone wanna go for a walk or something?" Kala asks.

"Yeah," I shrug, because I really need to distract myself from the blow in my sock.

Bryan looks at me and grins. I don't get it.

"I'll be right back," Kala tells me and runs upstairs.

I turn to Bryan. "What're you smiling about, dickface?"

"You know she's still way into you, right?"

"Who?"

"Kala, you fucking stoner."

Kala appears again and I follow her to the door, glancing back at Bryan. He just winks at me.

We're alone on the street. I watch Kala walking barefoot, the frayed legs of her jeans dragging on the pavement. It's kind of sexy for some reason. If she's so into me, why did she hook me up with Val?

"So what happened with you and Val?" she asks.

That doesn't mean anything.

"Nothing. Haven't talked to her in a long time."

"You just didn't call her, huh?"

"Yeah."

"Greg…"

"I know, I'm a dick."

"You're developing a pattern," she says.

"I know."

"So there's nothing going on with you two?"

That might mean something.

"Uh-uh."

"Mm."

Does that mean something?

"So you still think about Laina a lot?" she asks.

This is a tough one. I still think about Laina. I still miss her. But do I want to tell Kala? I look at her. Would I want to be her boyfriend again? She is pretty cute, and she is a lot of fun, and I do know her really well, but maybe we've come too far to go back to the girlfriend-boyfriend configuration we never fully explored. Could I have sex with her without a relationship? Maybe. But there are already enough people who think I'm an asshole because I've been an asshole. Was her ass always that nice? Bottom line: I'm interested, but not convinced. I need to keep the option open with a response to her question that simultaneously lets her believe there's a chance I'm into her, but in no way commits me to anything.

"I guess. I don't know. Not really."

Good one.

I don't know how we got here, but we're at the little park on Fremont Ave that has those weird pastel cement thumbs sticking up out of the grass by the playground. I look at the thumbs in the dim light from the street and wonder whose idea they were and what illicit chemical substance that person was under the influence of at the time of artistic inspiration.

"So are you coming back to school this year?" Kala asks me.

I look at her in the dark and kick a rock into the grass. "Yeah."

"Good," she says. "You just kinda disappeared."

"Yeah, but it's gonna be weird going back," I tell her. "I think I'm gonna feel really out of place."

"Why, you're friends with everyone."

"Yeah, I guess, but I don't really talk to any of them anymore."

"So start again."

"I don't know if I really want to."

Kala looks at me. "Why not?"

"I don't know," I shrug. "I'm just sick of the whole scene. I think that's kinda why I left last year."

"What scene?"

"You know, all the partying and the drugs and the drinking and shit."

"What, are you gonna quit?"

"I kinda want to."

Kala stares at me for a second and erupts into laughter.

"Yeah, I know," I nod.

She bites her lip and punches me in the side. "We should probably go."

Kala continues her intermittent bursts of laughter as we walk to her car and drive back to her place. I guess I'm funny. I follow her into her room and she sits in the big chair in the corner.

"Where's God?" she asks me, looking around the room.

I find the TV remote and hand it to her. Instead of sitting on the couch, I sit down on the floor in front of Kala and lean back against her legs. I'm not sure why I'm doing this. After staring at the television without actually watching it for a while, I suddenly realize Kala is twirling a piece of my hair around her finger.

"I'm so glad you're growing your hair out again," she says softly.

I turn slightly to look up at her. She has a dreamy look in her eyes, raptly watching her fingers in my hair. I don't know what to do. Should I kiss her? No. Yes. Do I want to? Yes. No. I don't know what I want. I know she wants me to. She's not being subtle. But I can't. Look at her, she's beautiful, look at the way she's looking at me. I should kiss her. I want to kiss her. Do I want to kiss her?

"I should go."

CHAPTER FOUR

And here I am again. Real school.

Fuck.

I look around the room. We've graduated from prison deskchairs and stained plywood walls and have been relocated temporarily to a portable building in the back parking lot of the school while our former classroom is being remodeled. Prison deskchairs and painted foam walls.

"Hey Greg," Julie smiles.

"Hey back."

For the last few weeks, Julie's been invariably gravitating to the desk next to mine without explanation. Julie has replaced the absent Brandi as the most beautiful girl in the universe. I don't know why she's been so flirtatious recently, but I don't really care as long as she pays attention to me and lets me delude myself into believing there's a possibility we may have sex at some unspecified point in the near future. Unfortunately she has a boyfriend at another school who I've been told is a great deal larger than I am. I watch my step.

"I really love it," Julie tells me, rolling the necklace I gave her last week between her fingers. I don't watch my step that closely.

Enter teacher. Actually, let's get this straight. Ms. Lake is a student teacher from Stanford, but our real teacher has clearly decided her student is fully qualified because we don't see her more than five minutes a day, during which time she does nothing that could be mistaken for monitoring or evaluating her student. Ms. Lake is young and passionate and not yet jaded by the everyday mundane toil and utter lack of recognition and appreciation teaching provides. And I can see I've become her special project this year. Her Stanford education doesn't make her any less transparent than anyone else.

From my behavior in the two hundred fifty minutes a week she sees me, Ms. Lake has made a fully conclusive assessment of my entire life. I'm connected with all the most popular groups, yet still a sort of outsider, most likely by choice, because of a lack of interest in these friends who do not satisfy my elevated expectations and intellectual capacity and emotional maturity. I'm distant and quiet and always seem depressed. Perhaps I'm from a broken home and Mom and Dad don't give me hugs when I need hugs. Maybe I have a chemical imbalance that requires medication. Or perhaps because of my poor body image and resulting low self-esteem, I'm just very shy and self-conscious.

The reason is incidental, really. What matters is that in her classroom I seem removed, dislocated, depressed. She knows I'm wise beyond my years, an underachiever only because I'm not being challenged by conventional pedagogy, a bright young man who's lost his way and is in desperate need of inspiration. She feels I have no one with whom to connect, no one with whom to share my feelings and thoughts, my hopes and dreams, my fears and failures. I'm afraid of exposing the sensitive, understanding, passionate, intellectual young man I keep hidden within myself.

And she's going to fix me.

I was right when I told Kala I'd feel out of place coming back to school. In the year I was gone, everything changed. People have different friends, different lives, and different hairstyles and outfits to match. My drug use and drinking of stale urine are no longer distinguishing characteristics. Even the most well dressed and makeup-ed girls drink urine now. They just call it Keystone Light. I'm not sure where I fit into the picture anymore. I'm not sure I want to fit in at all. The clothing fashions may have shifted, but we're all still reading the same basic cable television movie script. I avoid contact as much as I can with everyone but Kala. She's the only one I can talk to anymore. It would appear from casual observation that I still have a lot of other friends, but I find myself struggling with a relentless feeling of discomfort in their presence. I don't know how to function with them anymore. This is why I don't talk in class, why I stare at the wall and try to ignore the noise. I might even be willing to explain this to Ms. Lake if she were more direct.

"Greg," Ms. Lake says, "can you stay after a few minutes?"

What the fuck did I do?

"Yeah, sure."

I wait at my prison deskchair as everyone else files out of the room. Julie gives me her standard I'm-going-to-continue-to-make-you-think-I-want-to-have-sex-with-you-as-bad-as-you-want-to-have-sex-with-me-but-never-give-you-the-chance-because-owning-you-like-this-provides-me-far-more-pleasure-than-sex-with-you-ever-could smile as she leaves. Some guy straight out of a bad college band walks in and hugs Ms. Lake. Who is this guy and why am I here to see this grossness?

"Greg, this is my friend Andy," Ms. Lake says.

What the fuck is she doing?

I stand up slowly and shake College Band Andy's hand.

"Ms. Lake says you climb," he says.

Ms. Lake has apparently decided to find me a connection with the world through one of her sweater-wearing poetry-writing college friends to assure me I'm not all alone in my emotional struggles. I start to laugh, but my curiosity overpowers the urge.

"A little," I tell him. "Not much anymore."

I glance over at Ms. Lake and catch her observing me interact with this jack-off. She quickly drops her eyes and pretends to be looking through the papers on her desk. She must think she's so clever. Is this the kind of shit they teach at Stanford? I have to say something.

"Look, Ms. Lake, I know what this is."

She looks up at me innocently. "What?"

"I'm not retarded. It's pretty transparent."

College Band Andy's smile is fading rapidly along with Ms. Lake's.

"I don't—"

"Look, I appreciate it, but you really don't need to do this."

"I just—"

"I know, you just wanna help, but you have no idea what you're helping.

Just because I don't smile all day long doesn't mean I need a guy from a bad college band to come talk to me after class about rock climbing."

College Band Andy looks at me.

"No offense there, Andy."

Ms. Lake is struggling for words. "I didn't—"

"Right, I know," I interrupt. "Look, my next class is on the other side of the parking lot, so I better get moving." I hit the door and turn back to look at them. "Hey, maybe someday we can all hang out and jam."

□   □   □

I follow Kodi into the small laundry room off the kitchen and watch him unwrap a square of aluminum foil. Cutting the strip of acid with a pair of scissors, he takes one half and I take the other. Kodi's parents are out of town, and being the responsible young men we are, we're taking advantage of the opportunity and using drugs in the safety of his home.

Kodi calls Jimmy. "Hey. We just dropped."

We've coordinated our ingestion of acid with Jimmy's to ensure we'll peak together. This is the cornerstone of the team hallucinogen experience.

Kodi and I sit down at his kitchen table. He's found one of those metal disks that make trance-inducing rhythms of shifting hologram shapes as they spin. In combination with acid, this toy is remarkably dangerous, possessing an unrivaled ability to erase time in large increments. So far it's only been an hour for us.

"Do you hear that?" Kodi asks me without taking his eyes from the spinning disk.

"What."

"Those dogs."

I listen, still staring at the spinning shapes. I can hear three or four dogs barking and howling in the distance. It's a little unsettling. "Yeah, I hear em."

"Fuck, that's weird."

The front door opens and Kodi's girlfriend steps in, walking over to the table and saying something to him. He just nods and keeps watching the disk. I don't think he understands what she's saying either.

"Do you hear that?" Kodi asks me.

"What."

"Those dogs."

"Yeah, what the fuck."

Kodi's girlfriend stares at us. "That's on the CD, guys."

"What?"

"The dogs," she says. "They're on the CD that's playing right now."

I slowly put it together. We put in Pink Floyd's *Animals* a while ago. The song *Dogs* is playing right now. The barking dogs are in the song.

"That's weird," Kodi says. "I totally thought those were real dogs."

Jessica says something to Kodi again, but I can't listen and watch the spinning disk at the same time, so I ignore her. I think Kodi is doing the same. Finally she kisses Kodi quickly and leaves.

"What the hell was she talking about?" I ask him.

"I don't know," he shrugs.

We go back to the disk.

"Do you hear that?" Kodi asks me.

"What."

"Those dogs."

"Yeah."

"What the fuck, whose dogs are those?"

"Wait, maybe it's on the CD."

"Yeah, maybe."

I have to work tomorrow morning at the bike shop, and I know I'm not going to sleep tonight, but at least we're not out on the streets where we can get into any real trouble. After stumbling out of a laser show last week on a large amount of acid and too stoned to really talk, we found The Beast—recently inherited by Kodi from his brother—and didn't even make it across the street and all the way down the freeway on-ramp before we were pulled over. Highway Patrol officers approach vehicles on the passenger side to avoid being hit by passing cars on the freeway. I happened to be occupying the passenger seat with a duffel bag containing a large amount of assorted drugs and related paraphernalia, items generally not appreciated by law enforcement officers. I rolled down the window and stared straight ahead as the cop shined his flashlight in on us.

"License and registration."

Kodi handed him the paperwork over me. I kept my eyes diverted and staring through the windshield. My pupils were probably the size of nickels. When the cop returned, I quickly passed the paperwork to Kodi without turning my head.

"You guys been drinking tonight?" he asked.

"No sir." Full disclosure is for real estate agents.

He thought for a moment. "You know why I pulled you over?"

"No sir."

Dramatic pause. "You don't have your headlights on."

Shit.

Kodi looked at the dash. "Sir I just forgot you know the street's lit up so much right around here I couldn't even tell I'm so used to driving my mom's car she has those automatic headlights that turn themselves on you know I just totally forgot I wasn't even thinking about it it's just that I'm not used to this car my brother just gave it to me I haven't really even driven it that much I'm just used to my mom's car with the automatic headlights that come on by themselves when it gets dark."

I clenched my jaw and waited to be instructed to exit the vehicle with my hands in clear view. Kodi had just spit out the most nervous, incoherent, speed-induced monologue I'd ever heard. It was exceedingly obvious he was not capable of safely operating a motor vehicle.

"Tell you what," the cop said finally. "You turn your lights on right now and I'll let you off."

OK, maybe not exceedingly obvious to people who don't have the same extensive personal experience with illicit chemical substances we do. Kodi snapped the headlights on and we drove home to get clean underwear.

The front door opens and Jimmy bursts in wearing the ugliest tie-dyed shirt I've ever seen. "Dude, I'm already trippin nuts!" he yells.

"Yeah," Kodi and I say without looking up from the disk.

"What the hell're you guys staring at?" Jimmy walks over to the table and freezes when he sees the disk. And now he's stuck on it too.

Finally I break my stare and spin around so I can't see the disk. "Fuck, man, we've been sitting here for like six hours."

I stop the disk from spinning and Kodi and Jimmy slowly look up at me. The sound of yelling outside suddenly catches our attention and we all turn to see Jake let himself in, still yelling something I don't understand. I fucking hate this guy. He's pulled himself up from being that little shit in elementary school everyone picked on and put in trashcans by selling drugs. One of the most arrogant jerk-offs I've ever had the misfortune of knowing. I don't think he'll ever understand his friends are only in need of his connections. I refuse to buy from him. Even if it means I have to pay a little more or go a little farther, I will not do business with him.

"What's up!" Jake yells as he slaps Kodi and Jimmy's hands. He turns to me with his hand out. "What's up, man!"

I just stare at him. Jake laughs uncomfortably. I keep staring at him until he backs away and sits down at the kitchen table, opening his backpack and pulling out a rolled-up sock stuffed with about half an ounce of weed, followed by an electronic balance. This guy is fully mobile.

"What're we doing, an eighth?"

Kodi and Jimmy are at the table immediately like starving dogs scrambling into the kitchen at the sound of the cracking dog food can. It suddenly strikes me how pathetic we are. All the excuses and justifications are so transparent. It's embarrassing to realize the only way we can interact with each other anymore is while intoxicated, while speaking about being intoxicated, or while planning to get intoxicated.

Weighing out the eighth and bagging it, Jake stuffs the rest of his gear into his backpack and stands up. "I gotta go do some more business. You guys take it easy."

"All right, man," Kodi says, shaking his hand again.

I stare at the motherfucker until he leaves.

"Dude, you know what?" Jimmy says. "We should candyflip."

Candyflipping is taking acid and ecstasy together. Right now this seems like a good idea.

I smile. "I'll call Danny and get some caps."


I can't move. I'm not trying to move, but I think if I tried to move, I couldn't move. It seems like I can't move right now. I don't know how long I've been sinking into this couch. I think I've always been on this couch. Is this couch purple? I think it's purple. I'm sinking into this purple couch. Why is this couch purple? I've never been so comfortable in my life. This is better than sex, I think. Better than disappointing sex, at least. That sex where you finish and just look up at the ceiling and all you can think about is taking a shower and going to sleep and the physiological satisfaction suddenly doesn't seem worth it anymore because now you have this extra body in bed with you and you can't stretch out and sleep like you usually do, like you want to so badly, and you have to compress yourself into a tighter package and your bad shoulder starts aching so much and you can't lie still and you can't get comfortable and this other body wants to be pressed right up against you, but it's hot in the room and you're still overheated and sweating from the sex, which wasn't even good because she had no rhythm and she was bouncing all over the place and making an excessive amount of noise and corny moans and comments straight out of the low-budget pornographic films on which she obviously models her technique that turned you off so much you had to concentrate on an exceedingly obscene fantasy with another girl with a bigger ass just to maintain an adequate erection, and you just want to be alone, so you do your best to maintain a comfortable distance to cut down on the transfer of body heat without offending the owner of the other body too much. Holy shit I can see the blood pumping through the veins in my forearm.

Kodi drops his ass down on the purple couch next to me with the candyflipping grin on his face and shakes my hand. This is not an ordinary pump-it-once-and-pull-it-out handshake. Our fingers end up intertwined and twisted like temporarily homosexual lovers. Imagine cracking your knuckles and having an orgasm in your hand. It's like that.

"Dude, Jessica's coming over," Kodi tells me. "We're gonna fuck!"

"Don't do it, man."

"Why not?"

"Because, think about it," I shrug. "You fuck like this and sex'll never be any good again. It'll never compare to this."

"Dude, I gotta do it once."

"You're gonna regret it, man."

"No way."

"Besides, you're gonna hurt yourself when you come."

"Dude, I don't care," Kodi says defiantly. "I'll die coming."

"OK, man, don't say I didn't warn you when you can't ever get a boner again."

□     □     □

The chronic absence of Kala's otherwise indifferent parents has made her house the center of our social world, the vast majority of our time outside of school and work being spent on her back porch in green plastic chairs that we've discovered break surprisingly easily upon landing after being launched forty feet into the air. I've never been sure whether Kala encourages this particular view of her home or simply accepts it. The same maternal instincts that inspire her to scold me for doing stupid things to myself also compel her to ensure none of us strain ourselves with unnecessary domestic responsibilities like picking up our bottle caps and cigarette butts. She seems to be in a perpetual state of cleaning and fixing and making sandwiches motion. The nature of her living situation and her own personality have pushed her to the apex of our social structure, making it possible for me to communicate with her almost exclusively without noticeably altering the apparent nature of my relationships with anyone else. It's rather convenient.

"Come hang out," Kala says when I answer the phone. "My parents are in Boston and we're all shrooming."

"I don't wanna trip," I tell her.

"So dri—"

"I don't want to."

"Then at least come smo—"

"No."

After reaching a new level of disgust with myself last month smoking weed at 5:00 in the morning on Kodi's porch with that shithead Jake, I finally decided to quit. Weed makes me slow and lazy and stupid and fat and tired and more like that guy than I'm willing to be. I'm done with it. If I'm going to spend money on drugs, I'm going to be a smart investor. No more of this lightweight hippie shit. I'm going huge. No more beer. I'm only drinking whiskey, straight from the bottle, and I'm going to drink it until I lose consciousness and only stop then because I haven't yet learned how to drink when I'm unconscious. And no more weed. I'm going to yank endless lines of blow until my nose freezes and bleeds and gets so congested I can't breathe and my throat is so numb I can't swallow and my hands are shaking too much to cut any more lines. If I'm going to kill myself, I'm not going to fuck around.

"Fine," Kala surrenders. "Just come hang out with us."

"I'll be there in a while."

I hang up the phone and look around my room for my eighties shoes. I'm reluctant to go to Kala's. Evidence would suggest I'm not exactly a model of self-control. I find my shoes and head out to the scratched-up 1987 Honda Prelude I just bought for some inexplicable reason. It's exceedingly impractical. But I guess it beats the silver four-cylinder 1986 Volvo station wagon with blue vinyl interior it replaced. I park on the street in front of Kala's house and walk through the door.

"Greg!" Shannon is on me before I'm even all the way inside. He can't stand up straight, so suddenly all six-feet four-inches of him are hanging on me. Maybe a little more intimately than usual.

"You E-ing?" I ask him.

Shannon laughs and glances around cautiously like it's a secret. "I'm E-ing balls!" he whispers.

Ecstasy is not one for the homophobes. The straightest of guys will be all over each other, hugging and rubbing and shaking hands for entirely too long, anything that proves sensually satisfying, which is everything with enough ecstasy. It can make those who are a little insecure in their own sexuality uncomfortable. I don't really mind. I'm just uncomfortable because he's heavy and presently using me as a crutch.

"OK, man, let's go back here," I tell Shannon, half-leading and half-carrying him back to Kala's room. Dumping him in the big chair in the corner, I walk out onto the deck and sit down in one of the green plastic chairs that hasn't been broken yet.

Kala sees me and jumps into my lap. "You came!"

"I said I was coming."

"Yeah, but it's you," she reminds me. "Are you sure you're not doing anything tonight?"

"Yeah."

Kala makes an exceedingly dramatic frown to express her disappointment in me, then lights up suddenly with a brilliant idea. "Gimme a back massage!" she says.

Demonstrating my pathological inability to deny an attractive girl anything not requiring irreparable self-mutilation, I obediently rotate Kala on my lap and begin massaging. Mike walks out from Kala's room and stands in front of the door, staring at us silently. Mike is one of those bruisers who fixes cars and beats people up. Like he told me once, "He threw my backpack, so I punched him in the face."

"What's your problem?" I ask him.

"I'm trippin nuts!"

I don't think Mike has ever done anything but drink and smoke weed like most bruisers, who may be tough on the football field and thoroughly capable of beating the shit out of guys like me, but are complete pussies when it comes to fucking up their brains with real drugs.

"I wanna go to a rave," Mike says, making a repetitive bass beat and moving his hips to the rhythm with his hands still jammed in his pockets, because he wants to go to a rave and this is what a rave would be like. The beat is obnoxious, but at least he's not punching anyone in the face.

"Mike," I say finally.

Mike looks at me, still raving.

"Stop."

"Sorry." Mike walks back inside to rave.

My massage slowly tapers off and Kala spins in my lap so she's sitting across my legs and leaning back against the wall to my side, her hand curled lightly around the back of my neck. I feel a drop on my arm and look up into the black sky where I assume it came from.

"It's raining," Kala explains.

Crushing out his cigarette, Jason expresses his displeasure with a string of profanities and leads everyone inside. Kala and I stay, tucked up under the short overhang of the roof. The rain begins falling harder. It's silent and dark except for the tiny white lights strung up around the edge of the roof above us, now glittering with water. I smell the rain. The wet dirt, the wet grass, the wet wood. Kala's jeans are soaked and cold under my hand. I glance down at her. She has that dreamy look in her eyes again. I guess it could just be the mushrooms. I turn back and stare across the small yard at the fence, the rainwater seeping down unevenly through the wood. Kala's hand moves from the back of my neck to my ear, slowly tracing the ridges. Should I kiss her? I should kiss her.

I look down at Kala. "We should go inside."

□   □   □

I smile and wave to Ms. Lake as Julie and I exit the classroom. Let her think she fixed me. At least I won't have to shake the sweaty hands of any more college band members. I don't even want to think of where those things have been. College band members don't get many dates.

Julie and I have been spending a little more time together than I imagine her boyfriend would like. He would appreciate even less the fact that our conversations consist almost exclusively of flirtatious reminiscing and Julie's continual complaints about him and the way he treats her.

"I went on the pill for his birthday, and he never even thanked me," she tells me.

Most people say the dog is man's best friend, but most people are stupid. The pill is man's best friend. And having your inconceivably gorgeous girlfriend go on birth control so you don't have to wear a rubber glove when you have sex with her is probably the greatest gift I can imagine, maybe second only to the gift of her virginity, which I'm actually not entirely convinced is a gift since it may be the most uncomfortable event a girl ever experiences next to childbirth, and I don't particularly wish to be associated with discomfort.

Julie and I leave the sunlight and walk into a dark hallway in the 500 wing, stopping in front of our neighboring classrooms for our routine parting conversation.

"So how's your boy?" I ask her, hoping she'll tell me he died or left the country or is in some other way no longer relevant to the situation.

"Fine, I guess," she says. "He just pisses me off sometimes."

"Well, you know, if you ever wanna have sex or anything, just gimme a call," I shrug.

"OK," Julie laughs. "I will."

I lean back against the pillow in the corner of my room and glance around dully. I come home during my lunch break from school instead of going out with everyone. It's just one more meager and thoroughly ineffective attempt at maintaining my righteous independence. But now I'm bored and have another half an hour before my next class.

Logical solution: Drugs.

I dig through the drawer against the wall and pull out the little tin box to which I've assigned the duty of storing all things inappropriate and illicit, provided of course they're small enough to fit in a little tin box. Pulling out what's left of a half-ounce of blow, I shake a pile out onto a CD case and look at it. Then I shake out a little more. With a flat side of my ATM card, I smash the little clumps of coke, careful not to send any of it flying onto the floor. The bigger pieces broken, I use the edge of the card to cut it into finer and finer powder, routinely scraping the spreading particles back together into a tighter pile to be cut again. Satisfied with the consistency, I slide the card through part of the pile and draw it into a couple thick lines.

Rolling a small piece of paper into a tube, I lean over and snort each line with a different nostril to balance the damage, straightening up again to sniff any lingering powder as high as I can. It tastes like stinging mint in the back of my throat. I dust the rest and scrape the scattered remnants into a pile, sticking the powder to my finger and wiping it on my lower gums. They immediately begin to tingle and slowly numb.

The effects of coke for me have become almost non-existent. Initially, a quarter gram made me feel like God for a couple minutes. That lasted about as long as my first gram did. I pull thicker and thicker lines now, more at a time, more frequently, but I can't get that God feeling anymore. I tell myself I need to stop for a while so my body can readjust, stay clean all week and then go huge on the weekend, but suddenly my weekend ends on Tuesday and starts again on Thursday and I still don't feel like God. So I maintain a continual stream of cocaine into my nose. When I can't breathe anymore and the nasal decongestant won't decongest anymore, I roll cigarettes full of coke or break out the aluminum foil and smoke it straight.

I'm not addicted. I'm dedicated.

No one knows I do this. It's something I've always done alone, off a smooth bathroom counter, off a CD case on my bed, off whatever I've had at my disposal when I've felt the brilliant flash of narcotic inspiration, which has become more of a steady starving glow. I don't know why, but I go to great lengths to keep it a secret. I guess I'm ashamed. I guess I'm afraid to admit I've lost control.

I sit back and my nose begins running immediately. I sniff it up. I don't want to blow my nose because I don't want it to bleed, and more importantly, I don't want to eject any cocaine before it's fully absorbed. I sniff again and check the clock. The problem with cocaine is that it never gets you high enough, it never lasts long enough, and you come down hard. You crash into the worst depression you can imagine and nothing can distract you from that hunger, that need for more, that aching knowledge that the only thing that will ever relieve your pain is more coke. I don't want to be sitting in class with hundred-pound cocaine eyeballs contemplating suicide.

So I need some more drugs.

Ecstasy would be my first choice. Its external effects are minimal and relatively easily concealed in public, and what a profound metaphor in combination with something as unendurably heinous as school.

But I don't have any ecstasy. I'll have to settle for acid.

I tear off a single gel tab and drop it under my tongue. I don't want to take too much. The last thing I need is to try to explain my behavior to one of our security guards when I freak out. Within twenty minutes I can feel the effects. Vibrating with the restless energy, I walk back across the street onto the campus. Kala sees me in the quad and cuts me off in the middle of the grassy corner.

"Hey," she says.

I look at her and smile. I can't stop smiling.

Kala watches me. "What's wrong with you?"

"Nothing."

"Greg..."

"What?"

"What'd you do?"

I shrug.

"You're on acid again, aren't you?"

"Yeah."

"How much did you take?"

"Just a little."

Kala shakes her head at me. "You're pushing your luck."

"Totally."

I walk into the classroom and sit down quickly in my prison deskchair. I have to be cool. I can't be doing anything stupid and obvious. I glance down at my foot. It's tapping nervously on the floor tile. I stop it and try to sit still. I can't. My foot is tapping again and my hands are finding itches everywhere. I strain to concentrate and control myself, but it's impossible. This must be how Tom Arnold feels. The bell rings and this guy I think I know comes sprinting into the room, sliding across the dusty floor and into the desk next to me.

"Hey man," he says.

I stare at him. I know I know this guy. I know I talk to him all the time. He gave me some pills last week. I still don't know what they were. I took them anyway. He's always chewing on his fingernails. He's chewing on them right now. I know I know this guy. But who the fuck is he?

He looks at me like Kala looked at me. "What's your problem?"

I try not to laugh. Then I laugh. He knows exactly what's going on. He leans back in his chair and starts laughing too.

"Hey," our teacher says. "Quiet."

I glance up at her, not at all surprised that her stare has managed to single me out from the two equally culpable parties. I don't think she likes me. She actually threw a pen at me once.

The guy keeps laughing quietly. "Sorry Mrs. C, Greg just told me something funny. You know what a jokester he is."

"Well get with the program," Mrs. Caulin snaps.

"OK," he nods soberly. "Go Team USA."

Leaning forward in my desk and clamping my hands together, I struggle desperately not to laugh, clenching my jaw and looking down at my lap to try to get myself under control.

My pants are really funny.

The repressed laughter explodes from my chest and the guy makes it worse by laughing with me. I glance up at Mrs. Caulin. She's glaring down at us with her fists on her hips, apparently not enjoying this as much as we are. I try to ignore her and look over my shoulder, but everyone behind me is laughing now, and their faces are even funnier than my pants.

Finally I manage to relax a little and the laughter slowly fades. I raise my eyes cautiously. Mrs. Caulin hasn't shifted from her pose. And now her mouth is moving. Is she speaking English? I glance at the guy for a little assistance. He just shrugs.

Slowly Mrs. Caulin steps to the other side of the room to the overhead projector, glancing back at me suspiciously before going on with whatever the fuck she's doing. My foot is tapping again. I stop it and push my ass back in the chair, leaning my forearms on the desk with my fingers intertwined tightly. I will sit still and stare at the floor. I will not laugh. I will not speak. I will not mo— Fuck, my foot. OK, I will not move. I will not draw attention to myself. The only reason I'm still here and not being interrogated by a security guard is that Mrs. Caulin is presently convincing herself that no one would be stupid enough to drop acid before class. She apparently doesn't know me very well.

□   □   □

I can smell weed from outside the apartment. Bryan fumbles with the knob and finally manages to open the door. I step into the place and I'm enveloped in the haze. Bryan returns to his chair in the corner and I sit on the couch next to him. He directs his attention to the small table at his side and I move to the edge of the couch and watch him weigh out chunks of hash for distribution.

"Check this shit out," Bryan says, handing me one of the little gram bags.

I inspect it under the lamp. I haven't smoked anything in what seems like forever. It probably hasn't been more than a couple months, but for a guy who's accustomed to smoking one to four times a day—before school, during school, after school, any time I had nothing better to do than get high, which was the majority of my typical day, or any time the better thing I had to do would be either enhanced or not severely adversely affected by being high, which was the majority of better things I had to do—a couple months is an eternity.

"You want a gram?" Bryan asks me, zipping another bag shut.

It's been a long time. I have no reason start again now. I hate weed. I think of a smoky room full of fat, sweaty, longhaired stoners who smell like feet and I feel ill. I don't ever want to smoke that weed bullshit again. But this isn't weed... exactly.

"Yeah." I pull a twenty from my back pocket and lay it on the table next to the scale.


I pull up in front of Kala's house and kill the engine. We've both apparently decided that night in the rain never actually happened. Defining the nature of our relationship has been problematic since our first attempts at junior high school romance. It seems wise to just back off and not push square pegs into round holes. I'm sure there will be other holes for me to push my peg into.

"I told Laina we'd come pick her up," Kala tells me when she opens the door.

"We?"

Laina and I still haven't really spoken since the night I called her and tried unsuccessfully to apologize. In the last year, she's been absorbed by this crew and is now Kala's closest friend, putting us in constant close proximity. But instead of perhaps taking advantage of the opportunity to attempt reconciliation, we've employed the skills we developed our freshman year to completely ignore each other.

"She's not gonna beat you up, Greg."

"Are you sure?"

"Shut up, come on."

I drive quietly. There's really nothing more I can do to repair the damage between Laina and me. I apologized the only way I knew how, and I know an apology is nothing more than a way to forgive yourself in front of someone else. I wrote her a letter last week trying to explain something I can't explain, but I never gave it to her because I don't think I should ask for forgiveness I don't deserve. I folded the letter up and tucked it into my phonebook.

Parking along the sidewalk below Laina's apartment, we see her appear from the dark and run across the street. Kala gets out to let her climb into the backseat and I pull away from the curb.

"I got some Coronas for you," Kala tells her, then turns to me. "Are you drinking with us tonight, loser?"

"I don't know," I shrug. I merge onto the freeway and glance in the rearview at Laina. She looks up and catches my eyes. I turn away.

Kala shifts in her seat and kicks my phonebook. "Clean up your damn car," she says, grabbing the phonebook and tossing it into the back seat.

"Sorry," I say, not sorry.

Laina grabs the phonebook and starts flipping through the pages. She's like me, always needing something to occupy her hands; except unlike me, I don't think she was ever likened to a rat by her eighth-grade Spanish teacher with fake bar fight teeth while methodically tearing away tiny pieces of her binder's cover during class like a crank addict silently immersed in an epic project.

"What's this?" Laina asks me, finding my letter and holding it up for me to see. I guess I'm giving it to her now.

"Uh. That's for you," I tell her.

She slides the letter into her pocket without saying anything.

The freeway widens into five lanes as it becomes Grant Road and I slow for the red light. Kala apparently believes this is the proper moment to flip on my car's hazard lights. Unfortunately, once depressed, my car's hazard lights button does not release. I yell a brief explanation of the situation through the open window to the concerned law enforcement officer alongside of us and glare at Kala as we pull away through the intersection.

"Sorry," she squints.

Kala continues to simultaneously apologize to me and insult my car until we finally pull up to her house. I pop the hood and pull fuses at random until the lights stop flashing.

"I'll work on the button later," I tell Kala, because I totally know what I'm doing.

Shannon is waiting for us when we walk into Kala's room. As usual, a collection of guests has arrived in her absence.

"Hot tub later," he smiles.

"Indeed," I say.

I walk out onto the deck and take my customary plastic chair in the corner. Jesse and Mike nod in acknowledgement of my presence and return to their pipe as Laina and Kala reappear with their beers.

"Remember that night we were all shrooming here?" Kala asks me, lighting a cigarette. "Like an hour after you left, we couldn't find Mike anywhere. So I come out here and his feet are over there sticking out from under the deck."

I glance at Mike. He just shrugs.

"He was lying on his face halfway under the deck!" Kala laughs. "I thought he was fucking dead!"

Mike grins vacantly. "I didn't even know where I was."

"Good one," I tell Mike, believing it was a good one.

I glance at Laina. She's sitting quietly in the far corner of the small deck sipping her Corona, staring off into space. There wasn't enough time for her to read the letter already. But I don't think she has to. I'm really not that hard to figure out. Laina slowly shifts her gaze and catches mine. I can't look away. There's a beautiful sadness in her dark brown eyes. A calm satisfaction with her life, a gentle acceptance of the truth. She always looks at peace within herself. The eye of the storm, untouched by the chaos in her life.

I drop my eyes slowly and my nervous hands find the hash in my jacket pocket— I have hash. I pull out the gear and surreptitiously place the sticky ball in the pipe. I'm not in a sharing mood. Dropping my head, I bring the small glass pipe to my lips and suck the flame of the lighter into the bowl. The smoke fills my lungs and I cup the pipe secretly in my hand, blowing a tight stream of smoke above me. I glance down at the hash. A few small trails of smoke trickle lazily from the glowing red center. It seems a shame to waste it. I cup my other hand around the pipe and pull it to my mouth like a harmonica, inhaling deeply, exhaling, breathing in again through the pipe. I don't need oxygen. I need this. The growing crowd of people on the deck and their noise fade slowly into the blurred background as I breathe the smoke rhythmically, the world slipping away until I forget everything but the warmth of the pipe in my hands and the smoke in my chest.

I open my eyes and raise my head slowly. Everything is thin and distant. I see their mouths moving, but the words are lost in the emptiness. Their movements are blurred and delayed like my own. I watch Shannon sit down next to me. It takes at least five minutes.

"What's your problem?" he asks me.

"Huh?"

Shannon nods at the pipe still cupped in my hands. "I thought you quit smoking bud."

"I did..."

"Then what's that?"

"Hash..."

"How much did you smoke?"

"A gram..."

Shannon laughs at me and shakes his head. "You are fucked up. You coming in the hot tub with us?"

"I can't get up..."

"All right, man, let me know when you're back on Earth."


I'm back on Earth. I guess. The initial weight of the hash has lifted and left me with a constant nervous trembling. Expecting to fall, I get up from my chair carefully and stagger through Kala's room into the kitchen where Shannon is digging through the refrigerator.

He spins around with a beer and sees me. "Hot tub!"

"Hot tub," I repeat obediently.

I stumble into the bathroom and find the pair of board shorts I leave over here for convenience. Pulling my shirt off, I catch myself in the mirror over the sink. I look like a junkie. Imagine that. Making sure the bathroom door is locked, I slip a neatly folded piece of paper from my wallet and open the little envelope carefully. I brush the counter clean with my palm and slowly shake out a pile of coke, staring at it in the fluorescent light. It almost glows. With ritualized precision, I cut it up patiently, lost in the familiar and comforting motions. I draw it into a series of thick lines and dust them one by one, trying to clear my deteriorating nasal passages in between.

After going through a second pile, I clean up my gear and continue sniffing while I splash water on my face and carefully wipe away the traces of powder in my nose. They'll never even know. Trying to catch my breath and force my uncontrollably shuddering heart to calm, I pull on my shorts and walk through the living room onto another deck. Kala and Jesse are already in the hot tub, beers in hand.

"I was starting to wonder about you," Kala says as I slip into the steaming water.

"Huh?" My nose is frozen and the back of my throat is numb from the coke. It makes it hard to swallow.

"I thought we lost you."

"Uh-uh." I sniff gently, hoping my nose won't start bleeding into the water.

I try unsuccessfully to not appear acutely concerned with the way Laina looks in her black bikini as she and Shannon walk around from the other side of the house. The two of them slide into the hot tub and Laina shifts into the corner across from me, leaning her head back on the edge. I haven't heard her say a word since she asked about the letter in the car. I don't know what to think. If she hates me, if she loves me, if she doesn't care. Or if she's quietly plotting my murder with zip-ties and obscure dental tools.

Jason wanders around from the other side of the house and sits on the edge of the hot tub. Jason is younger than the rest of us, a year or two maybe. I don't really know much about him. I can't even explain his presence. One day I just noticed him here. He has dark eyes that never fully open and a quick temper that gets him into a lot of trouble. And I think the kid has some kind of genetic propensity for drug use. His capacity is unbelievable. I've watched him drop three doses of vodka-cut acid without even noticing. Kala looks up and smiles sweetly at him. Something is going on with those two. I guess I don't really care. I've had my opportunities to try something again with her and I've never stepped up. I was probably just intrigued by the idea of having sex with her like I am with every other girl I meet.

I lift my hand from under the water and watch it trembling as the steam drifts from my skin. I just smoked a gram of hash. And then added half a gram of blow. Forty bucks for some more brain damage, the shakes, and the predictable maintenance of a reputation I never meant to create for myself. I drop my trembling hand back into the water and look up at Kala and Jason. There's definitely something going on with those two. I've seen that look in her eyes before.

Kala stands up and grabs a towel. "I'm getting too hot."

I look at Jason. He's wearing the that's-right-we're-going-to-go-do-it-now smile. Fucker. He stole that one from me. "That's mine!" I yell.

Shannon looks at me. "What?"

I point at Jason. "That's mine!"

Jason is looking a little uncomfortable. I guess I'd be uncomfortable too if there were a skinny white guy in a heated puddle of communal filth pointing and yelling at me for no apparent reason.

Shannon laughs and raises his beer to me. I flip him off.

Jason follows the dripping Kala into the house and closes the sliding glass door behind himself. I'm sure they dismissed my outburst as just another drug-induced lapse of mental stability. I'm well known for them.

"Fuck, man, I'm getting kinda hot too," Jesse says.

"Pussy."

Jesse disappears inside and I glance from Shannon to Laina. She still hasn't said a word. Just sat there in her corner silently drinking her beer and staring up into the sky. Shannon looks at me and indicates Laina with a subtle nod. I think he's asking me what our deal is. I shrug. I don't know what our deal is.

"Uh, I'm gonna go in," Shannon says finally, winking at me before Laina looks. I guess he thinks he's helping me out somehow by leaving me alone with Laina in a hot tub. He dries off quickly and slips inside.

Laina leans back and looks up into the sky again and I sink down in the water to rest the back of my head on the edge of the tub. The sky is framed by the black silhouettes of the young redwood trees around us, the white stars glittering in the emptiness. I drop my eyes and watch Laina closely. She's gazing up at the stars, moving her eyes slowly among the constellations, her hair tied up loosely, a few stray ends wet and dark.

I have no idea what time it is. The streets are dark and still, the backyard quiet. Everyone else must have stumbled inside to surrender consciousness to biomechanically incorrect positions with their nearly empty bottles balanced precariously on body parts not suitable for balancing bottles. I lift my hands from the water and stare at them in the dark. I'm not shaking anymore. I drop them again and glance at Laina. She's looking at me.

"We should probably go in," I say quietly.

"Yeah..."

I watch her as we dry off and follow her inside. She slips quietly around the corner and I step over an anonymous body into the bathroom with my clothes, squinting in the yellow light as I dress.

Clothed and chlorinated, I head for Kala's room and sit on the edge of her bed. The room is littered with bodies, most less than conscious. Kala looks up at me from the couch and starts waving.

"I'm gonna take off," I tell her.

"OK," she waves.

I get up and wave back at Kala before slipping into the dark hallway.

Laina steps out from the bathroom, pulling her hair back. "Are you leaving?"

"Yeah... You need a ride home?"

She nods and pokes her head into Kala's room to say her goodbyes. I open the front door and follow her to my car.

We drive in silence. Laina pulls the folded letter from her pocket and I watch her uncomfortably from the corner of my eye as she holds it at an angle to read it in the streetlights. Her face is expressionless. She finishes reading and carefully refolds the letter along the creases.

I turn onto Laina's street and glance at her. Her eyes just gaze through the window into the dark as I pull up alongside the curb and kill the engine. She doesn't move.

"I just don't understand what happened," she says finally. "You just disappeared."

"I don't know," I mumble. "I guess I just didn't have my shit together back then."

Laina looks up at me slowly. "Do you have your shit together now?"

I don't even know what shit we're talking about let alone have it together, the reason I chose the word shit instead of explicitly defining whatever shit is. "I think so," I shrug.

Laina opens the door slowly and looks back at me. "Walk me up?"

In front of her door, Laina turns to face me and looks into my eyes with that familiar peacefulness. I step forward slowly and kiss her, feeling her hands on my shoulders, her fingers curling around my neck.

"Does this mean we're gonna try again?" I ask her.

"Yeah," she says quietly, smiling for the first time all night and leaning her head against my chest.

□　□　□

Laina and I walk across the dark soccer fields to the other side of the park and sit together on a wooden bench under twin redwoods. We're sick of all the noise and the chaos, of all the bodies and the spills, all the smoke and the stale beer breath. This is the only way we can really be alone. It's been a few weeks and things seem to be working out with us. Maybe I do have my shit together. Or maybe it's only been a few weeks.

Laina leans against my shoulder and I wrap my arm around her, slipping her long hair behind her ear with my other hand. This is perfect. Sitting here with Laina in the dark, alone and quiet, running my fingers through her hair and smelling her skin. It's all I really want. Aside from frequent oral sex.

"Remember that night in the hot tub, when it was just you and me?" Laina asks. "That was perfect."

See?

Laina kisses me quickly on the cheek and puts her head back on my shoulder. "Look at the stars," she says. "Do you ever think about fate?"

"Sometimes."

"Do you believe in it?"

"In a way."

Laina is quiet. "I think what happened with us was fate."

Maybe it's my default genetic male fear of commitment, or maybe something a little less trite related to my own personal psychological deformities, but suddenly I'm a little uneasy. What is the term of this agreement and what are my options for termination? All of Laina's qualities suddenly seem a little faded and worn. Maybe I've been lying to myself about her. Maybe she's not who I think she is, who I want her to be. Maybe I was only drawn to what I thought I could never have again.

"I think somehow I always knew we'd get back together," Laina tells me softly. "We were meant to."

CHAPTER FIVE

I spin the wheel in front of me and watch the fluorescent lights reflecting in the spokes. It's my first day back at the bike shop and I'm a little disoriented after spending two months in Los Angeles in a complete social vacuum. I've been home for a week and I still haven't talked to Laina. I'm pretty sure I should have called her.

"Wake up, man," K says.

I glance at him vaguely and nod.

After shamelessly bullshitting my way through five application essays—one specifically concerning my code of ethics—I was accepted by Prescott College in Arizona, about the furthest thing from a traditional college I could find. I have no desire to attend college, but I know a degree is the easiest way for people with no skills to find employment. I deferred my enrollment a semester to allow myself a few months after I graduate to change my mind and get a job pumping gas, selling drugs, or removing my clothes for drunk middle-aged women.

"Hey man, you got a visitor," K tells me quietly.

I look at him. "Huh?"

He motions out the window onto the sales floor. Laina.

I wipe the grease off my hands slowly and toss the rag onto my bench. She watches me shuffle out onto the floor with my hands in the pockets of my apron.

"What happened to you?" she asks softly.

"What?"

"Where've you been?"

"I don't know," I shrug, looking at my feet. "Working."

Laina forces a thin smile. "I wanted to see you," she says.

I nod and jingle the tools in my pockets. "Well, look, I'm kinda busy with repairs, you know..."

"Yeah..."

"I'll call you tonight."

I'm still a liar.

◻    ◻    ◻

I pull up in front of the gym and check the glowing clock in the dash: 4:57 A.M. The place doesn't even open for another three minutes because they're pussies and don't stay open from Monday at 5:00 A.M. until Sunday at midnight like the gym I went to in LA. The unnecessarily masochistic habit I developed this summer of forcing myself into the gym in the still-dark hours of the morning has yet to be broken. I have to be at school at 7:00 A.M. to TA for my former math teacher, which I've decided requires I be here at 5:00. But I don't actually have to be here. I could do what conventionally sane individuals do and work out in the afternoon, but I can compile a concise list of reasons I don't. The first is that the place is packed like a contemporary cattle ranch at any other time of day. The rest of the reasons are extensions of the previous: I don't like people, I don't like waiting, and I'm entirely too insecure to put myself in such an exposing position in front of such a dense population. Instead I sleep thirty hours a week.

I've made a conscious decision this year to clean myself up a little. I haven't defined any quantitative parameters, but I'm operating under the assumption that it means cutting back on the drugs and alcohol in both frequency and quantity. I'm guessing my habits are probably not extraordinarily conducive to my efforts in the gym. I seem to be doing reasonably well by utilizing my growing hatred of the general high school population—which I guess includes me—as fuel for my personal motivation.

I also offer to drive as much as possible when we go out to limit my opportunities to drink, which works in theory but is rarely successful in practice. I'm definitely done smoking, but that leaves coke and acid and mushrooms and ecstasy and alcohol and anything else I can manage to absorb without smoking. And a little counterproductive to this new resolution is my purchasing of another ounce of blow last week. It's like telling yourself you're going on a diet and buying a case of Twinkies to get started.


Kala and I walk into the newly remodeled classroom and sit down in the back next to Jesse and Shannon. English. Always my favorite class. The lack of irrefutable facts and absolute answers makes the time a little more bearable. I can argue my points until I'm recognized as correct, or at least until I exhaust the teacher into surrender. Either is satisfactorily gratifying with a high school audience. I slide all the way down in my prison deskchair to assume proper slacker positioning and glance around the room. Looks like the usual gang of misfi— Fuck.

"Laina's in here," Kala laughs at me. "Have you still not talked to her?"

"Uh-uh."

"What's your problem, anyway?"

"I don't know," I shrug. "I don't wanna talk to her."

After almost four additional years of ostensible social and emotional development, I'm right back to the conclusion of my eighth-grade self-evaluation: I'm an asshole. I didn't have a revelation or anything, I just don't want to see or talk to Laina. I initially determined two distinct possible causes of my current asshole status: my repressed and unexercised feelings for Julie, or Laina's comment about fate's role in our relationship. But upon further consideration, I've concluded it's more likely a typically male combination of the two: Julie is the tangible representation of the abstract concept of outside female possibilities, and because I don't know her as well as I know Laina, I still believe she's perfect, which makes Laina relatively undesirable and the thought of some kind of binding arrangement with her unbearable. In the end, understanding or defining the reasons is thoroughly unnecessary; I still won't want to talk to Laina. Abandoning my futile reasoning, I shift my attention to the entering teacher and size up my new opposition.

□   □   □

The guy who lives here is out of town and one of his friends has a key, so he of course decided it would be a good idea to have some people over. I only know the guy with the key through some shady drug-related business, and I like him and his friends about as much as non-consensual anal sex, but some of us heard about the situation and decided we could put up with them temporarily for an empty house we weren't responsible for.

Kristi and I have been together for about a month—rapidly approaching my standard time limit. I met her when we were freshmen but dismissed her as just another cute girl I'd never have sex with—like I do with every other cute girl I meet—until finding myself involved in one of the most embarrassing conversations I can remember being involved in while sober.

"What's your problem?" she asked me.

"Nothing. Just thinking."

"About what?"

You without any clothes on.

I shrugged. "I've just always thought about us hooking up."

Kristi smiled at me and knocked the ash from her cigarette. "Hooking up like sex, or hooking up like girlfriend-boyfriend?"

"Well... Both, I guess."

She grinned while I waited for her to tell me what a jerk-off I was. "So have I," she finally said.

And now she's my girlfriend. This unspoken designation was confirmed around Christmas when she gave me a pair of flannel pajama pants—one pocket full of Hershey's kisses, the other full of condoms. Sweet girl.

Derek wanders outside with a slightly unstable gait and sits down next to me. "Where's Kristi?"

"Inside playing Quarters."

I was inside with her for a while, but I can't stand watching other people get drunk, especially by such inefficient methods as drinking games that require coordination and motor skills beyond raising a bottle to your lips.

"What're you guys doing after this?" Derek asks me.

"I don't know."

"Well come find me before you leave and let me know what's going on." Derek drains his beer and throws the empty can behind him into the dark because this isn't his house and he doesn't have to pick it up.

I lean back in my chair and watch him slip inside. He's immediately replaced with Kristi in the doorway. She steps outside onto the cement patio cautiously and straddles my lap, leaning in and kissing me. I can taste the alcohol on her tongue. It's not something I find extraordinarily pleasant.

"Let's go to my place," Kristi whispers in my ear.

I watch her. "Aren't your parents home?"

"Yeah... We'll just be quiet," she says. "They won't know."

I want to have sex with her. I do. I can't even quantify the magnitude of the erection she gives me. But I'm completely uninterested in trying to explain the situation when her underwear-clad father bursts into the room with something hard to hit me with. I watch her closely as she gropes me. We haven't slept together yet and she's drunk. I'm not going home with her like this.

"Come on..." she pleads quietly, kissing my neck.

If there's one thing I have trouble doing, it's saying no to a girl, even if she's asking me to mow her lawn with a pair of scissors. "I. Can't," I manage.

"Please..." she persists sweetly, still kissing me.

"I can't," I tell her again, trying to ignore the feeling of her ass grinding in my lap.

"Why..." she asks softly.

"Because you're drunk."

"So what..."

Fuck, she's making this hard. In every possible application of the word. "So I can't."

Kristi pouts quietly and moves her lips to my ear. "Please..."

I close my eyes and roll my head back as Kelly bursts through the door and almost knocks us both out of the chair before kneeling at my side.

"You know what'd be really good right now?" she asks, gazing up at me with her big brown eyes.

I glance up at Kristi and turn slowly back to Kelly. "What."

"Curly fries!"

Kristi ignores her. She leans in again to my other ear and kisses me. "Please..."

Kelly squeezes my arm. "Come on, let's go get some curly fries!"

If I sleep with Kristi, either her father lynches me or she wakes up the next morning and hates me for taking advantage of her. I can handle getting the shit beaten out of me by an angry father in his underwear, but I'm not that into disrespecting Kristi. And if I take Kelly, Kristi will hate me for it. But I don't want to disappoint Kelly. Kristi is still kissing my neck and Kelly is still squeezing my arm and I'm still stuck in the middle.

"All right," I finally tell Kelly. "We'll go."

Kelly squeals in delight and runs in to get Derek.

Pulling away abruptly, Kristi glares down at me. I catch one of her hands as she slides off my lap and turns away. She looks back, waiting expectantly for me to say something. I don't know what to tell her. We walk in silence out to my truck with Derek and Kelly and climb in.

"Why don't you just drop me off at home," Kristi says quietly.

"Yeah." At this point I think my best option is to just shut the fuck up.

I pull up in front of Kristi's place and she slips out of the truck without saying anything. She turns back to look at me and says it all without a word: I want to say *fuck you*, but we're not alone and I'm too mature and in control of myself to start an ugly scene in front of our friends. I'll call you when I feel like it.

Damn it. I even like her when she's mad at me.


Kristi sits on the wooden bench next to me and leans in against my shoulder. "Look, I'm sorry about the other night," she says. "I was drunk, I shouldn't've been mad at you."

I shrug. She shouldn't be the one apologizing.

Kristi glances up at me and drops her eyes again, her slender fingers softly petting my arm. "I'm glad you didn't come home with me." She laughs a little. "Not that I didn't want you to. But it means a lot to me."

I kiss the top of her head and look up at the pale sky over the bright city hall building in front of us.

"You like Kelly, don't you," Kristi says softly.

"I don't know."

"You can tell me, Greg, I'm not mad at you."

If anyone deserves the truth, it's Kristi. She's been nothing but sweet to me, given me more than I ever gave her. Not that that's ever really prevented me from being an asshole before. But I must reform my wayward ways.

Besides, girls can see through bullshit better than polygraphs.

"Yeah," I tell her quietly. "I guess."

Kristi nods against my chest. "I can't say I'm happy," she says. "But I'll live. Just promise me we'll still be friends."

I kiss her forehead and rest my cheek in her hair. "Yeah."

I know I fucked up. I love being with Kristi. But despite everything I love about her, there was something in me that wanted out. Something in me waiting impatiently for the end. Maybe it was Kelly, or even Staci. Maybe it was Laina again. Maybe it was just The Julie Concept. Or maybe I need to quit contriving complicated excuses and just admit I'm a stereotypical dick owner who can't stay with one girl for very long before needing to find an easy yet infallible exit requiring no direct confrontation with her for the sake of pursuing new vaginas.

Kristi sits up and looks into my eyes. She's beautiful. Smiling softly, she shrugs and leans in to kiss me. "It was fun while it lasted."

□   □   □

K looks out the window onto the sales floor and sighs with boredom. The bike shop is dead. Apparently people don't ride their bikes when it's cold and raining.

Pussies.

No one's riding, so we have no bikes to repair. No one's buying, so we have no bikes to build. We've been reduced to entertaining ourselves with juvenile and moderately dangerous activities. Correction: Now we have more time for our juvenile and moderately dangerous activities.

I pry out the handlebar plugs from the bike in my stand and grab the air compressor hose. Our compressor tops out around 120 PSI, more than enough to propel a plug from the end of a handlebar across the shop at a velocity capable of producing a considerable dent in the drywall. But tradition bores me. Noticing a can of cheese-puffs on the shelf over K's bench, I grab one of the glowing orange balls and slide it into the barrel of the handlebar.

Stuffing the nozzle of the compressor hose into the other end of the bars, I spin the barrel to the wall over K's bench. He wisely steps aside. I squeeze the trigger of the compressor and the cheese-puff explodes from the bars, disintegrating against the wall. K and I stare in awe at the fluorescent orange circle now painted on the dirty white wall. Performance art.

"Smoke break!" K yells.

Our newest hire Phil grabs his cigarettes and follows us outside. Phil typically comes to work spun out on crank and tweaks around in the back at my old bench quietly building bikes and sniffling constantly like one does when one frequently snorts things into one's nose. After tiring of our routine harassment of new employees and giving him a chance, K and I realized we actually like the guy.

K and Phil light their cigarettes and I stuff my hands in the pockets of my apron and jingle my tools. The sky is dark and grey, the air filled with the lingering smell of wet pavement. I look down into the puddle at my feet and remind myself what an asshole I am for blowing it with Kristi. And Laina. And Staci. And Kala. And Val. And pretty much everyone.

"Hey, you have any doses?" Phil asks me.

I look back up. "Yeah, I still have some of those gels. What do you need?"

"Ten."

I open the door of my truck and reach under the center console, pulling out the plastic bag with the acid. Carefully cutting a strip from the side with my knife, I stick it in a gum wrapper for Phil. "Twenty for you," I tell him.

He unwraps a corner and peaks at the orange gels, then hands me a twenty from his wallet. "How are these things?"

"They're pretty much double that blotter shit."

Phil nods and drops his butt in a puddle. Glancing inside the shop, he pulls the solitary wrinkled cigarette from his breast pocket and grins. "Time for a magic cigarette."

I was under the impression that I used drugs at inappropriate times pretty frequently until I met Phil. He lights the cigarette and passes it to K. I look down at the bag in my apron pocket and contemplate the acid. Fuck it. I have no conflicting responsibilities. I quickly tear a dose from the grid and drop it under my tongue.

K catches me and laughs. "Did you just drop?"

"Sure."

I toss the bag back into my truck and sit on the painted white curb near the dumpster fence. The acid slowly melts under my tongue into a sticky wad of gel on the uneven backs of my lower teeth. K and Phil finish smoking and the three of us walk casually back inside, not at all surprised by the still empty sales floor. I lean up against my bench and unenthusiastically spin the pedals of the bike in front of me.

"Are you coming on yet?" K asks me.

"No."

K puts a new CD in the stereo above his bench and looks back at me. "Are you coming on now?"

"No."

"How about now?"

"No. Stop."

K looks disappointed. I survey the damage to my workbench my lack of productivity has somehow managed to create and decide I need to clean it. My exemplary cleanliness and organization at work has yet to spill over into any other area of my life. I'm not sure I completely understand feeling a greater need to clean a workbench than my own bedroom, but since it apparently doesn't bother me, I don't commit a great deal of time to contemplating the situation.

"Are you coming on yet?" K asks me.

"No."

"How about now?"

"No. Stop."

The painted white surface of my bench is scarred with Super-Glue residue. What began simply as a boredom-inspired routine of gluing a few unimportant tools to absent employees' benches has rapidly progressed through competition and retaliation to an epic adhesive war involving the calculated gluing of every tool present, as well as any spare change, scrap metal, or trash that happens to be available. An empty Triscuit box was glued to my bench last week. I left it on for a few days as an artistic comment on American consumerism or something.

"Are you coming on yet?" K asks me.

"Yes."

"How about— You are?"

"Yeah, fuck."

Those gels come on fast. I can feel the tension in my jaw and the walls are vibrating in a fine boil. I hear the hum of the automatic doors sliding open and I glance at K. Together we turn and look out the window onto the floor. We have a customer.

"I got it," I tell K.

He watches me skeptically. "You sure?"

I just laugh and shuffle out front to assist the woman standing at the register with her bicycle leaning precariously on its kickstand, a horrible invention of which I'm determined to rid the earth forever.

"Can I help you?" I ask her.

Successful salesmen avoid yes-no questions, engaging their customers in natural conversation and deceiving them into believing making a sale is not their first and only priority. But I've never been a good salesman. I really don't care if I make a sale and I really don't like talking to customers. I ask yes-no questions whenever possible and hope for a no, my implicit release from service.

"I'm looking for those things that go over the tires and keep water from spraying up on you," the woman tells me.

"Fenders?"

"I think so," she shrugs.

"Allow me to show you your options."

She smiles and I duck into the back. K watches me dig through several boxes and pull out three sets of fenders. I walk past him and grin. My opinion of sales is rapidly improving.

Placing the fenders neatly on the display case in front of my valued customer, I explain in depth the various benefits and drawbacks of each model using large Latinate words, complex sentence structures, and references to construction techniques and materials to impress my customer and convince her that I'm the foremost authority on bicycle fenders, when really I'm making half the shit up and confusing details between the models.

"I'll just take these, I guess," the woman says, pointing at the least expensive model.

I smile and nod like I'm pleased with her choice while I silently curse her for choosing the most difficult model to install, knowing she's about to ask me to install them for her.

"Can you put them on for me?" she asks.

See?

"I would love to, ma'am," I tell her. "It'll be just a few minutes."

I roll her stupid kickstand-having bike back to my bench and throw it up into my stand. Tearing off the plastic packaging, I contemplate the fenders. These things must have been designed by a bunch of third-graders for a class project or something. I look at the bike and the rack over the rear wheel that's going to make the job about ten times more involved and wonder if I can go tell the lady I don't want to sell her fenders anymore.

The acid is really pumping through me now. I dump the bag of bolts onto my bench and watch them roll, staring at the light reflecting in their polished plating. I unstick myself from the distraction and start unbolting the rack. It promptly collapses over the wheel and I toss it carelessly onto my bench. Sliding the rear fender into place, I tighten the bolts and inspect it for balance and proper positioning. Perfect.

"You forgot to put the rack back on," K says.

I look at the rack on my bench. "Fuck."

K laughs at me as I unbolt the fender and struggle to position the rack while holding the fender in alignment and reinstall the bolts.

"Hold this, fucker," I tell him.

K holds the rack while I work, still laughing at my inability to control my finer motor skills and my continual dropping of items and tendency to find my fingers caught in the tight spaces between the rack and the tire. Finally tightening all necessary components, I inspect my job with the satisfying relief of completion.

"Front," K says.

I look at the front fender waiting patiently on my bench to be installed. K returns to his stereo, flipping through radio stations while I pick up the fender and stare at it. Which is the front end? Glancing up, I catch my customer peering in through the service window curiously, watching me like the proctor of an examination I'm currently failing.

After finally installing the fender, then removing it and installing it again properly, I smile proudly and spin the wheel. The tire rubs on the fender supports.

"Fuck!"

"Grundle it," K says.

K and I have developed a local reputation for fixing what others have deemed unfixable utilizing unconventional methods often involving seemingly destructive component modification and the construction of our own custom components using the large supply of parts we've collected from our repairs. Somewhere along the line, an unknown party for unknown reasons dubbed the method *grundling*. Our excessive exposure to toxic lubricant fumes decided for us to adopt the term without question.

Checking to make sure my customer isn't still watching me—one of the fundamental rules of grundling—I grab my channel locks and clamp down on one of the fender supports, bending it out away from the tire. Repeating the procedure on the other side, I spin the wheel again. No more rubbing.

I finally figure out how to use the cash register and ring the woman up as fast as I can. She smiles at me sympathetically, probably assuming the shop performs an admirable community service by hiring the mentally handicapped. Dragging my feet on the way back to my bench, I start putting away my tools slowly. My 10-mm won't move. I look at K. He just grins and shows me the bottle of Super-Glue in his hand.

□   □   □

Phil's house is disturbingly crowded. It would appear the fire marshal is not in attendance. Phil recently moved back to the Bay Area and in with his grandparents, who apparently fail to notice the increase in property damage after each weekend they leave for vacation.

Phil stands up from his chair and shakes my hand.

"This is Bryan and Shannon," I tell him.

Phil acknowledges them slightly. "Party's on this side of the house," he says.

I drop my ass into the chair next to Phil and admire the built-in bar. Bryan and Shannon start working on their beer while I look around the room at the people filing in and out. I only recognize a few. A blonde girl whose ass is a little too fat and white for her tight black Dickies walks in and smiles deliberately at me. [To clarify: I don't dislike big asses. In fact, it is my opinion that big asses are quite possibly the most wonderful physical attribute women can possess. But there are two primary stipulations: 1) Women with big asses must have some skin color; white girls can pull off the big asses, but they need decent tans. 2) The big ass must contain underlying muscular structure to provide shape for the surplus fat to augment, not replace. It should be noted, however, that each ass must be evaluated independently in order to allow the consideration of additional factors not contained within these stipulations, including personality, face, voice, hair, laugh, dress, political inclinations, and other non-ass-related elements that may contribute to a woman's overall sex appeal, which have the potential to drastically affect the result of an ass's evaluation. In this case, the blonde has failed unequivocally to meet either stipulation, and appears upon cursory observation to offer no potentially redeeming qualities, and therefore must not be indulged.] I look away without returning her smile. Can't accuse me of misleading her.

Bryan wanders back over and leans against the wall to my side. "Deanna's here."

"Deanna," I think. "As in cheerleader Deanna?"

"Yeah."

Deanna was two classes ahead of us at Kodi's high school and is now apparently a cheerleader for a certain NBA team. Kodi introduced me to her casually a couple years ago, but I can think of no logical reason for a beautiful professional cheerleader to remember me.

Deanna and a friend who only increases Deanna's beauty by relativity push their way through the door and sidle up to Bryan. Her blond hair is now tightly cropped, presumably to prevent unwanted movement during the leading of cheers, and imaginably convenient during various other activities with which I'd very much like to be involved. Bryan reintroduces her to me and I quickly resume my conversation with Phil, being debilitatingly shy in the presence of Deanna's overwhelmingly beautiful blue eyes and having nothing to say to her that doesn't include the words *sex*, *have*, *we*, and *can*.

"Phil!"

Phil turns to the yelling bartender. "What!"

"We're outta juice, man!"

Phil turns back to me and shrugs. He's not concerned. He's discovered the wondrous beauty of straight alcohol and its stunning efficiency and has no interest in childish diluted drinks.

"I'll go get some," I offer, demonstrating my attractively unselfish nature for Deanna.

Phil nods and disappears to make a bill collection while I walk to the bar and ask the guys what they need. Suddenly aware of a human presence at my side, I turn to see the blonde with the fat white ass smiling intently at me. Phil reappears and slaps a stack of money in my hand. Counting it quickly, I slide it into my back pocket and push off from the bar.

The blonde stops me. "Are you going by yourself?"

"Yeah…"

"Can I come with you?" she smiles.

"Sure…"

I drive less than carefully the few blocks to the store, braking hard and accelerating quickly, cutting turns too sharply for the height and weight distribution of the truck. I am one with the universe and its fundamental physical laws do not apply to me.

"Are you drunk?" the blonde asks me, wondering if I'm drunk.

"No."

And sometimes I just don't feel like observing traffic laws and break them simply to remind myself and those around me that laws are nothing more than words in a book, which also do not apply to me.

The blonde and I step into the fluorescent bath of the store lights and wander through the aisles looking for where it is these silly fools hid the big bottles of refrigerated juice since they're not located where I would place them were I to be assigned the task. Our conversation is comfortable, although a little slow and thoroughly hollow. She seems like a perfectly wonderful young lady with a lot to offer the world. I just don't want to see her naked. Finally we find what we're looking for and load up.

Back at the party, I drop off the juice and change at the bar and head straight for the urine depository at the end of the hall. I hear unfamiliar female voices through the thin door and get the feeling I'm the subject of conversation. Whatever. It seems only natural that girls talk about me while I'm urinating. I shake off and head back out.

A few girls in a tight circle ten feet away freeze and look at me briefly before returning quietly to their conversation. I recognize a piece of the circle as Phil's girlfriend, whose name I don't know because I wasn't paying attention when she told me what it is and Phil has never once referred to her as anything other than *My Girlfriend*. They glance at me again as I slip past them into Phil's room.

Somehow my chair next to Phil has remained available and I resume observation position. Bryan and Shannon sit on the edge of the bed across from my chair.

"Dude, that girl you took to the store?" Bryan says.

"Yeah?"

"She's gross."

My Girlfriend sticks her head through the door and waves Phil over.

He stands unenthusiastically and wanders through the swarm of bodies, slipping out of sight around the corner.

"I'm going outside," I tell Bryan and Shannon, imagining Deanna will somehow notice my absence, realize I'm outside, find me, and fall in love with me in the time it takes for her to walk the distance between us.

I push through the room and into the hall. Phil is leaning back against a washing machine with his cup tipped back at his lips, his eyes diverted from My Girlfriend.

"Hey," he says to me. "Come here."

I stand between Phil and My Girlfriend and wait for him to take another drink.

"You know that girl you took to the store?" he asks me. "She wants to fuck you real bad."

I nod and contemplate Phil's remark. My memory pulls a few files and I examine the girl in the various poses I've seen her in tonight: walking next to me in the parking lot playing with the strings on her jacket; standing next to me at the bar; sitting in my truck asking me if I was drunk while I violated assorted traffic laws. There's a subtle fondness to my memories, and it has been a while since I've done anything but dry-hump a drunk girl who didn't really care who I was in a hot tub, maybe I should just— Standby, incoming files: her fat white ass squeezing out of her black Dickies while she dances with three far more attractive girls; showing Deanna pictures of all the guys she's fucked, which judging by the current situation is probably an extensive list; side-by-side mug shots of her and Deanna. The fondness quickly fades and is replaced with an unsettling surge of stomach acid.

"No way," I tell Phil.

"Come on, dude. If you go in there," he tells me, pointing to the vacant bedroom in front of us, "she'll be there in five minutes."

"Would you fuck her?"

"Hell no," he laughs.

"Right."

□　□　□

I roll a page of my textbook and tuck it into another upside-down teardrop shape in the series I've diligently spent the first half of the class period working on. My usual lack of interest in school has reached the level of absolute metaphysical absence today. I am not here. I'm stumbling around in my own head among ridiculous pastel romantic fantasies involving Deanna and a less embarrassing physically enhanced version of myself.

"Dude," Bryan told me on the phone a couple weeks ago. "You know Deanna?"

"How many professional cheerleaders do you think I know?"

"Yeah, well I just talked to her."

"So what."

"So she wants on your nards."

"That's very poetic."

"She wants to see you."

As soon as my desire to see her naked finally overwhelmed my fear of rejection, I called Deanna and convinced her to stop by Shannon's place. We spent the night talking about nothing of consequence and comparing tattoos as a clever but obvious way to show each other a little more skin.

"So you wanna go to Monterey with me tomorrow?" I asked her, trying to think of an excuse to see her again immediately.

"Sure."

I stared at her. "Really?"

Within an hour of finding K at one of the bike races in which I competed regularly before the onset of my current motivation deficiency, we were all drunk. K provided me with an uninterrupted supply of sample beer to complement the two-liter bottle of Seven & Seven I repeatedly struggled to hold in my teeth while urinating. There was something about Deanna that let me forget her intimidating profession and overwhelming beauty and feel at ease. I said what I wanted to say and did what I wanted to do. The excess of cheap alcohol might have been a contributing factor.

I notice people packing up their books and binders and the bell rings. Pulling all the pages in my book straight before I close it—because I respect school property—I dive out into the wave of students filling the hall.

"Greg!"

I turn as Shannon catches up with me. "What's up."

"You going to the dance tonight?"

"Fuck no," I tell him. I don't believe in participating in school functions. They exist solely for people who rely on the high school social structure to provide them with a life, the same people who effectively die when they graduate. In case this condition is infectious, I avoid contact as much as possible.

"Come on," Shannon says. "Shawna wants to go with you."

"So what."

"So she has huge tits," he reminds me. This is standard male logic.

"I have a girlfriend, dude," I remind him. Who also has huge tits.

Shannon nods with a grin. "What're you guys doing tonight, watching a movie?" he asks, humping the air. *Watching a movie* is apparently Shannon's euphemism for fucking. It's a pretty good one.

"Hopefully," I shrug.

"Hey," he grins. "You wanna pierce my ear in English?"

"What?"

He pulls out a small piercing gun with a stud already loaded in it. This was not spontaneous. "Up in the cartilage," he says. "You're good at it."

I guess he's basing his evaluation of my ear-piercing skills on the ten holes I've managed to collect in my ears, nine of which I pierced myself, and—what he's apparently failed to notice—nine of which are not good.

"OK," I say. "Gimme the thing."

We step into our English class and I follow him to a seat in the back corner instead of taking my customary seat by the door. The bell rings and the remaining half of the students wander casually into the room. Our teacher has wisely given up on trying to get them here on time and waits patiently. Finally she starts talking about something like teachers always seem to do when they're teaching, but Shannon and I are busy whispering in the back of the room.

"OK, just sit straight and look forward," I tell him.

He turns and I position the piercing gun on his ear. I can see him cringing in anticipation through his grin. Waiting until the teacher turns to write on the whiteboard, I quickly squeeze the gun and feel the pop of the stud piercing the cartilage.

Shannon jumps. "Ah!"

The teacher spins at his outburst and looks immediately at the two of us. We are usually responsible for outbursts. "What was that?"


I can still hear the water splashing against the rocks in the riverbed below my carefully parked 4Runner, a vehicle far easier than a Honda Prelude to have sex in. Deanna and I were wandering around by the river for a little while with the lingering twilight, but we both knew exactly why we came up here and decided not to waste any more time being indirect. Deanna is capable of exhibiting more class than any girl I've been with, dressing sharply for dinner and behaving accordingly, but equally capable of shedding the refinement and exposing her tattoos along with the more grounded, straightforward aspect of her nature. It seems like such a cable television cliché to be fucking in the back of a car in the hills, but our options at this point are limited and abstinence is not among them.

Deanna pushes me onto my back and swings her leg over me, leaning down to my lips. I begin lifting her shirt, but stop abruptly when a pair of headlights bounces off the rear window. The car pulls up behind my truck and stops. Like a cop.

"Fuck."

Deanna slides off my lap with obvious frustration as I sit up. I can't see anything out the window but headlights. I scramble to climb into the driver's seat and turn off the stereo while I roll down the window, waiting for what I know will be a short cop whose son I used to dump in trashcans. Deanna slides into the passenger seat and glances at me. I check the side mirror. We seem to be popular with the law enforcement crowd tonight: two sheriff's patrol cars.

One of the deputies walks cautiously up to the side of my truck with her flashlight resting on her shoulder. Reaching my window, she shines the light in and makes a careful inspection of the vehicle. I still have an eighth of mushrooms and a couple grams of coke in here. Fortunately, this vehicle is equipped with abundant drug-concealing interior features.

"Can I see your license and registration?" the deputy asks me, finally lowering the light.

I hand her the paperwork and watch as she inspects it closely.

"You're a long way from home, aren't you?" she asks.

"It's a ten minute drive."

The deputy ignores my answer and leans in and looks at Deanna, then back at me. "What're you guys doing tonight?"

"We were walking around by the river," I tell her.

"Doesn't look like you're walking around by the river."

"We *were*," I repeat more clearly.

She's not amused. "Why don't you step out a minute and go stand back there with my partner," she tells me.

I slide out onto the dirt and walk back to the cruisers. Another deputy is standing in the headlights.

"You having fun tonight?" he asks me.

"We were trying to." I fold my arms across my chest and wait to be excused. I hope that lady's not rooting through the truck and finding things she shouldn't be finding.

Finally she returns and hands me my paperwork. "All right, look, here's the story," she says. "We got a call about a suspicious vehicle up here. I wanted to separate you two to see if she was all right."

"OK."

"You might want to go somewhere else," she says. "Understand?"

"Yeah."

The two cruisers swing around and disappear down the road as I climb back into my truck and slam the door.

"She was asking me if I was all right," Deanna laughs. "She thought you were raping me or something."

I shake my head. "Is the idea of me having consensual sex that incredible?"

□   □   □

I slip a CD into the stereo above K's workbench and turn up the volume. "She was just bugging the shit outta me," I tell K, concluding in my typically indifferent manner my typical discourse on the typical failure of my typically ephemeral relationship with Deanna. "She just always had to see me, always had to talk to me, all the time, it was too much."

K nods. "She wanted to be married, man."

I broke up with Deanna. Let me rephrase that: I pulled my typical bullshit and forced Deanna to break up with me because I'm an asshole and I didn't want to do it myself.

Everything about her repulsed me. The same glimmering blue eyes in the same beautiful face, the same lean body with the same curves, the same voice, the same words, the same slender hands on my skin: everything that used to make me believe I could love her. Until this point, I've had no trouble ignoring logic and assigning blame to the girl for my loss of attraction to her. But I know Deanna is no different than she was the day we met.

"I finally call her back after she's been paging me for a couple days," I tell K, "and she's crying, says it's obvious it's not gonna work out with us. I just agreed with her and got off the phone as quick as I could."

He shrugs. "Fuck it."

"Yeah," I agree. "I need to just stay away from girls."

K nods in agreement and we go back to our repairs because they don't involve girls.

"Dude," K says suddenly, leaning back against his bench. "I can't believe this is your last day. Who the fuck is gonna entertain me now?"

"I don't know," I shrug.

"Who am I gonna throw shit at?"

"I don't know."

"Whose gonna do all the shitty repairs I don't wanna do myself?"

"I don't know."

"Who's gonna do the monkey dance while I'm on the phone with a customer and make me laugh?"

"I don't know."

"Whose gonna help me fuck with new guys until they quit and have to hire therapists?"

"I don't know."

K looks at me and shakes his head. "Damn, man."

□    □    □

I walk into the photo classroom and step around the darkroom wall. Laina is at the back sink developing negatives while the instructor addresses her students between us. The recovering hippie who formerly taught this class was replaced last year with a bitter, frustrated failure of an artist who has, according to convention, become a critic—only instead of professionally, on a personal level with her unmotivated students. I spent my fair share of time last year arguing with her.

"Hey Ms. Parks!" I yell and wave at her.

She stops mid-sentence and looks up. It seems I've interrupted her. The students spin around to look at me and Laina laughs from the sink, still turning the film slowly.

"Hello, Greg," Ms. Parks grins despite her obvious effort to appear sternly displeased.

"I'm sorry, am I interrupting something?" I ask innocently.

"Yes. My class."

"Oh!" I lift my hand to my mouth in apologetic surprise. "I didn't realize you were busy. I just dropped in to assist my associate there," I say, nodding at Laina. I wave my hand over the students approvingly. "Proceed."

Ms. Parks glares at me as I stroll past her casually to the sink, but fails to conceal her smile. She's probably imagining me naked. I consider grabbing her ass just to see what she'd do, but decide I don't need the complications that might arise from either disciplinary action by the administration or from encouraging her to pursue a sexual relationship with me I don't want to have with her.

Laina glances back at me and smiles. After a couple months of being involuntarily within close proximity of each other due to our class schedules—which were apparently created with retribution for my mistreatment of her in mind—we once again managed to fall back into our old routine. My past failures have apparently been forgiven again—if not completely, enough to allow friendly interaction between us.

"How's it going?" I ask Laina quietly.

"Fine," she shrugs, nodding at a plastic bottle over the sink. "Wanna grab that for me and hold it while I pour?"

□   □   □

I stagger into my former math classroom on four hours of something vaguely resembling intermittent sleep and collapse into the chair behind the teacher's desk. Being a TA for my old math teacher was the easiest way to get the rest of the units I need to graduate. Kristi TAs with me, but she only shows up once or twice a week—not including special occasions like my birthday when she brings me cupcakes with those fucked up candles that don't go out and starts a small fire in the hallway outside the classroom. The bell rings and the remaining students shuffle into the room.

Kristi walks in fashionably late and pulls up a chair next to me. "Morning, Sunshine," she beams.

"Yeah." I hand her a stack of papers and lean back in my chair.

Mrs. Adams steps over to the desk for her notes. "Morning guys," she smiles at us.

"Morning."

I look back down at the homework papers as Mrs. Adams begins her lecture, but my concentration quickly fades and shifts as it always seems to in idle moments to my most recent series of failures. When I turned eighteen, I tattooed my back as an undeniable promise to myself to stay clean. Turns out I'm still a liar. It didn't even last a month. I was right back to it all, losing myself in the blur, in the pulsing swarm of slurred words and forgotten nights. It's a voice you can't hear, pulling hands you can't feel. It pushes you into the corner and laughs when you crumble and slide down the wall, when you can't hide anymore, when you give in and let yourself slip away. You wrap your arms around your knees and watch your hands tremble in the fading light. It won't let you go. It won't let you stop. You search the mirror for someone you know, but all you find is a cold distance and eyes that have lost all their tears. You fall back into the only arms that never pulled away and left you shivering in the grey rain. You shake with your restless heart and try to blink the world from your eyes. You need more. You always need more.

It owns you. You don't feel anything anymore but an untouchable, tearing need, a frozen burning in your trembling hands and your empty chest. It brings you to your knees and makes you crawl. It steals the thoughts from your mind and breaks your will. You find yourself on the floor, scratching at the glass, crumbling with the weight of your own weakness. You breathe the glittering trails of need and roll your head back to pull it deeper. It puts lies in your mouth and fear in your dreams. You feel the cold sinking in so deep your heart shivers in your chest. Every minute without it feels like forever. You clench your jaw and grind your hands into fists and wait. The need swells and consumes you. It pulls the grey over your eyes and whispers in your ear, telling you all the lies you need to believe until everything else is silent and distant and unreachable. You come back again and learn the same lesson you forget the moment you leave. You learn to never trust yourself.

You spin endlessly down the hole you swore you'd left behind forever, still scraping the dried blood and dirt from under your fingernails. The light fades above you and the cold settles in as you kneel alone on another grey afternoon and let it fill you with the same emptiness that shoves you back down to your knees again. You know the emptiness will never leave you, know you'll never find the answer at the bottom, but you can't escape it long enough to find what you're waiting for. It knows you'll never tell them. It knows you'll always be back.

Eventually you quit fighting and give in to the pull. No matter how far up you look, there's no end. And everything you know, everything you recognize and love and need is waiting at the bottom for you with open arms and familiar smiles. You close your eyes and let the welcoming comfort consume you in its warmth.

I can feel the damage crawling in my blood. I can see it reflected in my friends and their lives. We graduate next week. I don't know what's going to happen to them. I don't know if I care. Sometimes it seems like Kala is the only friend I have left, and the distance between us is growing as she slips further into the hole and closer to Jason. I can't do this alone. I want to yell and shake her and shove her face into the mirror, but I know I can't change her. She has to open her eyes if she wants to see.

□　□　□

The more concerned members of the school's administration have organized an all-night graduation party for us in an attempt to keep us sober and alive, neither of which most of us were at the graduation ceremony. I've declined the offer to attend in favor of a party without the unnecessary adult supervision. Shannon begged me to eat acid and trip with him at the last possible school function as some kind of political statement he has yet to articulate, but fuck that. I do not participate. And I'm staying sober tonight.

I pick up a hemp anklet and roll the bead between my fingers. I'm going to tell her tonight. Kala. I'm going to tell her I love her. I think I love her. I can't handle watching her with Jason anymore. I can't watch the way she hurts herself because of him anymore. I can't watch her make my mistakes anymore. And I can't do this alone. I need her. Tonight I'm going to give her this and tell her I love her. I slip the anklet into my pocket and head out to my truck.

K is waiting on my driveway. "I threw a present for you in the front seat," he tells me.

I open the door of my truck and pull out a two-liter bottle of Sprite. The seal on the cap is broken. Apparently it isn't just Sprite.

"I know how you drink that Seven & Seven shit," K says. "There's a bottle of Seagram's in there."

I unscrew the cap and sniff it. "Holy shit."

K grins. "Have fun, man."

"Yeah, thanks," I say, rubbing the burning sensation from my nose. "I'll come by the shop in a couple days when I wake up."

I drive to Kala's house in deep focus. I am not going to drink tonight. I have two liters of Seven & Seven and I am not going to drink it. I am strong and disciplined and capable of maintaining sobriety.

Kala answers the door and hugs me. "Hey."

Jason appears with a twelve-pack and we all pile into the truck and pull away. Somehow Jason ended up in the front seat, and right now he's showing me how little fat he has on his forearm.

"Look at that, dude, I can hardly pinch anything."

"Yeah," I say, not really looking.

"Remember that night when your parents were in Boston?" he asks Kala. "When we were all shrooming?"

"Yeah, I remember," Kala says from the back seat.

"Man, I was so pissed." Jason shakes his head. "I totally thought you were into Greg."

Kala makes a soft noise of acknowledgement and I glance back at her in the rearview mirror. I did not want to hear that. I would have preferred a passionate assertion of her love for me. But what I heard was an utter lack of protest, a completely indifferent verbal shrug.

I pull up in front of the party and Jason and Kala climb out. Together. I look down at the bottle of Seven & Seven. Fuck her. Grabbing the bottle defiantly, I march up to the house and plow through the crowd without acknowledging anyone. I find a chair out back on the porch and assume the drinking position, smelling the alcohol as I lift the bottle to my lips.

Some blonde girl looks at me curiously. "Are you drinking Sprite?"

I hold out the bottle for her to smell.

She pulls back quickly and makes the stale urine face. "Holy shit. You're getting trashed tonight."

I nod vaguely and go back to the bottle.


When you accept no interruptions or distractions, it's amazing how quickly two liters of warm alcohol can make its way into your stomach. I crush the empty bottle in my hands and throw it into the backyard. I need to piss.

Mike stares at me incredulously. "You drank that whole bottle already?"

"Yeah."

I push my way through the house to the bathroom and lock the door behind myself. The fluorescent lights in the ceiling make my flushed face orange in the mirror. I look away and take care of business. The weight of the whiskey suddenly hits me and I lean against the counter to wait for my balance while I listen to the water swirling in the toilet. I don't even know why I'm here. Fuck everyone. Kala's the only reason I came. She's the only reason at all. Finally I figure out how the doorknob works and stumble back down the hallway with my hands on the walls to keep myself upright.

"What's up, Greg."

"Fuck you."

I don't even know who that was, but fuck him. Fuck all of them. I stagger through the crowd and make it outside onto the driveway. Slipping through a couple parked cars out onto the street, I walk unsteadily along the dark road until I see my truck.

I reach the tailgate and fumble with the key trying to slide it into the lock to roll down the rear window. Finally managing to open the gate, I climb in and carefully twist onto my back. My eyelids fall shut and the world begins spinning uncontrollably. If I move at all I'm going to puke. I need to—

I blink my eyes. Was I just passed out? I hear yelling down the street but I can't lift my head to look. It sounds like the cops are chasing someone.

"Fuck you, pigs!" I yell. Fucking pigs.

More voices. They're getting closer.

"Greg!"

That sounds like Mike.

"Greg!"

I lift my head enough to see Mike at my feet. "Huh."

"We were looking for you, man, what the fuck're you doing?" Mike says. "The cops just arrested Drew, we gotta go."

I don't move. I can't move.

Mike laughs and starts yanking on my leg. "Get up!"

Oh Mike, that was the wrong move. I jump off the tailgate and about three gallons of partially digested something ejects from my throat onto some nice people's front lawn.

"Oh!" Mike laughs.

I would have guessed it wasn't physically possible to simultaneously laugh and vomit, but I'm doing it right now. Mike is standing right behind me laughing in the infectious way Mike laughs, and I'm laughing with him through the shit pouring from my mouth.

"Oh!" Mike laughs. "That looks like rice!"

Rice? I didn't eat any rice. Why does it look like rice?

"That's what you get, fucker!" Mike yells.

He keeps laughing while the watery puke finally tapers off. I spit a few times to clear my mouth and grin at Mike.

"Fuck, man, what'd you eat?"

I shrug and stumble without even walking.

"I guess you're not driving, huh."

I shake my head slowly. It seems I've failed to fulfill my commitment again.

"I'll drive you guys," Mike says. "Gimme your keys."

I hand him the keys and climb into the back of the truck with Kala and some girl I recognize but whose name I can't remember. Jason gets in front with Mike so he can show him his forearms. I lean back against the side window and stare at the cars behind us. I think I know those people. I flip them off and spit stomach acid. Fuckers.

"Are you OK?" Kala asks me.

I nod and look away. Fuck you and your junkie boyfriend.

We bounce into a driveway and park. I lean my head on the tailgate and listen to the muffled voices around me.

"Greg?"

Someone's saying my name.

"Greg?"

I look up. It's the girl whose name I don't remember.

"I got you some water," she says quietly, handing me a bottle.

I slur something like thanks and take the bottle.

The girl watches me drink. "Are you OK?"

I spit a mouthful of water to my side and take another drink. "Yeah," I mumble. "Thanks."

She touches my arm and smiles softly.

I drop my eyes again and watch her feet as she walks away. I don't know why she's being so sweet to me. I don't even remember her name. I want to have sex with her. I think she's only sixteen, but I don't care. She's beautiful.

She's my angel. I think we should have sex. But we should probably wait until I quit puking first.

Eventually I feel Kala next to me and realize the truck is moving again. Looking up from the tailgate as we stop, I watch Kala and Nameless Girl crawl out of the truck through my blurred eyes.

"Come on, Greg," Kala tells me. "We're going up to Laina's place."

I glance around. Jason is standing next to Kala now.

"Come on, man," he says.

I don't want Laina to see me like this. Like myself. She's one of the only people I know who hasn't seen me this out of control. And she's one of the only people whose respect means anything to me anymore.

"I'm staying here," I tell them.

"You can't just sit out here by yourself," Kala says.

"Yeah I can."

Jason steps up. "Come on, man."

"Get the fuck away from me."

He puts his hands up and backs off. "OK, man, I don't wanna get my ass kicked. We just don't wanna leave you out here like this."

"I'm fine."

Kala watches me closely.

"I'm fine."


I hear voices and lift my head slightly. They're coming back. I don't know how long it's been. I don't even know if I've been conscious the whole time. I'm not sure I've ever been conscious anymore.

Kala's face emerges from the dark. She looks at the pavement by her feet and back up at me. "You puked more?"

"I guess."

The girls climb in and Kala pulls me into her lap. I feel her fingers running comfortingly though the short hair over my ear and the truck lurches away from the curb. Why is she doing this? She reaches down and pulls my hand into hers. It's so soft and warm. I look up at her and she smiles and squeezes my hand tightly. I want to say something to her, but I can't find the words. I can't even talk. I need to tell her I love her. I do, I love her. I know it now. She's all I want anymore. I have to tell her tonight.

The truck stops and I look up at Kala for an explanation.

"We're at my house," she tells me. "Let Mike take you home so you can sleep."

I nod slightly and roll off of her so she can get out. I can't even sit up. The anklet.

I keep her hand in mine. "Wait…"

"What?"

"Wait," I tell her again, reaching into my pocket for the anklet. It's not there. I search frantically. I need to give it to her, I need to tell her. I need to tell her I love her. "I can't find it," I mumble.

Kala watches me. "What're you talking about?"

"I can't… I need…"

She kisses my forehead. "I'll call you tomorrow."

"Wait…"

Kala pulls her hand from mine slowly and she's gone.

## CHAPTER SIX

Summer. I'm a high school graduate. And nothing's changed. I glance down at the thin margarita in my hand and over to Laina. Her face is as blank as mine, her eyes glassy. Summer invariably reminds us how little we actually do other than go to school and work: drink, use drugs, and have sex if we're lucky. I'm not very lucky. But I make up for it with more drugs.

Kala walks back into her room and stares at us. We stare back. She just falls onto her bed languidly.

"So are you gonna get a training job?" she asks me finally.

"No." I have a serious problem with continually involving myself in conflicting pursuits. Last week I completed my personal fitness trainer certification: not a particularly sensible career move for a junkie.

"Why not?"

"Because people suck."

I don't like people. They tend to be stupid and dependent and lack any sense of reason or discipline, which makes them less than ideal clients. So fuck all of them. I'm going to sit on my ass and drink.

I empty my glass and stare down into it as it rests on my leg. I never told Kala. With a little distance from the whiskey and her lap, I realized I was wrong. I don't love her. I just want to. I just need to. I'm just grasping for anything to hold onto because I know I can't hold onto myself anymore. Kala has been anchoring my life for too long. I continue to strip away the layers and she always remains. She's always there for me to fall back on.

Laina shifts on the couch listlessly and leans against my side. I don't know what's going on with us. We've been following a pattern of constant motion since we met. The lines we draw fade and blur and leave us stumbling. I know I've hurt her. I know I hurt her every time she lets herself trust me. I know I've never wanted to. But I know I always will.

"You want another margarita?" Kala asks me.

I consider my empty glass again. "No, I'm gonna take off. I need to get some shit done."

Laina sits up so I can stand and watches me. "Are you coming back later?"

"I don't know," I tell her. "Maybe."


I don't have anything to do. But sometimes this cold distance seeps into me and I can't be with anyone anymore. Our nights are a shaky video recording repeating endlessly on a flickering screen across the room. It's always the same. We're all the same.

The doorbell rings and I decide I should probably answer it because whoever it is may become upset and decide to vandalize my car. I open the door and Laina looks up at me.

"Hey," she says shyly.

"Hey, what're you doing?"

She shrugs. "Didn't feel like seeing all those people at Kala's."

She follows me upstairs into my room and sees the cards on the floor. "Oh my god, you're actually playing solitaire."

Laina and I spend an unhealthy amount of time arguing about which one of us is more of a loser based on how frequently we play solitaire. I think I win.

"You're such a loser," she says.

I shrug and sit back down on the floor by the cards.

Laina sits next to me and leans back against the side of my bed, pointing out a move I missed. "Don't you hate it when people play over your shoulder?" she says.

"Yes. Stop."

Laina suddenly reaches out and smears the cards all over the carpet. I yell and grab her wrists, trying to wrestle her away from the cards, but she manages to swipe at a few more before I push her onto her side and hold her down with my weight.

"Get off me, fat ass!" she screams.

"You're fat!"

"You are!"

Laina grabs the waistband of my boxers and pulls it like a ripcord. A vision of little Dave hanging from a doorknob by his tighty-whities flashes through my head and I suddenly realize it's not as funny from on the doorknob. She laughs and pushes me off of her while I extract my boxers from my ass. Finally I give up resisting and Laina straddles my waist, pinning my wrists to the floor. She smiles over me, her dark hair swinging down around her face as she waits to catch her breath.

We stare at each other silently. What exactly are we doing? Laina looks like she's asking a few questions of her own. I feel her grip on my wrists begin to loosen and she slowly lets go and leans back, still watching me closely.

"Look," she says. "I should probably get back to Kala's."

"Yeah..." I agree reluctantly.

Slipping off me, Laina straightens her shirt as she stands. "Call me," she says. "OK?"

"Yeah."

Laina glances back at me one more time and walks out the door.

I drain my beer and set the empty bottle on the table, spinning it weakly in my fingers. I'm bored and out of alcohol. Fuck drinking anyway. Pushing back from the table, I wander into Kala's room and drop myself into the corner chair, leaning my head back and slowly closing my eyes.

Shannon's voice wakes me up again. "What're you doing?"

"Exactly what it looks like," I tell him.

"I'm still E-ing a little, dude, you wanna tr—"

"Yes."

I walk outside and lean through the window of my truck to reach under the center console. I find two plastic bags: one filled with leftover scraps of gel tabs and the other with collected mushroom shake. Stepping back inside, I toss the bags on the kitchen table in front of Shannon. His smile grows.

"There's a few tabs worth of scraps, plus all that shake," I tell him.

"Well," he says, looking up at me. "Let's eat it."

Gina walks into the room while I start dividing the drugs into equal portions. "What're you guys doing?"

"Drugs."

"Oh." She sits down next to me and watches.

I start chewing on my mushrooms. They're dry and stiff and chewing them doesn't really do anything.

Shannon gets to work on his share and makes the stale urine face. "Uhh. I need something to drink."

"Pussy."

Shannon sits back down with a glass of orange juice and washes down the rest of his mushrooms. I swallow everything and drop the acid scraps under my tongue.

"Drink more," I tell Shannon, nodding at his empty glass. "We need Vitamin C."

"Why do you need Vitamin C?" Gina asks me.

"Makes it work better."

I'm not a big fan of Gina. She's obnoxious and arrogant and probably wouldn't have sex with me. I don't even know why she's here. She's not usually part of this crew. But I'm an attention slut, and she seems exceedingly fascinated with me and what I'm doing right now.

Gina looks at the electronic balance Jason left on the table. "Let's weigh stuff," she says.

I stare at her. "What?"

She turns on the balance and picks up a bottle cap. "How much does it weigh?"

Shannon is immediately enthralled. "One gram," he says enthusiastically.

Gina drops the cap on the balance and they anxiously watch the digital display. "Two grams," she announces.

Shannon swears and looks for something else to weigh.

The speed in my acid has kicked in and I'm getting restless: we've run out of things to weigh. I finish my fourth or fifth serving of orange juice and rinse the glass out in the sink.

Shannon follows me. "I think Kala wants to go bed, dude. We should probably go."

"OK." I set the glass down. "Where."

"I don't know."

"What time is it?"

"It's only like 11:00," he says. "Let's just go to the park and walk around or something."

Shannon grabs his keys and we climb into my truck. I eventually figure out how to start the engine and we peel out down the street. My passion for driving at night when I'm on acid has proven to be less than safe. I find myself staring in my side mirror at the pretty colored lights reflecting in the dark puddles behind me instead of through the windshield at the stationary cars in front of me.

I pull up to the sidewalk in front of Cooper Park and we walk out to the playground. Shannon unwraps a piece of gum and carefully refolds the foil.

"What're you doing?" I ask him.

"Keeping the wrapper. I bet you in a few hours I'll find it again in my pocket and it'll be really cool."

We wander over to the sidewalk again after unenthusiastically kicking the swings awhile and stop by a streetlight. There's a bright circle of yellow light painted on the sidewalk, defined sharply by the surrounding darkness. I sit on a wide wooden post that seems good for sitting on and watch Shannon kick around a rock that seems good for kicking around.

"Dude," Shannon says suddenly. "Remember that part in *Alice in Wonderland* when they go from Nighttime Land to Daytime Land?"

"Not really."

He ignores my response and points at the sharp circle of light on the sidewalk. "Look at that. Just look inside the circle and not around it. Everything is light, like in daytime. That's weird, huh."

"Yeah."

Shannon steps over near the light and stares down at it. "Dude, right now I'm in Nighttime." He steps into the light. "And now I'm in Daytime." He steps back out into the dark. "Now I'm in Nighttime again," he grins. "That's crazy, huh."

Shannon freezes suddenly and looks at me. "Dude, let's go to the beach!"

he smiles. "What time is it?"

"Like 2:00."

"Let's go to the beach!"

We head back to my truck and climb in. I stare at the dash and try to remember where the key goes.

"Are you cool to drive?" he asks me.

No.

"Yeah."

We pull away and I notice my truck making an unusual noise. It sounds like something important is fucked up. I shrug and turn up the music until the noise goes away.

Highway 17, the winding four-lane highway that runs through the Santa Cruz Mountains, is widely regarded as one of the most dangerous roads in the country. The lanes are narrow, there's no shoulder, the turns are unexpectedly sharp, and the average speed of traffic tends to be far beyond the posted limit.

"Dude, we're going to Santa Cruz," Shannon laughs, because driving to Santa Cruz at 2:00 A.M. on drugs that significantly reduce one's driving abilities is fucking hilarious.

The grade begins to level and the sign for the summit flies past us. I feel the road begin to descend and I'm suddenly blinded, enveloped in a sheet of brilliant grey. I can barely make out the road directly over the hood of the truck.

"What the fuck!" Shannon yells.

Fog. It must be fog. But why is it so bright? I become conscious of my foot planted on the gas pedal. Maybe I should slow down. I downshift and let the engine begin to slow the car.

"Whoa, dude, what?"

We find the answer to our blindness. A grove of CalTrans's work spotlights has sprouted on the backside of the summit, the blazing white light reflecting off the cement dust thickening the fog.

"Oh shit!"

I slam on the brakes as I see a parked highway patrol car and smile politely as we pass, hoping the cop notices my nice haircut. He glances up from his newspaper briefly and goes back to being bored and in dire need of a mobile pastry distribution unit. CalTrans has closed off the northbound lanes entirely and has redirected the traffic into the inner southbound lane.

We're now separated from oncoming traffic by nothing but intermittent orange cones that I have an overwhelming urge to slalom through at sixty miles an hour.

I look around in sudden confusion. I don't recognize this road. "Dude, are we still on 17?" I ask Shannon.

"I don't know, dude..."

I glance at him. He's leaning forward and staring out the windshield, trying like me to orient himself.

"I didn't turn off, did I?"

He rubs his hair in a slow circle. "I don't think so..."

"Then I guess this is still 17," I shrug, flooring the gas again.

"Go left here," Shannon says.

I turn and coast down the street. "That's not it."

"Shit. Turn right here."

I turn again.

"No, this isn't it," he frowns.

We're somewhere in Santa Cruz. I have no idea where. Apparently Shannon doesn't either.

"Dude, we're on the wrong side," I say. I point behind us. "The ocean is that way."

He looks at me and back at the road. "Are you sure?"

"Not really. But apparently it's not over here." I spin the wheel and head back to the last main intersection. "Which way?"

Shannon shrugs. "Right?"

We roll through the deserted streets looking for anything familiar.

"This is it!" Shannon yells. "Turn right up here!"

Shannon finally manages to direct me to the harbor and we walk through the sandy parking lot onto the wall of enormous cement jacks separating the small harbor from the beach. We stop and kick at the jacks, trying to move them even though we know they probably each weigh more than my car.

"Dude, how do you think these things got here?" Shannon asks me, kicking one of the jacks.

"A crane." I tend to ruin other people's acid fantasies.

"Maybe it was a giant playing jacks on the beach," Shannon says, ignoring my more practical response, "and he just forgot them when he left."

I laugh and we walk down the cement ramp to the sand.

Shannon freezes and grabs my arm. "Dude," he says, pointing to something dark creeping out from a crack in the ramp by his feet. "What the fuck is that?"

We squat down to get a closer look.

"I don't know," I shrug.

"Is it moving?"

We stare at it thoughtfully. Everything is moving right now.

"Touch it," Shannon says.

"What? No, dude."

"Come on, dude."

"You touch it."

"No way, dude."

Shannon gets on his hands and knees and lowers his face to the ground. "Oh, dude. It's a plastic bag."

Standing up again, he brushes the sand off his palms and the two of us walk out onto the beach. A massive piece of driftwood is still smoking in the sand from an earlier bonfire. I walk to it and stare at the glowing embers in the core.

"Dude," Shannon says. "Last time I was here, we were walking back to the car and I stopped to pee in those bushes up there, and I'm peeing, right—I'm frying nuts—and I look down and I'm peeing on a guy! There was this guy passed out in the bushes and I was peeing on him!"

"Did he wake up?"

"No!"

"So what'd you do?"

"Finished the pee and shook off!"

I laugh and look up at the moon. It's deep blue and almost full. The white foam of the small waves running up and down the shore glows in the soft light. I inhale deeply and smile at the gentle scents of smoldering wood and saltwater, the peace—

"Dude!" Shannon holds out his hand. "I still have the gum wrapper!"

I nod and watch him inspect it intently in the moonlight.

He finally looks up again. "You wanna go somewhere else?"

"OK."

We walk back along the shoreline and up the cement ramp, past the plastic bag and back onto the jacks. Stopping on the path above the harbor, we look down at all the moored boats rocking with the waves.

"Dude, what is that shit?" I ask Shannon, pointing down to the water at a collection of indiscernible black spots.

He looks. "Rocks, dude."

I look closer. "No, dude, they're floating."

"What? Nuh-uh, dude."

"Yeah, dude, look."

Shannon strains to see in the dark. "Shit, what are those things?"

I squint and concentrate. "Are those ducks?"

"What? Nooo, dude."

"Yeah, check it out."

"Dude, they're rocks."

"They're floating!"

"I don't know, dude, ducks?"

"Dude, I swear, look. Those have to be ducks."

Shannon thinks. "Throw something at them."

I look by my feet for a rock. No rocks. The two of us scour the ground for any kind of projectile. We're not leaving until we figure this out.

"Wait, here we go, dude," I say, finding a rock and winding up. "Watch." I let it fly. It lands in the middle of the little black things, which proceed to sprout wings and scatter.

Shannon stares in disbelief. "Whoa, dude, what the fuck?"

"See dude, I told you those were ducks."

Someone got ahold of a beach house for Kala's birthday tonight. The girl who brought me water when I was drunk and puking on grad night is here. I still don't know her name. But she's been leaning on my shoulder all night, so it seems a little late to ask. We left midnight behind a couple hours ago and a few of the lighter-weight guests have faded away or slipped surreptitiously into bedrooms to fuck. And apparently Kala has forgiven Jason for whatever it was he did earlier tonight to send her running into the street in tears while he sat laughing on the couch with Steve.

I spit over the fence and screw the cap back onto my bottle. I don't even feel like drinking tonight. I'm not finding anything interesting but my persistent thoughts of Laina. I haven't even seen her in at least an hour. I've just been sitting out on the porch staring into an empty parking lot being not drunk.

"Hey."

I turn. It's Nameless Girl. "Hey back."

She sits down next to me. "Are you drunk?"

"No." I hold up the bottle. It's only down a few fingers.

"Everyone's going to bed, but I don't want to," she says. "You gonna stay up with me?"

"Sure."

Nameless Girl glances behind her at the house. "Let's go for a walk. We can see if that weird lady is still out there."

Nameless Girl talks breathlessly while we walk. I listen and nod occasionally. She's not annoying, she just isn't interesting. She just isn't Laina. I throw out a word or two when necessary and she just laughs, bumps her hip into mine occasionally, and keeps talking about nothing. We walk to the beach and sit on the cement retaining wall between the sidewalk and the sand.

Nameless Girl looks out past the jetty and frowns. "The weird lady's not there anymore," she says.

"Maybe she drowned."

"That's mean."

"I didn't say I hope she drowned, I just suggested drowning as a reasonable explanation for her absence."

"OK," she nods.

I glance at Nameless Girl. Is she trying to encourage me to make a move, or is my dick making assumptions for me again? Maybe she just wanted to walk to the beach and I was her only available company. Either way, I'm not drunk anymore and she's not my angel.

I finally slide off the wall and look at Nameless Girl. She gets the hint and follows me. We walk back to the house and I drop back into my chair on the porch while Nameless Girl slips inside. The yellow glow of the crime lights on the liquor store wall makes the parking lot look fake and distant. I think about the whiskey in the freezer but decide against it. It's almost 3:00 in the morning.

Nameless Girl reappears and looks down at me. "I can't find Laina," she says nervously. "I just looked everywhere."

"Was she drinking?"

Nameless Girl shrugs. "I don't know, I think so."

My stomach sinks. She's drunk. She drove home. Drove back over 17 drunk. That little cement median is covered in rubber and paint from previous failed attempts. And Laina is the kind of girl who would do it. She would get up and leave without telling anyone. But she's not stupid. I know she's not stupid. She wouldn't try to drive that road if she were that drunk. But if she were that drunk, it wouldn't seem like a bad idea.

I stand up to grab my shoes from inside the door and Laina suddenly emerges and almost runs into me.

"Hey," she says casually.

I stare at her. "Where were you?"

"Walking on the beach." Laina sees the confusion in Nameless Girl's face. "I came back in through the other door," she explains.

I start breathing again and sit down next to her. That sucked.

Nameless Girl looks at the two of us and sees she's not as welcome as she used to be. "Uh... I'm gonna go to bed."

"Night," Laina says over her shoulder. She turns back to me and shakes her head at my concern.

"What?"

"Nothing," she smiles.

I watch her closely. "You scared the shit outta me."

"Why?"

"Cause, I thought you drove home drunk."

She shakes her head again. "You worry too much."

"I guess."

Laina laughs softly and takes a drink from her water bottle. I keep my eyes on her face.

"So where're you sleeping?" she asks me.

"Nowhere, now."

"What do you mean?"

"I was planning on just drinking too much and passing out under the kitchen table, but I'm not drunk and I don't feel like sleeping."

"Good," Laina smiles. "Let's go down to the beach and wait for sunrise."

She grabs a blanket from inside and we walk slowly to the beach without talking. Lying in the sand, I roll onto my side next to Laina and wrap the edge of the blanket around myself.

"Cold?" she smiles.

"Yes," I finally admit to her for the first time.

Laina pulls closer to me. I can feel the heat radiating from her body. I want to put my arm around her waist and push my face into her soft brown hair, but I can't. I don't want to push her away. We talk softly with the crashing waves, laughing with each other like we used to and watching the sky grow light. My eyes burn with exhaustion, but I don't want to sleep. The sun finally breaks from behind the hills and clean white light creeps slowly up the beach toward us. I hear distant voices and doors opening and brooms sweeping the sidewalks in front of the small shops down the street. Rolling onto my back, I stare up into the pale blue sky.

"You wanna go?" Laina asks me quietly.

"Sure."

"I mean leave here," explains. "Ditch them and go home."

I look over at her and smile. "Yeah. Let's go."

□    □    □

Brandi is in town this week. That's why my shirt is so small. It accentuates my thick chest and bulging arms. I mean it creates the illusion of a thick chest and bulging arms being accentuated. This is important because girls like thick chests and bulging arms and it will encourage Brandi—who is a girl and likes thick chests and bulging arms—to have sex with me.

Brandi turns off the television in Kala's living room and lays her head on the couch. The room is dark and everyone else has finally left or fallen asleep. I lean back in my chair and try to telepathically encourage Brandi to take her clothes off and climb into my lap.

"I'm gonna get woken up so early by Kala's mom," she sighs. "I just wanna sleep."

I pull my keys from my pocket and stand up. "You can stay at my place if you want."

Brandi looks at me in the dark. "Are you sure?"

"Yeah. Come on."

She follows me back to my house and we step quietly up the stairs into my room. I close the door behind myself and kick off my shoes.

"Take the bed," I tell Brandi. "I'll hit the floor."

Please ask me to get in bed with you.

"I can sleep on the floor," she says.

Damn it.

"Take the bed," I tell her again, pulling my shirt off and lying down on the carpet.

"Fine. At least take a pillow."

"No."

I will refuse any comfort or unnecessary sleeping accessories and this will encourage Brandi to have sex with me because she is at the mercy of her natural selection instincts and men who refuse pillows and comfort are strong and capable and must be mated with. Brandi slides under my sheets and I stare up at the ceiling and wait for my theory to be proven.

"So what's with you and Laina?" she asks quietly.

"I don't know."

"Are you guys gonna get back together?"

I laugh quietly.

Brandi peeks over the bed at me. "What."

"Laina hates my guts."

"No she doesn't. I saw you guys together."

"Yeah she does," I assure her. "I don't blame her, either."

"Yeah. Kala kinda told me what happened."

I roll onto my side facing the bed. "So you have a boyfriend?" [Read: Are we going to have sex tonight?]

"I did," she says. "We broke up a few months ago. I just wanna focus on school and dancing right now." Brandi is silent. "I'm still a virgin," she says softly.

"No you're not!"

"Swear."

We're not having sex.

"Why?"

"I don't know, I guess I just haven't found the right guy yet," she says. "What about you?"

I look at her in the dark. "Am I a virgin?"

"Yeah."

I should say yes. Maybe it would make her feel comfortable enough to finally express the intense and undeniable sexual attraction she feels for me. Or maybe I should say no. Maybe she wants a guy with experience for her first time.

"No."

"Mm."

I knew I should have said yes.

"So what about you and Kala?" she asks.

"What about me and Kala."

"You two should just get married."

"What?"

"Oh, come on," Brandi laughs. "It's so obvious you two are in love with each other."

"You were just talking about me and Laina," I remind her.

"Whatever," she says. "You know I'm right."

"If Kala's so in love with me, why is she with Jason?"

"Because she doesn't think she can have you. She's been trying for years and you keep backing out."

I shake my head at her. "You're fulla shit."

"OK," Brandi shrugs. "Whatever you say."

I drop a couple capsules into my hand and screw the lid back on the bottle. Shannon watches me, sitting on the edge of my bed chewing on a mouthful of mushrooms. He makes the stale urine face and takes a drink of orange juice.

"What is that shit?" he asks me.

I swallow the pills and toss him the bottle. "Vanadyl sulfate. It increases cell membrane permeability."

Shannon stares at me.

"It makes your body absorb things you ingest more quickly and completely," I explain. "Take it with mushrooms and it makes you trip quicker and harder."

I eat my bag of mushrooms and we drive to Whitey's place. In his naturally excessive friendliness, Shannon mistakenly promised we'd stop by and unintentionally gave Whitey the impression we wanted to spend quality time with him.

Slipping out of the truck, Shannon looks at me. "Let's get in and out, dude."

Whitey lives in a former garage with a dirt floor covered incompletely with assorted scraps of carpet. There's little light and everything is coated in greasy dust. I'm afraid to touch anything. I don't want hepatitis. I position myself in the cleanest part of the room and stand very still.

Bryan looks up at us from his chair. "What's up."

"Nothing, dude..." Shannon says quietly, trying to find the second cleanest part of the room.

Krist, that vanadyl sulfate worked faster than usual. I'm already feeling the mushrooms. The walls are swelling and everything I look at is unstable. Whitey suddenly bursts into the room yelling an incomprehensible string of profanities apparently focused on someone named That Fucking Bitch.

"Whitey," Bryan interrupts, "shut the fuck up for a second. What're you talking about?"

"That fucking bitch," he starts again to explain. It appears Whitey's mushroom connection has fallen through.

"Can you get any?" Bryan asks me.

"No," I lie, trying to conceal my elation and look sympathetic.

Bryan reaches for the phone. "There's one more guy I can try."

"All right, well, we need to get outta here," I say, taking advantage of the opportunity to escape. "Just page me later if you get anything."

Bryan nods.

"Late..." Shannon says, following me out the door.

I glance back toward Whitey's place as we reach my truck. I stop walking and start laughing because I can't do both.

Shannon looks at me. "What's your problem?"

"I'm trippin nuts already."

"I'm starting to." He looks at me. "Dude, let's walk to Kala's."

I lock the truck and we start down the street. I reach up to brush the hair off my forehead, but it's not on my forehead. My ear itches. I scratch it. I scratch it again. My hair is back on my forehead, but it's not. I brush it away and itch my ear again.

"Fuck, dude, we've been walking forever," Shannon says.

"Yeah, this is the longest two blocks I've ever walked in my life," I agree, brushing away the hair that's not on my forehead. I scratch my ear. My palms feel moist. Am I bleeding? There's blood on my palms. I wipe them off on my pant legs, but they're still wet. I brush the hair off my forehead and wipe my palms again. Shit, I just walked through a spider web. I rub my face trying to get it off, but I feel it tickling me again every time I drop my hands.

"Dude," Shannon says, "we're still walking."

"Yeah, fuck." I swipe furiously at the spider webs and my hair and wipe my palms again. Fuck! My hands are bleeding and there's shit all over my face!

Four hours or five minutes later we finally stumble up to Kala's house. It looks dark.

Shannon looks at me. "Shit, dude, is anyone here?"

"I don't know... Everyone's cars are here..."

"Maybe we should go around back," he says.

"Yeah."

Shannon fumbles with the latch on the gate and cautiously pushes it open. I step through and close it quietly behind myself. It's pitch-black back here. I take a step forward and bump into Shannon.

"Sorry."

I hear Shannon start moving and I step carefully through the blackness. There's a loud metal crash and I run into Shannon again.

"What the fuck was that?" I ask the shadow in front of me.

"I think I just knocked something over, dude."

We stand still, waiting for the silence to help us navigate the darkness.

"Hello?"

"Kala," Shannon says. "It's us."

A light flips on. I squint and look down at the bike lying on its side by Shannon's feet. He looks back at me and grins. We walk around the corner of the house onto Kala's porch and everyone stares at us curiously.

"Why'd you guys walk around that way?" Kala laughs.

I shrug. "It seemed like a good idea at the time."

I sit down in a vacant plastic chair and jump to my feet again because my crotch is vibrating. Grabbing at my shirt, I pull the pager from my waistband and look at the screen. I keep looking at it. I look at it again.

Finally I hand the pager to Laina. "What does that say?"

She reads me the number and hands it back to me.

I look at it again and think. "Whose fucking number is that?"

Laina shrugs. "I don't know."

I shake my head and slide the pager back into my pants.

Shannon jumps through the doorway and grins at me. "Dude. We're watching *Alice in Wonderland*."

The movie ends and I look around the room at everyone. My eyes stop on Laina, then jump to Kala, then wander back to Laina. I don't know these people anymore. They're like memories with forgotten names. Everyone is so different, so distant, so unrecognizable. Maybe it's just the drugs.

My crotch starts vibrating again and I grab my pager and stare at the number in confusion. Finally I just give up thinking and slide the pager back into my pants. Kala flips on the light and I squint as my eyes adjust slowly. Who the fuck are these people?

Laina glances at me and stands up, pulling out her car keys. "I'm going to bed."

Kala waves and I watch Laina leave. The rest of the strangers file out one by one until Shannon and I are the only ones left. For a minute I forget where I am.

"You wanna go?" Shannon asks me.

"Where."

"I don't know," he shrugs. "Walk around."

"Yeah."

Shannon jumps onto Kala's bed and hugs her. "Bye Kala!"

"Bye," she says breathlessly from underneath him.

I just stand in the doorway watching her silently, feeling the distant unfamiliarity.

Shannon and I walk back through the side yard and I pick up the fallen bike and lean it against the wall on my way out the gate. Stopping in the middle of the empty road, we look at each other.

"Where should we go?"

"I don't know."

I look down the road to where it dead-ends against an ivy-covered fence. "Let's go that way."

"It's a dead-end," Shannon says.

"It's a fence, dude, not the edge of the world."

We walk to the dead-end and contemplate the fence. The ivy is too thick for us to see through to the other side.

"What's over there?" Shannon asks.

"I don't know," I shrug. "But there's nothing on this side."

We posthole through the ivy on the ground and I grab ahold of the chain-link fence. Shannon tries to use his height to peek over to the other side, but the ivy is too high. I jump and push myself up to straddle the fence, quickly swinging my second leg over and dropping down on the other side. My feet are stopped by cement. I look up as Shannon drops down next to me. We turn slowly to see where we are.

"Parking lot," Shannon says.

We walk along the back of a dark building cautiously. We have no idea where we are.

"Dude, it's like we're in another world," Shannon says quietly.

I nod and stop by a dumpster. There's a large piece of mechanical equipment sitting on the cement next to it, broken and neglected. I kick it curiously. It doesn't do anything. The two of us pace back and forth contemplating the machine. This is important.

Shannon kneels down next to it and brings his face in close. "Dude, what do you do?"

I laugh and kick it again.

Finally we give up on the unresponsive machine and walk through a narrow alley to the front of the building. I stop and look up and down the street. I know where we are.

"Dude, this is Altos Oaks," I tell Shannon.

His face lights up. "Yeah."

I kneel down and grab a handful of gravel from the side of the building and clench my fist, slowly grinding the rocks against each other. I grab more gravel in my other hand and keep grinding.

"Dude, what're you doing?" Shannon asks me.

I open my hands and show him the little rocks. "Feels cool."

Shannon picks up some of his own gravel and we wander out into the road. There's a dim light glowing inside an office across the street. We walk slowly to the plate glass window and gaze into the empty waiting room.

"Dude, I've been in there before," I realize.

"What for?"

"To get blood tests. My white blood cell count is way low."

"Why?"

"Apparently this whole thing with using a lot of drugs and never eating or sleeping isn't that healthy," I tell him. "I'm probably gonna die."

We stroll back down the sidewalk and stand in the middle of the empty road. Sliding my hands into my pockets, I find the gravel and begin grinding it again. Shannon tosses his rocks one by one down the street.

"Dude, you know what's crazy," he says. "I'm moving to San Diego on Saturday."

I glance at him. "Yeah..."

"We're all just leaving."

I nod and toss one of my rocks.

"It's crazy," he says, shaking his head. "We've all been friends for so long and now everyone's leaving. You think we'll all still see each other and hang out and shit?"

I shrug and Shannon throws the rest of his rocks. I toss a handful up into the air and watch them rain down onto the pavement.

"I don't know," I say finally, rolling my last rock between my fingers. "I don't know what's gonna happen."

□   □   □

My eyes burn in the flickering blue television light. Laina is asleep on the couch with me, her face buried in my chest, her long brown hair soft against my neck. I watch my fingers run softly over the tanned skin on her lower back and remember the thrill of touching her for the first time. I shouldn't do this. She shouldn't let me. I know I don't deserve another chance. I know I never even deserved the first.

I look over at Kala sleeping in her bed. The blue numbers on the clock behind her head glow in the dark. Past three in the morning. Laina stirs and I watch her wake slowly and look up at me.

"We should go," I tell her quietly.

Laina sighs in exhaustion and lays her head back down against my chest. I cautiously run my fingers through her hair. Finally exhaling heavily, she pushes herself upright and sits against me, holding her face in her hands as she struggles to wake up. I hear Kala shifting and look over as she rolls onto her side and brushes the hair out of her face.

"Are you guys going?" she asks.

I stand up and grab my car keys from the floor. "Yeah."

"Could you make sure the front door's locked?"

"Yeah, go back to sleep."

Laina stands up next to me and heads for the door, waving to Kala as she steps into the dark hallway. I stop and lean against the doorframe at the foot of Kala's bed.

She rolls onto her back and props herself up on her elbows. "Are you guys OK?"

"Yeah, go back to sleep," I tell her. "I'll call you tomorrow."

Kala smiles in the dark and I slip out and quietly shut the door, following Laina outside into the street. She leans back against the side of her car and watches me.

"So what're you gonna do now?" she yawns.

"I don't know." I sit down on the pavement and wrap my arms around my knees, leaning back to look up at her. "What about you?"

She shrugs. "Probably read awhile."

"Read?"

"Yeah, read. You know what reading is?"

"Yes I know what reading is."

She laughs softly and shifts her weight. "So you're just gonna go home?"

"I guess." Am I supposed to have other plans? I scratch the back of my neck and look up at her. "Come over for a while."

Laina drops her eyes and uneasily shifts her weight back and forth, searching for comfort she can't find. Slowly she sits down a few feet away from me, knocking her key chain nervously against the pavement. I watch her closely. Her eyes wander apprehensively, carefully avoiding the question in mine.

"We can't do this anymore…" she finally whispers. "I can't let myself get close to you like this again." She looks up into my eyes and drops her gaze.

I turn and face the darkness. "I know," I nod finally, looking back at Laina as she stares at the ground. "I know."

She's silent. I listen to the breeze rustling in the bare tree branches above our heads. I should have kept my distance. I was stupid to believe I'm any different from the one who's hurt her every time she's let me.

"You meant more to me than anyone else ever has," she says. "No one's ever hurt me as much as you did. I love being with you, but when we're together, I start to forget about the past. And I can't let myself forget."

I look up at Laina's beautiful face as she searches for words. Her dark eyes glow in the faint moonlight.

"I don't think I could ever forgive you for everything that happened," she says softly.

I nod slowly and stare at the cracks in the pavement. "I never expected you to forgive me. I never thought this would happen again," I tell her quietly. "I wish it could be different, I really do. I never meant to hurt you."

Laina shakes her head and sniffs. "I don't understand you. I never understood you. Nothing that happened ever made any sense to me and it still doesn't."

"It doesn't really make any sense to me either."

"I tried," she says. "I really tried to forgive you and be your friend again. But I can't forget our history."

"I know," I tell her quietly. "But I can't change it now."

"So what am I supposed to do?"

I shrug slowly. "I don't know."

Laina looks at me carefully. "I really thought we had something, even when we first met. I really thought it was gonna work. I thought it would last."

"It did last, in a way," I offer weakly. "I've never been with a girl as long as I've been with you."

She laughs. "Is that supposed to make me feel better?"

"Well, no. I don't know."

"You've never been with another girl that long, but you've never hurt another girl as much, either," she reminds me.

"You're right," I shrug. They've never let me. "You're right. But what do you want me to say?"

"I don't know," she says quietly.

I drop my head. Laina picks at the cracks in the street with one of her keys. I feel a light raindrop on my arm and glance up into the black sky.

"What about her," Laina says finally, nodding at Kala's house.

I stare at her. "What?"

"I know you still have feelings for her," she says. "I still see something between you two."

I shake my head. "That ended a long time ago."

"It never ended," Laina tells me.

"I don't know," I say, glancing at the house.

"I think you do." She stands up slowly. "You always have. All the girls you've been with in the last few years: you've just been looking for her. She was always right in front of you." Laina shakes her head slightly. "I was never what you really wanted."

I watch my feet. "I never wanted to hurt you," I tell her again.

"I know," she nods.

"For whatever it's worth, I'm sorry," I tell her quietly. "I wish I could change things, but I can't."

"No, you can't." Laina opens her car door and turns to face me. "Look, maybe it's good that you're leaving," she says. "I don't think I wanna see you anymore."

I nod slowly, knowing I should just let it go. There are no last words. I walk past Laina silently to my truck and she slips into her car and pulls away, her taillights disappearing sharply around the corner. My eyes burn. I'm never going to see her again.

My immediate reaction is to slam my forearm several times into the passenger seat because violent demonstrations of rage are far easier for me than expression of the genuine emotions for which they substitute. Eventually I realize that beating the shit out of my own car probably won't accomplish a great deal for me and I start the engine without exerting an excess of force to the ignition.

Driving home slowly, my mind wanders to Kala as it always seems to when everyone else rejects my mental approaches. Maybe Kala is the reason I hurt Laina so badly. Maybe she's the reason I'm never satisfied, the reason I'm never able to stay with a girl. It seems to make sense. Even Brandi saw it. Kala has always been what I've really wanted. I'm going to write her a letter and explain. A long letter. But not too long. Exceedingly long letters generally indicate obsession and other weirdness involved with stalking and are not well received. But I have to tell her everything. I have to tell her I love her.

I park in my driveway and kill the engine, looking at the dark house. Sometimes I'm afraid to sleep. Each night I lie alone silently and it consumes me. All the fear, all the uncertainty, all the panic swallows me in the stillness. Every night I slip further away from myself. And I'm so tired. I'm so tired of making excuses. Two blood tests showing severely low white blood cell levels and I'm still doing this to myself. I knew from the start what was happening. But I couldn't stop. Clenching my jaw, I seethe at the thought of the time I've wasted, the thought of everything I've done to myself. I think of the endlessly swelling string of lies I've fed myself and everyone that ever mattered to me. I think of the sleepless nights, the uncontrollable binges, the shamefully hidden addictions. I lie to myself every time I look in the mirror.

But I've tried to escape before. I've been trying to escape from the moment I fell in. And I've never made it. I've always slipped on the edge. I've always fallen back to what I know. It's the only thing I've ever had that I knew would never leave me. They're always waiting to pull me back in when I need them to save me from myself. I can't shake loose. I always fall. I always let myself fall. And they're always waiting for me at the bottom. Waiting to watch me give in again and crawl.

Laina and Kala were my life. And now Laina's gone. Kala is the last thread between my fingers, the last hand around my ankle in the dark below me. But it's a mistake. Everything I let myself believe. I'm not in love with her; I'm afraid of myself. It was always a lie. I clench my jaw and breathe the cold air deeply. It's over now. I have to get out. I have to get all the way out.

CHAPTER SEVEN

I set a crate down on the table and start laying out the parts boxes in front of me. It's been a month since Laina told me she never wanted to see me again. I quickly escaped to LA and haven't looked back. I haven't seen or spoken to any of my friends. I haven't touched a grain of coke or a scrap of acid. And I'm through with it. I'm through with them, with that life, with all of it. Every day my vision is clearer. They never meant anything to me. They were only distractions and comfortable options in a package deal I never intended to buy. No one has ever experienced the kind of pain I have. I now actively reject all comfort and social interaction. I need nothing. I am so intense now.

Grabbing a valve body, I begin methodically assembling the sensing head while my mind wanders from the cold cement walls. It's here with my newfound vision I construct my most profound insights into life, which invariably manage to remind me how intense I am. Like this one: These valves are like people. Watching them, their complexity seems overwhelming. But when you finally break them down and step back, you see the incredible simplicity. They're all the same. Weights, colors, textures, names, it doesn't matter. They're all the same. And not one is as intense as

I am.

"Greg!"

I look up from my valve at David and he holds out the phone to me. I walk over to the wall and take it.

"Greg," the receptionist says, "your mother's been trying to get ahold of you. You want me to dial her for you?"

"No, I'll call her later." I hang up and return to my valve philosophy.


I unlock the door and step into the apartment. Geoffrey, a former employee and close friend of my grandfather's who took over his business when he died, has been generous enough to give me the spare room in his apartment along with a job. He's a well-dressed and unbelievably charming Englishman who drives a new Jaguar and manages to inspire women forty years his junior to fall in love with him before I can even finish my first drink. Unfortunately, his dedication to the company translates into little free time, and I'm unable to learn his secrets with my limited exposure to him. He does, however, insist I drive the Jaguar when we go out, which, along with my tightly cropped hair, chronic lack of a smile, and various other visible manifestations of my intensity, has had me mistaken several times for his bodyguard, a role I'm more than honored to play. In seeming contrast to his professional lifestyle, he's a devoted keeper of a balcony garden, to which he recently added what he believed to be a small lemon tree. When we realized it instead produced small oranges, we resourcefully began substituting them for the lemons in our gin and tonics.

"It's a lovely drink," we agreed.

My days here are routine and unvarying: wake up in the dark to a piercing alarm, say the word fuck approximately seven-to-fifteen times, hit the deserted gym, back to the apartment to shower, drive to work, think about how intense I am while I build valves, come home, eat something with HP sauce on it, have a few gin and tonics, read, watch TV while I stretch, go to sleep. [I know, I'm still drinking. Alcohol will be the last substance rejected since it seems to be relatively benign, and, more importantly, it's effectively impossible to cohabitate with the English without drinking. Once I leave LA, I'll have gained sufficient control over my urges and will have no problem abandoning alcohol permanently in order to achieve peak intensity.] I don't mind the monotony. I've quickly grown accustomed to it and actually find comfort and satisfaction in the numbness. It makes me feel alive to work long hours in a cement-floored warehouse, to walk the unfamiliar streets alone, to have no one.

I rub my eyes slowly. Sometimes I try to sleep. I don't think I ever really do. Walking back to my room, I see Geoffrey in his office, his face glowing in the blue light of the computer screen.

"Your mother called for you," he tells me. "I think you should probably call her tonight."

I watch him closely. Something's wrong. I duck out of the office and dial home. "Jamie's in the hospital," my mother tells me. "She overdosed on her meds last night."

"Why's she still in the hospital?"

"She's on a respirator."

"Well is she gonna be all right?"

The line is quiet. "They don't really know," she says finally. "I just thought you should know what's going on."

"Yeah…"

"I'll call you with any news, OK?"

"Yeah."

I hang up and Geoffrey walks out from his office. He knows.

"I thought you should hear it from your mother first," he tells me quietly.

"Yeah," I nod. "Thanks."

"Fix yourself a drink," he says.

"No, I don't— Yeah."

I pull a bottle from the cupboard and mix a gin & tonic for myself. Drinking it quickly, I stare at the glass and pour another. Goddamn it, Jaime. I have a third drink and rinse the glass.

"Look, I'm going to bed," I tell Geoffrey. "I'll see you tomorrow."

He nods slightly and heads back to his office.

Closing the door behind myself, I sit on the edge of the bed and stare at the yellow lights out the window. I see my sister in a brilliant white hospital bed with a tube down her throat, machines coldly monitoring any trace of life. I see the wild, unfinished map of scars underneath her arms, remember the sounds of frightened whispers and her distant indifference the first time my mother noticed the sharp grey marks. Finally undressing, I lie down and stare unmoving at the books on the dresser.

I snap the sheets off suddenly and find my notebook. Lying back down and turning to a clean page, I stare at the thin blue lines. I've tried to write before. It was never anything more than scattered, pedestrian, retrospectfully embarrassing drivel. But with my newfound intensity and rage, I'm confident my literary creativity will now be unrivaled.

□　　□　　□

I worked late tonight and I can't face the apartment. Jaime was released from the hospital yesterday. Her voice was rough and strained over the phone from having a tube down her throat for so long. We talked like nothing had happened. I'm sitting in my truck on the side of Magnolia Street with the window open, listening to the sounds of the passing cars mixing with the music. The cool night air feels so real in my chest. The night makes everything clean again. The traffic noise quiets the noise in my head sometimes. I pull on my sweatshirt hood and watch the people walking out of the office building across the street. Each time a woman walks out, I look away. I'm afraid she'll think I want to hurt her.

I start the engine and pull away from the curb. Turning right onto San Fernando, I drive by all the brightly lit stores and the coffee places, watching the people sitting outside with their friends and their cigarettes. It's the only contact I have with anyone anymore. I don't want to get any closer.

□　　□　　□

I glance around my old room from my seat on the floor. The wall glows a soft orange in the setting sun. Nothing left but a futon and the notebook in my lap. I write now. I write in this notebook, scribbling endlessly with this sharp black pen, scratching at the paper, scratching at the ghosts and the silent films flickering behind my eyelids. I close the door on the rest of the world and try to tear it all out. In a month I'll be thirteen hours and a lifetime away from this wreckage. I need to step out of this suffocating grey and begin again in black and white, with straight lines and sharp angles. I need the isolation to rebuild. Holy shit I am so intense.

I pick up the ringing phone slowly and walk to the window. "Yeah."

"Greg?" Silence. "It's Staci…"

"Staci," I repeat quietly. "Shit."

She laughs cautiously. "How've you been?"

"I've been all right," I lie. No one wants the answer to that one.

"It's good to hear your voice again," she says. "Can you meet me somewhere?"


Driving slowly through the parking lot, I scan the tables in front of the coffee place. I see a smooth sheet of black hair and swallow. That's her. Parking out of sight, I sit in my truck and watch the traffic on El Monte. I don't know what Staci expects from me. I don't even know why I'm here. I don't know what I'm going to say to her. Hey, I don't speak to any of my friends anymore, I don't drink, I don't use drugs, I harbor an unhealthily severe hatred for most of the human population, I'm becoming partially psychotic from sleep deprivation, and I sit in my room alone seething all day and writing absolute shit no one will ever read. Do you want to have sex?

Taking a breath, I finally slip out and walk slowly to Staci's table. She smiles when she recognizes me, standing up and wrapping her arms around my back. I hold her weakly and find myself fixated on the unfamiliar feeling of her soft hair against my skin.

Staci looks at me as we sit down. "Do you want anything?"

"No, I'm OK."

We watch each other uncomfortably for a moment.

"So this is the last thing I expected to be doing tonight," I tell her finally.

"Yeah," she laughs. "So how've you been?"

Any psychiatrist would be immediately convinced I'm mentally unsound and in need of indefinite commitment. I only decided to see you because I'm subconsciously entertaining the possibility of sleeping with you, the current extent of my emotional availability.

"Pretty good," I shrug.

Staci gazes at me. "God, what's it been, two or three years?"

"Yeah, almost three years."

She pulls her chair closer to the table. "I didn't know if you were gonna be at your old number or not."

"I wasn't. I just got back from LA last week."

"You were living down there?"

I consider the question carefully. "I was working down there."

"So what're you doing now?"

"Just waiting to get outta here," I shrug.

Staci laughs. "Where're you going now?"

"Going to school in Arizona. Leaving on the first."

"As in January first?" she frowns. "Why're you leaving so soon?"

"Soon? I've been waiting to leave forever."

"Yeah," she smiles, "but it's soon to me."

"Sorry."

"Wait—" Staci says suddenly with a disapproving face. "Arizona?"

"Prescott. It's not what you're thinking," I assure her. "It's up in the mountains."

"OK, good," she nods. "What're you doing there?"

"Wilderness search and rescue."

"You're crazy."

"Sometimes," I shrug. "What about you?"

"Am I crazy?"

"No, what're you doing now?"

"Oh." Staci reaches into her purse and pulls out a pack of cigarettes. "Just working and going to school. I'm a music major."

"Really?" I squint. "Where do you work?"

"I teach piano."

"Are you serious?"

"Yeah, I'm serious," she laughs, looking playfully insulted.

"No, I didn't mean it that way, I just didn't know you even played the piano," I explain. Our relationship was somewhat lacking in communication.

Staci narrows her eyes at me.

"What?"

She laughs again, shaking her head and finally lighting her cigarette. Letting a breath of smoke roll out of the corner of her mouth, she slides the cigarettes back into her purse. "You have a tattoo?" she asks, noticing the ink creeping out from under my left sleeve.

I nod, lifting my sleeves to let her see. Anyone as intense as I am needs tattoos.

Staci knots her brow slightly. "Those things are creepy. You have any more?"

"Just one more on my back."

She nods. "So are you doing anything for New Year's?"

"Yeah. Packing."

"You're not going out or anything?"

"Don't do it anymore," I shrug.

Staci looks at me in quiet confusion. This is not congruous with her memories of me.

After an interminable hour of slightly awkward conversation—I'm unable to express any emotions that may be misinterpreted as happiness because of my overwhelming intensity, and I've managed with my isolation in the last few months to completely lose any social skills I ever possessed—Staci glances down at her watch and frowns. "I gotta go," she says. "I have to teach."

I guess we're not having sex tonight.

Staci drops her cigarette butt and grinds it out under the table. "Let me give you my new number."

She reaches into her purse and tears a small piece of paper from her calendar, neatly writing her name and number and sliding it over to me. I look at it briefly and push it into my pocket while I stand. She leans in against me and I hesitantly wrap my arms around her lower back.

"It was good to see you again," I hear myself tell her, slowly realizing I mean it.

"I'll call you later tonight," Staci says, pulling away to look up at me. "I wanna see you again before you leave, OK?"

"Yeah."

She smiles and quickly kisses my cheek.

☐ ☐ ☐

Staci turns the page of the photo album in her lap, looking down at the sharp granite peaks and the dark blue sky. "When was this?"

"September," I tell her, staring at the floor.

"God, it's beautiful out there." Staci looks closely at the empty piercing holes in my left ear. "You don't wear earrings anymore?"

"I don't wear anything anymore," I tell her. "I don't want shit hanging off me." I finally realized what earrings are: decoration. Polished metal rings whose sole purpose is making you more attractive than you really are. I don't want to trick anyone.

"I remember when you had so many earrings," she says. "I like you without them, though. You look older."

"I am older."

Staci laughs. "You know what I mean, smart-ass."

I shrug. I do know what she means and I am a smart-ass.

She looks back at the photographs. "Who were you with?"

"Me."

Staci turns another page and glances up at me. "You were alone?"

I nod. "Didn't see anyone the entire week I was out."

"I don't think I could do that."

"Yeah, it leaves you a lot of time to think," I nod. "Maybe a little too much."

She closes the album slowly and looks at me as I take it. "I wish you didn't have to leave so soon."

I set the album back down on the floor and slide my notebook out of the way with my foot.

"You hate it here, don't you?" she asks softly.

"Sometimes."

Staci looks down at the floor and nods at the tattered notebook by my foot. "What's that?"

I pick it up and look down at the irregular black writing. I was given a C in handwriting in third grade. Apparently my teacher didn't appreciate my style, which admittedly involves omitting the last two or three letters of every word.

"It's a book," I tell her, immediately regretting my honesty. I don't know if I can explain this one.

"You're writing a book?" She looks back up at me. "How long've you been doing that for?"

"I don't know, a couple months," I tell her. Ever since I got so intense.

"What's it about?"

"It's not really about anything," I shrug uncomfortably. "Just writing."

"What, like a journal?"

"Kind of. I don't know."

Staci looks at me. "Can I read it?"

"No, you don't wanna read this," I tell her, closing the notebook and dropping it back onto the floor. "I'll send you some of it when I finish typing it up."

Staci pushes me playfully. "Come on..."

I laugh a little, shaking my head. "No, it's all scattered and shit. Wait till I do a few rewrites."

"Come on!"

I look over at her. "You couldn't read my handwriting anyway. I can hardly read it."

"Fine," she surrenders. "But you have to let me read it when you're done."

□   □   □

I assured Staci watching me have my tattoo retouched would be less than thrilling, but she insisted I bring her along anyway. Maybe seeing how tough I am while being repeatedly poked with a needle will stimulate her primitive natural selection instincts and she'll realize it's absolutely imperative she have sex with me immediately.

We follow Robby back to his little cubicle and I pull my shirt off and sit in the dentist's chair. Staci sits on a chair in the corner and takes my shirt into her lap. I hear the gun buzz a few times and turn to watch Robby carefully adjust the rubber band. He leans in again with the buzzing gun and I feel the needle in my skin. Staci cringes to make up for my blank face. I spent my junior high school career preparing for this by burning myself with cigarette lighters and carving large-breasted girlfriends' initials into my arm. I bet Staci totally wants to do it with me.

I shut the door quietly behind myself and my skin tightens in the cold air. Everything is still in the late night darkness, a streetlight glowing pale blue across the road in the thin mist. I can feel Staci looking at my eyes, but I keep mine on the ground at her side.

"I'll write you soon," she tells me, her breath clouding faintly. The weak light glimmers in her smooth black hair.

"Yeah."

Nodding, she looks down at her feet and back up at me. "Call me when you get there, OK?"

I glance into her eyes and nod. "Yeah."

"I'm gonna miss you," she says.

Staci wraps her arms around me and I hug her weakly. I can feel her soft hair under my chin. I want to hold her tighter, hold her forever, never let her leave. I want to push her away and never see her again. Pulling back, she looks up at me silently. I watch her dark eyes glisten, full of words she can't speak, words I can't understand. Leaning in, she kisses my cheek softly and stands back to look into my eyes again.

"Bye," she whispers reluctantly.

"Bye."

Staci watches me. I let my stare fall again to her side. Wrapping her fingers around my forearm gently, she waits for my eyes. I look up at her again, her lips pressed tightly together as she stares back. I don't know what she wants. I don't know what I have to give her. Dropping her eyes and solemnly nodding her head, Staci walks silently to her car and pulls away, turning to look back at me before she slips around the corner. I step inside again and lock the door. I don't need her.

□   □   □

The weathered Prescott town limits sign finally emerges from the dark on the side of the highway and I downshift as signs of civilization begin to appear. Driving slowly past the endless string of bars on Whiskey Row, I turn up the hill to the place I'm renting, a tiny dive of a guesthouse on a dirt alley a block from downtown.

I find the unlit driveway and park on the side of the alley. Small patches of snow are still melting on the gravel next to the house. Carrying my things in wearily, I dump them on the floor and look over the sparse collection. I only brought what fit in my truck. Intensity dictates minimalism. I throw the thin futon mattress into the bedroom and push it into a corner. It almost covers the entire floor. Back in the main room, I build a desk with a rough piece of plywood and four milk crates. Aside from the mattress, it's my only furniture. I guess I should find a chair for it.

Stepping back into the bedroom, I drop a clean notebook on the floor by the mattress. I decided to end the book last night. I don't know what I'm going to do with it, but I've now written a book and deserve recognition and praise from beautiful young women and the sex by which it is of course accompanied. Deciding I'm finished for the night, I undress and slip into bed, sinking quickly through the mattress onto the hard cement under the carpet. I smile in the dark. This is what I need. I have to keep myself lean.

I plug in the phone and pick it up. No dial tone. I fuck with the plug and the phone because I think pushing buttons that don't work will eventually make them work. Still no dial tone. I guess I have to call the phone company. But I don't have a phone to call with. I guess I'll go do something that doesn't require a phone.

Cautiously leaving the safety of my house, I climb into the truck and find a hardware store because hardware stores contain everything one could possibly need to survive. I wander through the aisles somewhat aimlessly, quietly enjoying the presence of nuts and bolts and things that fix things, and notice an aisle with chairs. I look for the cheapest price tag—$12.00— and grab the folding metal chair attached to it, then find a few more little items I could probably do without but require to maintain a minimal sense of cleanliness and order.

Dropping my purchases off in the truck, I walk back to a payphone and call the phone company. "My phone doesn't work," I tell the operator, giving her all the information and listening to her typing at her computer. I wonder how many ears have been on this phone. I probably have hepatitis now.

"Well, I have no record of that service order," the woman tells me finally.

"Then why do I have a phone number?"

"I don't know, sir."

"So when am I gonna have a phone?"

"Well, we're gonna need ID and everything again."

I hate this woman. She gave me hepatitis.

"Are you kidding?"

"No, you'll have to fax us copies of everything," she says casually. "It'll probably be at least a week or two."

"Well fuck." I slam the phone down and walk back to my truck. I guess I won't have a phone for a while. Prescott College's new student orientation is a three-week backpacking trip. I have to be at some camp facility tomorrow morning to begin assembling gear with my group and being oriented. I'd rather pass on the trip and risk temporary disorientation, but it appears I haven't been given a choice.

I drive back to my hole and dump my new property on the floor. Maybe I should go find my mailbox. This is where I will collect fan mail. I walk down the alley and slip through a small apartment complex to the front house on Alarcon Street. I could shorten my trip by walking alongside the front house, but I don't want to risk encountering its residents. I'd rather remain anonymous. It increases the probability of a mystery-based romantic affair with the young divorced woman I'm sure lives there alone, just waiting to run into a handsome young man like me.

I open the little black box bolted to the wall of the house and pull out the mail, shuffling through it as I walk back to my place. Krist, I've lived here for a day and I'm already getting advertisements from television attorneys and supermarkets. The last envelope is hand-addressed.

Staci.

I lock my door and sit at my engineer's nightmare of a desk, dumping the uninteresting mail on the floor and tearing open Staci's letter.

*Foreverdeariss Greg,*

*This letter will probably get to Arizona way before you do, but I felt like writing you anyway. I'm glad we saw each other the other day. God, it's been a long time. I'm sorry we didn't talk to each other for so long. I hope we keep in touch while you're way over in Arizona. I want to try to come visit you sometime, too. I guess I'll talk to you later. I'll see you before you go to Arizona if you have time. I'll be waiting to hear from you.*

*Love & Friendship, Staci*

I glance at the date. The day after we met at the coffee shop. I don't know what to tell her. If she knew anything about me, she'd probably never speak to me again. She has no idea how intense I am. But I'm not going to lie to her. A primary characteristic of intensity is an unwavering commitment to the truth, no matter how ugly. At least when it complements the rest of the image. I grab my notebook from the floor and find a clean page.

□   □   □

Throwing my backpack into the master bedroom, I stumble into my well-furnished living room and collapse onto the floor. I've spent the last three weeks backpacking in the desert with my orientation group preparing for my approaching hippie college career and learning the difficulty of interacting with people who want to hug you all the time when you're too intense for social interaction and physical contact aside from casual sex. I have this strange feeling of being in kindergarten again. Only these kindergarten students are overgrown bearded boys and unshaven loose-breasted girls. I don't actually mind the swinging breasts, because swinging breasts can be nice, but their owners can be a little obnoxious and less than complementary to said swinging breasts.

But I'm back in my little house, my little hole, my little cell, my little escape. I don't think I ever want to leave it again. I can retreat into my isolation and work on the new book I've started, sitting on the hard floor in the cold scribbling illegibly in a notebook about the world's endless failures and my inability to escape myself.

After finally gathering the energy to shower three weeks of grossness off of myself, I check the mail and find another letter from Staci waiting patiently for me. I can smell her perfume on the paper. The more intense part of me dictates the letter be immediately disposed of without remorse, but the rest of me figures reading it may somehow make it possible for me to sleep with Staci. Locking the door again, I sit down at my desk and tear open the envelope.

*Hey, it's me again. Thanks for writing me back. I read the part of the book you sent and it made me think a lot. All the emotions and anger you talk about, I have them too, but I hide them. At least you're not lying to me. I never knew you felt the way you do.*

*You know how you asked me what I wanted from you? All I wanted was a friend. I wanted to be able to talk to you about anything and everything. I admit when I was talking to you I was just talking bullshit. But I just wanted to talk to you, just hear you talk. I don't know anymore. All those years I had feelings for you, I never told you how I felt, because I never thought you would ever feel the same way about me. So I kept it to myself. Until that night I saw you and... I can't explain it. To hear the words from your mouth, that you had feelings for me. I felt like my heart was melting and breaking at the same time. When you didn't come the next night I was devastated. I thought I was just lying to myself about you. After that week passed, I was so confused. I wanted to be with you, but I was too scared. If I had let myself love you, I would have never been able to pull myself away. And I didn't want you to have that burden.*

*The day we said our goodbyes, you were right when you looked into my eyes that what you saw was sadness and longing. When I hugged you, something didn't feel right. You didn't respond, you didn't hold me back. You just barely let your arms touch me and then you let go. I wanted to ask you not to leave, but what difference would that have made? You seemed so intent on leaving and you kept emphasizing how much you hated it here. I didn't want to get in your way.*

*OK, I'll stop this writing. I keep on thinking about you, and I can't help it or stop it. I hope one day I'll be able to talk with you. Please call me. And send me more of your book if you can.*

*Staci.*

I re-fold the letter and drop it on the floor. I need to forget her.

□ □ □

I step out of my telephone-booth-sized imitation of a shower and dry off quickly because it's February in the mountains and I refuse to use my heater. Heaters and the comfortable warmth they provide are unnecessary luxuries and a waste of fuel that could be put to better use incinerating unqualified and undeserving participants in the human experience. I pull my jeans on because I have to go to class and I don't think I'm allowed to attend naked.

The front door shakes in the frame with a knock—not because the knock is extraordinarily heavy, but because my front door is inadequately constructed and prone to excessive shaking—and I stare at it. I don't have any friends, I didn't order a pizza, it's not census time, and I don't think I have any outstanding warrants.

I zip up. It must be the mail lady.

I open the door and there she is: the same cute brunette who knocked on my door last week with a rejected manuscript accompanied by an abrupt but polite little postcard saying something about not accepting unsolicited and unrepresented manuscripts, printed specifically for ignorant hacks like me who have absolutely no understanding of the publishing industry but continue to make futile attempts at success with incorrect methods and unworthy material.

I glance at her hands. Along with a small package, she's brought me the battered stack of mail that's presumably been sitting out in my box for the last week not being collected by me because collecting it would require leaving the isolated safety of my house. What a sweetheart.

"Hi," she smiles.

"He-llo."

She hands me my gear with a cute little smile on her lips and I watch her carefully. This is not the standard postal employee courtesy smile. This is the I'm-a-lonely-thirty-something-woman-who-thinks-you're-really-cute-and-you're-never-wearing-a-shirt-when-I-come-to-your-door-which-is-why-I-come-to-your-door-so-often-when-thoroughly-unnecessary-and-do-you-want-to-have-sex-with-me smile. I check her out again. Those tight grey uniform pants with the black stripe running down each side are kind of sexy. I should ask her to come in. Just do it. You don't have to go to class and she doesn't have to finish her route right now. Casual sex is an obvious priority that supersedes any conflicting obligations. Invite her in.

"—" No, I can't.

"Uh. Thanks," I say.

She gives me her sexy grin again and starts walking away. But after a few steps, she stops and turns around, sliding her eyes down from mine and staring right at my stomach. She is not being subtle. Slowly she turns again and disappears through the gate.

I close my door and laugh. I'll get more mail tomorrow.


I am officially a college student. It feels remarkably similar to being a high school student. Despite most college students' claims to the contrary, college is nothing more than a four-year remote extension of high school. We have easier access to more dangerous things and less of the supervision we think we don't need but really do need because most of us have been living until this point under continual adult supervision and guidance while incorrectly believing we were independent and responsible for ourselves and are therefore ignorant and inexperienced and unable to manage our own lives with this new freedom.

This college's only distinction from my high school is its far smaller and depressingly homogeneous population. The reality is that the only students able to afford this school's tuition are middle to upper class whities, and the diversity among that demographic is slim and not apparent through casual observation. Their individuality is expressed in a conventionally unconventional manner: another brand of stylized decadence advertised on television and available for purchase in participating stores.

I walk up the wheelchair ramp behind a building on Grove Street and step inside. A year ago this was a furniture store. It's now the school's library and home to a few small and windowless classrooms. Prescott College is more conceptual than tangible: there is no campus. There are a few buildings in the same general vicinity on Grove and a few other facilities scattered randomly throughout town. We have no gyms, no pools, no playing fields. It makes sense, having no teams to utilize them. We don't even have a school mascot. It gets funnier when you see the tuition bill.

The students in the crowded hallway watch me pass curiously. I do not blend in well here. I don't think hippies are big fans of mine. I was a fan of hippies until recently when I discovered most of them are just as full of shit as anyone else. You can stop shaving and washing your hair and never wear shoes, but all that does is make you smell. Sitting on a big pillow in your living room taking bong rips and discussing the respective emotions elicited by your favorite colors accomplishes little more than pissing off the new guy with the military haircut who never smiles and speaks only in sentence fragments to minimize any personal interaction that may dilute his intensity.

I push through the dreadlocked patchouli patch to my classroom at the end of the building. First one here again. It's never taken me more than fifteen minutes to walk here, but I consistently leave twenty-five minutes before my classes start. We haven't yet covered more advanced concepts in my hippie math class. I sit at the end of the table nearest the door and rock back in my chair.

Eventually the rest of the students file in as a group. It's been like this from the beginning. They move in packs. I never see a hippie alone. They need someone else to hug and touch gently and carefully express their feelings to at all times. I stand out because I'm always alone. I wear earphones any time I don't have to be actively listening to someone. In between classes, I walk to an adjacent parking lot and sit on the curb watching traffic. No one talks to me and I don't mind.

The rest of the class sits down around me and the instructor appears with his backpack and an apple in his mouth. I reluctantly remove my earphones and try to look present. They call this class Writing Workshop. I'm not interested in learning how to write even though I acknowledge my complete lack of writing skill; I'm taking it because it's a graduation requirement and I want to graduate. As soon as possible.

□   □   □

I pick up each sheet of paper as it's pushed from the printer and carefully inspect it in the glow of the computer screen before placing it on my desk with the rest. Frustrated by the complete failure of my short series of random and weak attempts at finding the one publishing company representative I know is out there somewhere, waiting to discover this undeniably powerful work that's been ignored and rejected because of a general inability to comprehend the profound and revolutionary meaning contained within the unconventional writing and its deceiving appearance of simple mediocrity, and limited by my complete lack of understanding of the procedures and practices of the publishing industry, as well as the suspected but still unconfirmed poor quality of my work, I decided to abandon my attempts and publish the book myself.

For weeks I experimented with book binding techniques and materials, finally settling on a horrible and tedious process involving an excessive amount of contact cement fumes that are probably eliminating quickly my few remaining brain cells. I've led myself to believe it's actually a good idea to make my writing easily accessible to the minds of people who remain grounded in the reality missing from my own critique of the work. I still somehow believe it'll be embraced as incredibly unique and universally meaningful by a vast number of readers from all points of the literate social spectrum, who will subsequently be motivated by their emotion to immediately transform their love of my writing to uncontrollable lust for me, resulting of course in an obscene quantity of somehow meaningful yet emotionally non-binding sex. I'm a little inconsistent with my manufacturing, but the good ones come out good enough and the bad ones come out good enough for people I'm not interested in having sex with.

Knowing the book will fail entirely unless it's believed to be the product of a legitimate publishing company, I decided I needed to create a name for the fictitious publisher to print on the books' copyright pages. I'm applying the same principles of independence, refusal to compromise, and employment of creatively unconventional methods that comprised the foundation of the Grundle philosophy back at the bike shop—not to metal and grease, but instead to paper and ink. And so with very little thought or consideration of future consequences, I arrived at the name: Grundle Ink. It made sense under the influence of contact cement fumes at 3:00 A.M. while I grundled books in my little house like one of those weird loners with the long beards who build bombs in their garages with common household items as some kind of distorted plea for women's affection.

Pressing the cover around the last book, I lay it flat on the desk and smooth my hand over it. "Nothing From No One," I mouth silently to myself, staring down at the title. It doesn't get much more intense than that.

Maybe I should give a copy to the mail lady.

□  □  □

Staci has discovered my inability to deny myself any opportunity for even the most minor sexual encounter, even if that opportunity requires I drive almost twelve hours back to the Bay Area to see her and temporarily forget I'm an intense and emotionally-tortured young man who's unable to interact with anyone. I hear her knock on the door and walk downstairs to answer it.

"Hi," she smiles. She's beautiful.

"Hey." I close the door and follow her upstairs.

Staci drops her purse and sits down on the edge of the bed. "How was the drive?"

"Fine, except for the last twelve hours of it."

She rolls her eyes. "Ha ha."

See, she thinks I'm funny.

"I've got something for you," I tell her. She eagerly watches me pull out a copy of my newly released book and hand it to her as I sit at her side.

"Oh my god, what's this?" she asks, glancing up at me.

"The book," I say, watching her thumb through it with wide eyes. "I told you I'd let you read the whole thing when I finished it."

Staci looks back up at me and holds the book out. "You have to sign it for me."

"No," I tell her, pushing it away.

She shoves it into my stomach. "Come on!"

"No!"

"Sign it!"

I shake my head, stealing the book from her and tossing it onto the bed behind us. "Some other time."

I pull my fingers through Staci's black hair and stare up at the ceiling.

"When're you coming back?" she asks me softly.

"I don't know," I shrug. "I've got a week off from school at the end of next month."

"That's like five weeks," she complains.

"I know, but that's as soon as I have the time."

Staci pouts quietly and nestles her head in tighter against my chest. "Stay here."

I laugh quietly. "You come to Arizona."

"Yeah right."

"Why not?"

"Cause," she says, "I'm in school."

"So am I."

"I know, but just move back here," Staci pleads softly.

"I hate it here."

"I'm here," she says.

I glance at my fingers in her hair. "You know what I mean."

Staci runs her hand down the center of my chest. "I wish you could stay," she whispers. "I miss you so much."

□   □   □

My phone is ringing because my phone line was finally connected and it does that now sometimes. I stare at it uncomfortably. I don't have any friends and I just talked to Staci. Maybe I should pick it up anyway.

"Yeah."

"Greg?"

"Yeah."

"This is Paul."

That little Christian bitch from the bike shop? How did he get my phone number and why is he calling me?

"What."

"I read your book," he says. "K let me borrow it. It's really good."

"Paul, half that book is dedicated to the insolent ridicule of Christians."

"Well, yeah," he says. "But the other parts I really liked."

This poor kid. No self-esteem.

"It's really descriptive," he adds.

It's two hundred forty pages of excessive profanity. There's nothing descriptive about it.

"OK."

"I do a little writing sometimes," Paul tells me. "Maybe I could send you some of my stuff and you could read it."

"Yeah, maybe," I exhale heavily. "Why're you calling me?"

"I have an idea for a book," he says. "And I want you to write it with me."

"You want me to write a book with you," I say, still struggling to absorb what's happening. This is a guy I almost made a career of tormenting for three years, a guy who represents something he knows I not only don't believe, but openly ridicule. And I'm having a friendly phone conversation with him.

"Yes," he says clearly.

"Why."

"Because you're a good writer."

"I'm not a writer," I remind him.

"But you write," he says. "And I need you."

"Why."

"Well let me explain the idea of the book and you'll get it."

"Please."

"I want to put two people with different backgrounds who don't really get along through some intense experience together and have them write during it to see the differences."

Not exactly well articulated, but I know what he means. It's a good idea. Fuck. I don't want to admit it, but it's a really good idea. And he's right about needing me. Black and white doesn't even begin to describe Paul and me. They need to invent new shades for the two of us.

"So what exactly did you have in mind for this experience?"

"I don't know," he says. "A backpacking trip or something."

"Have you ever been backpacking before?"

"Kind of once, only one night, with this church group."

"So no."

"Yeah," he concedes. "No."

I consider the proposal. I don't know if I could make it through any extended period of time in Paul's presence without hurting him physically or myself emotionally. But the finished product might be worth the damages.

"All right, I'll do it," I say finally, not actually believing I'll ever have to do it.

□ □ □

I'm supposed to register this week for next semester. For days I've been flipping through the thin schedule looking for anything other than the urge to break shit and knock some undeserving hippie's teeth out. I don't want to take any of these bullshit prerequisite classes. *Interpersonal Communication*? I came here to learn technical rescue skills, not how to share my feelings.

It's possible that my anger with the college and every single hippie on the planet, whether responsible for Prescott's course offerings or not, has been amplified by unrelated factors. I drove back out to the Bay Area again last week to see Staci. We'd made plans for me to stay the weekend with her in San Francisco while she was at a conference. She never called. I waited a day and left. I'm sure there are some genuine emotions somewhere within me as a result, but my new intensity has further stunted my already retarded emotional development and left me with only one recognizable and demonstrable feeling. I'm guessing I wouldn't normally be this enraged by a college schedule.

With the assistance of the emotional damage Staci has provided me, my new book is materializing at a disturbingly rapid pace. I supplement my life's experience deficiency with nothing more than endless hours of writing. It's become the only substitute for social interaction and my former drug abuse. I live in solitary confinement. Build a new prison cell every night. Crack the blinds with my fingers just enough to see outside. Sometimes I see the sun burning down on the empty dirt, the wilting plants, the broken, sagging fence, and I think I should be outside, but I have no reason to be.

The blinds stay shut all day and all night. I constantly feel watched. When I leave, I can't stay out long. I get lost. I do what I need to do and I come back and lock the door. Sometimes the girls smile at me from behind the counter when I walk into the store. I smile weakly and pretend I'm in a hurry. Sometimes they try to talk to me when they're cashing me out, but I have nothing to say. I can't talk to anyone. Staci was it. And now she's gone. I don't even know why. But I'm not going to call. I'm not going to ask her for something she doesn't want to give me.

The phone startles me. I blink Staci's face from my eyes and reach for it. "Yeah."

"Greg?" She pauses. "It's Staci..."

I wait.

"Look," she says quietly, "I'm sorry. I know I messed up. I really wanted to see you, I just couldn't. I knew you were leaving again, and I couldn't stand it."

I clench my jaw. I don't want to believe her.

"I mean it, Greg. I wanted to see you, I wanted to see you so much. I'm just so afraid of getting too serious with you and getting hurt."

I sit on the floor and listen. Staci tells me about the way her ex-boyfriend treated her, about finding out after three years he'd been cheating on her from the beginning. Even though I'm really intense, I can't help feeling somewhat sympathetic.

"I thought I was gonna die," she says. "I didn't know what to do. I'm just so afraid of getting hurt like that again."

"I don't know what to tell you."

"I've wanted to be with you for so long. I'm just scared."

"All I can do is what you let me," I shrug.

"Well, I wanna try," she tells me softly. "I really do."

The line is quiet. I don't know what to say.

"Can we talk for a while?" she says finally.

"Yeah, if you want."

Staci searches for a way to start. "Is school OK?"

"Not really. I'm probably leaving at the end of the semester."

"Why, what's wrong?"

"I'm just tired of it all," I tell her. "I have to register for fall next week and I can't get myself to do it."

"So what're you gonna do?"

"I don't know yet. I'm thinking about the fire academy and paramedic program in Butte County."

"Where's that?"

"About four hours north of you."

"So you're not coming back here?" she asks.

"No."

"But you could come down on weekends, right?" she says hopefully.

"Yeah, I guess."

"Are you gonna come home for the summer?"

"I don't know," I tell her. "I don't know what I'm gonna do."

Glancing up at the neon sign glowing in the second story window, I step onto the sidewalk and sit on the curb of a narrow alley. After a week of pacing around my place in Arizona all night wondering what the fuck I was going to do with myself besides beat the shit out of some hippies or those white trash gangsters that always hung out in the alley across the street, I decided to leave. I didn't know what else to do. I feel like a failure. I lasted five months. I didn't leave because I know what I want to do; I only left because I knew I hadn't found it.

I picked Staci up at work a few days ago and took her out to lunch. She told me she'd call that night. I sat and watched the phone like a death row inmate waiting for a call from the governor. It never rang. My sympathy for her dissipated quickly.

I turn and look up from my seat on the curb. Staci works in the building on the corner. She gets off in about ten minutes. I came here to tell her it's over face-to-face. I don't even know what I'm ending, but I can't do it anymore. I've put a lot of effort into preparing this. It's important I remain intense. I've already constructed the entire scene in my head:

I'll turn to see Staci walking down the steps, her black hair bouncing softly around her face. When she turns to walk down the sidewalk, I'll stand up from the shadows silently. Her shock will fade slowly to relief, then suddenly to concern.

"Greg," she'll say quietly. "What're you doing here?"

"I had to talk to you," I'll tell her. "You never called me."

"I know, I'm sorry," she'll stutter, brushing her hair from her cheeks nervously. "I just... I don't know."

"Look, this is never gonna work out," I'll say. "What you tell me and what actually happens… it's like you're two different girls. I don't understand what's going on with you."

"It just that… I'm confused," she'll stammer, shaking her head gently, her dark eyes full of pain. "I don't know what to say."

"You don't have to say anything," I'll tell her quietly. "I just came here to say goodbye." I'll look into her eyes as she stands silently, her mouth cracked as she searches for words. "All I ever wanted from you was what you said you wanted to give me."

I'll walk past her even if my car is in the other direction, letting my upper arm brush lightly against her shoulder to demonstrate my complete indifference.

"Wait," she'll plead softly, realizing her horrible mistake.

I'll keep walking and never look back. Cue music. Camera pans back into a widening aerial shot as my figure slowly disappears in the distance. Roll credits.

I nod to myself with satisfaction. That's how it'll happen. I glance at the steps in front of her building. If she ever shows up. I check the watch in my pocket: five after. So she got stuck on a call. She'll be out soon. I wait anxiously, watching anonymous feet pass me on the sidewalk, replaying the scene in my head, adjusting facial expressions and emphasizing different words for dramatic effect. Fifteen minutes later I walk out to the street and look up into the building. The windows are dark.

I guess she used the side door.

This is it. I'm actually going through with Paul's backpacking thing. I can't believe I agreed to this. When I said I would do it, I didn't really mean I would do it. I figured it was some unrealistic wet dream Paul had, some vision of selective fame and glory, writing a book for which his extended Christian family would embrace him, thus cathartically dispelling his personal anguish and emotional pain and drawing to him a nice Christian girlfriend with whom he can abstain from premarital sex. I never took him seriously.

But now I seriously have to do it.

I arrive to pick up Paul as agreed at 5:00 A.M. on less than three hours of intermittent sleep. His house is dark and silent. After knocking on the door for five minutes, I reluctantly ring the doorbell. A dog begins barking and heavy footsteps pound through the house. I'm going to kill him. I'm going to kill him out there in the mountains. It would be so easy. I'm going to kill him and roll his body into a lake.

Paul answers the door half-dressed and half-asleep. "Oh crap."

I stare at him. Yes, Paul, Oh crap. If you weren't so morally upright, your statement could be a little more appropriate, something along the lines of, "Oh fuck, Jesus Fucking Krist I'm a fuck-up, what a stupid piece of shit I am to sleep in like this when Greg is expecting me to be ready, because he is fucking awake and ready despite his severe sleep deprivation and not at all in the mood to wait for dumb motherfuckers like me to wake up and get dressed like little fucking speds, I mean shit, he doesn't even fucking like me as it is, and now this shit, me sleeping through my alarm like a fucking lazy dickhead. I should probably kill myself."

Finally Paul gets his shit together and we load up. I drive fast to make up for Paul's mental disabilities, watching the door out of the corner of my eye because I know it's going to shake right off its hinges, and we hit the trailhead just before noon. I'm still spun out from the seven-hour drive on top of the sleepless night and lack of food and the adrenaline high I'm experiencing while imagining Paul's murder, but within five minutes on the trail, we're both exhausted.

After sweating through about an hour of the brutally steep climb out of the rocky end of the valley, I suddenly acclimate and begin moving progressively faster. But Paul looks about ready to have a stroke after each footstep.

I look up from my feet and see two grey-haired men approaching us on the trail.

"You in the Marine Corps?" one of them asks me.

I don't get it at first, but then I remember I shaved my head a couple days ago. "No sir," I tell him.

I look back for Paul. He's staggering up the trail with his head down, wondering where the air is. I stop to wait impatiently.

The old men reach Paul and the Marine looks at him, then indicates me with a slight nod. "Good luck."


At night, Paul and I eat reconstituted dehydrated food with unnaturally long shelf lives and I clean the pot and my bowl with dirt. I think this strains Paul's sense of cleanliness, but I can see it impresses him at the same time. Cleaning things with dirt is pretty impressive. The evening seems to be the time Paul believes I'll be most receptive to his nonsense. He attempts unsuccessfully to engage me in conversation by traditional methods, then apparently realizes all he needs to do to make me talk is say something stupid, something he's remarkably capable of doing. Aside from the more superficial differences like our respective experiences with drugs, alcohol, and vaginas, I begin seeing the distinguishing quality in Paul that offends me even more than his chosen faith: his continual struggle to find and expose every inch of common ground we happen to share, using these similarities—which he fails to realize would exist in nearly any randomly chosen pair of young white males—to formulate ludicrous theories on life that ultimately support his religious beliefs. Too exhausted to verbally dissect his imagined profundity and raise my middle finger, I learn to just sit back and let him say whatever makes this particular chapter of his life more bearable.

We walk all day, Paul struggling with the thin air and the weight on his back. Every day I feel stronger. I walk until Paul is gone, and then I walk some more, and then I think I should probably stop and wait for him because he might be dead back there, but if he's dead, waiting here for him won't really be that helpful, so I walk a little longer, but finally give in to my restrictively hyperactive conscience and stop, picking at the rocky dirt with my walking stick until Paul stumbles into view. When he reaches me and thinks he's going to take a break, I stand up and start walking again.

I'm more of a wilderness guide than a co-author out here. I feel responsible for Paul's safety, and the problem is that I'm not confident in his fitness or technical skill and too often my concern for his well-being seems to temporarily disappear entirely. I have fleeting visions of him losing his footing and sliding down one of these steep faces and I start to laugh a little because Paul bouncing off sharp rocks is kind of funny, but then I stop laughing because I know I would probably feel bad if he actually died while trusting me to keep him alive.

We discuss our respective visions for this book we're creating, and I begin to wonder if I misjudged the merit of Paul's concept but decide it's a little late to back out at this point. Paul shares his idea of doing a reading at his church and trying to sell the book through that community. I tell him he's free to sell it in any manner and to anyone he sees fit, but I won't be accompanying him to his church events because I think I'd have a problem restraining myself and would say things I think shouldn't be said in a church only because my default general decency burdens me with an odd sense of respect for people's beliefs, even silly ones like institutional religion.

And then Paul finally manages to broach the topic that's apparently been troubling him for some time: He's worried about my profanity offending his Christian community and dissuading them from reading the book.

"Paul, that defeats the fundamental purpose of this book," I tell him. "Fuck."

"Not really."

"Yeah it does. You wanna show the contrast between us. Shit."

"Right, and there is a lot of contrast."

"But part of that contrast is that I say things like shit and fuck, and I write the way I speak, so I write things like shit and fuck."

"Yeah, but those people don't like that kind of language."

"Well I don't like those kind of people. Motherfucker."

"It'd just be easier to sell the books if the language were clean."

Finally I assure him my half of the manuscript will be acceptably clean when I read through my notebook and realize I haven't used any profanity in my writing, which is a little disturbing and makes me wonder if spending this much time with Paul is somehow damaging my brain.

Fuck.

□   □   □

The show doesn't start for another four hours. Naturally, K and I are already in San Francisco, stuck in traffic on Highway 101.

"I didn't know they put in a parking lot out here," I say.

K lights a cigarette and flips off the creeping cars to his left.

We have tickets for a sold-out Rollins Band show and we're ready. I've been preparing myself mentally to deal with large drunk guys who want to beat the shit out of me by imagining myself beating the shit out of them and going home with their girlfriends. Finally reaching our exit, we roll through the city to Eleventh Street and K parks a block from the venue.

"You hungry, man?" he asks as we head up the sidewalk.

"Yeah."

Passing the club and hitting the empty Mexican place on the corner, we get our food and sit up at the bar against the large window that looks onto Eleventh. From the elevated level of the restaurant, we quietly watch the city's movement. I finish one of my three tacos and look back across the street at a blonde who's been pacing the block since we sat down. She talks to someone for a few seconds and quickly moves on to someone else like she's looking to score.

"Hey," I ask K, "is that blonde really a guy, or just a fucked up looking junkie?"

K watches her for a few seconds. "I don't know, man."

The wind is blowing because it's San Francisco and the wind always blows in San Francisco. Stopping on the edge of the sidewalk, the blonde faces us with her arms folded across her chest, her sundress fluttering.

"Yeah, it's a guy," I nod when the wind blows the thin fabric tight against the front of her legs.

K shakes his head.

"Go get her digits, homo," I tell him.

"Fuck you."

We finish our food and stroll back down the sidewalk toward the club. I'm not sure I've ever strolled before, but we currently have about three hours to kill and only thirty yards to cover and strolling suddenly seems rather appropriate. The band's RV is parked against the curb. K lights a cigarette and leans up against the bricks across from it while I shove my hands into my pockets and glance around the street. The blonde appears from behind the RV and knocks on the door.

"What the fuck..."

We watch curiously. The RV's door opens and the blonde steps inside. I look at K and K looks at me. Whatever. Weird things happen in San Francisco.

A few minutes later the blonde emerges from the RV and disappears down the street. We continue hanging out: K leaning back with one foot up against the wall in a pose only he and the guys from Journey could ever pull off, casually smoking cigarettes and looking cool; me standing with my hands in my pockets not looking cool.

The blonde reappears from around the corner and stops next to us. "You know what time it is?" she asks me.

I look at K.

He checks his watch. "About 6:00."

"About 6:00," I repeat because I'm a smart-ass.

"Mm." She lights a cigarette and glances down the street. "What're you guys doing?"

"Listening to sound check and waiting to get in," I tell her.

"Yeah, they're sounding good."

I nod and check her out. Looking a little worn. She's not fooling anyone anymore. Fifteen years ago she probably looked pretty good as a woman, but she's looking a little haggard now. Stellar breast implants, though. I check out K. He's trying to ignore us and devote his complete attention to his cigarette. I think he's a little uncomfortable around the blonde.

"So what were you doing in the RV?" I ask her.

"Oh, I just wanted to say hi to Henry," she says. "I've known him for years."

"Really?"

"Yeah, we go way back. I was in a few punk bands back in the early eighties."

"No shit..."

K is suddenly not so afraid. She knows Henry. But he maintains a safe distance because he might be infected with the urge to wear women's clothing and get breast implants and have sex with boys.

The blonde reaches into her backpack. "I wrote a book about those days," she tells me, "the whole queen punk scene, mainly in San Francisco."

I take the book from her and flip through the pages. "That's cool."

"I'll give you that copy for three bucks," she says.

I give her the bills and flip through a few more pages.

"My name's Bambi, by the way," she smiles.

"I'm Greg and that's K," I tell her.

"Well here," she says, "let me sign it for you."

I hand her the book and she scribbles something on the front page. I take it back and look:

*To Greg and K.*
*To Henry and Ozzie.*
*Here's to glitter, glam, and punk rock daze.*
*Love Bambi.*

OK.

"So you know Henry, huh?" K asks bravely.

"Yeah," Bambi nods. "If you guys wanna hang out after the show, I'll introduce you."

I check for a wet spot on K's pants, but I guess he controlled himself.

"Yeah, that'd be cool."

"Well, I gotta go change," she says. "I've got this great black vinyl bra and these vinyl pants to go with it." Bambi slings her backpack onto her shoulder again. "I'll see you guys after the show."

Waiting patiently to regain our hearing, K and I scan the emptying warehouse for our transsexual liaison. The black floor is littered with trash and various pieces of clothing and probably assorted bodily fluids I'd rather not touch. Finally Bambi appears and waves to us. I check her outfit.

Bambi notices and poses out for me. "You like?"

"Totally."

"We should go out front and wait a little while," she says.

We walk back outside and K does the foot thing against the wall and lights a cigarette.

"You know this guy's a writer too," he tells Bambi, pointing at me.

Thanks K. You fucker.

"I guess," I shrug. "I've got one book done and I'm working on another."

"Are you gonna publish them?" Bambi asks me.

"I want to."

"Honey, you should do some readings at the Paradise," she says, pointing to the club on the corner. "My publisher is there all the time looking for new writers."

Nodding, I glance back at the club doors and watch two girls walk out together, a blonde and a brunette.

Bambi notices me noticing the girls. "Those bitches are total poseurs," she sneers. "They're just here for the scene. They don't even care about the music."

I laugh and shake my head. She's just jealous because they came with vaginas.

A young homeless girl walks up to us out of the dark, trying to stay warm under the beaten moving blanket wrapped around her shoulders. "You guys have any change?" she asks softly.

I watch Bambi and K ignore her completely. Maybe they don't understand the situation. Let's break it down. Homeless: Without home. No money, no worldly possessions besides the clothing on their backs.

"They should get a job," people say.

"Where?" I ask them.

"I see Help Wanted signs up all over the place," people say.

Do you really think that if you'd been wearing the same clothes every day and hadn't showered or shaved for a month that anyone would hire you? If you had no mailing address, no phone number, no anything? Think about how much time you've spent making yourself presentable for job interviews. Think of everything you had to fill out on your last job application. It's not as simple as getting a job. A couple years ago, I watched my coworkers at the bike shop laugh at a local homeless guy who asked me for a job application, completely sober and more polite and presentable than most of us. The store hired punk kids like me without a question. High school kids with no experience, no education, no references, nothing. Thieves, drunks, junkies, teenagers who regularly came in late because they were doing involuntary community service, even convicts who'd served five years in state prison for armed robbery—we were all in there. But the thought of this man getting hired was laughable.

I pull a five from my wallet and hold it out to the girl.

She stares at it and slowly looks up at me. "You serious?"

"Yeah I'm serious."

The girl watches me and cautiously takes the bill. Once she realizes I'm not going to steal it back from her, a bright smile spreads across her face. "Man, I'm gonna go get some food, get a bath, get warm tonight!" She shakes her head. "I was having the worst day until now."

"Why, what happened?" I ask her.

"Well just now, these guys walked by and called me a dirty nigger bitch."

I straighten up and look down the street. I will personally avenge all the world's injustices. "Who did?"

"Just these punk-ass whiteboys down there."

I scan the street for them. I want to find them. I want to find them so bad. I have a problem managing my anger and blood still full of residual adrenaline from the show. But the street is empty.

The girl sees me tense up. "Don't worry about it," she tells me. "It's no big deal."

I keep my eyes down the street.

"Don't worry about it," the girl says again. "They're gone."

They're gone. This is good. I don't care how intense and righteous and high on adrenaline I am: I can't take on six skinheads and expect to live.

"All right," I say. "Well take care of yourself."

"Yeah, you too."

The girl leans in and hugs me and I relax again because hugs are nice. Stepping off the sidewalk, she wanders away into the dark.

"That was really sweet," Bambi tells me, pretending that makes up for her bullshit. She glances at the club doors. "I'm gonna go inside and see what the hell those guys're doing."

I nod and Bambi disappears. Realizing I'm shivering, I manage to stop myself for a few seconds, but then start again because it's still cold. I have yet to grow out of the wearing-a-T-shirt-no-matter-how-cold-it-is phase of my life.

"Shoulda worn a jacket," K says.

"Jackets are for pussies."

K stares at me.

"I'm evaluating my body's response to mild hypothermia," I explain.

He drops his cigarette on the sidewalk and grinds it out with his boot, then looks up again and nods at something behind me. I guess I'm supposed to look. I turn around and jump back. The two poser girls are right in my face.

"You know that blonde's really a man, right?" the blonde one asks me. I can smell alcohol on her breath and she's a little unsteady on her feet.

"Yeah, sure," I say.

"OK, we just wanted to make sure you weren't getting yourself into anything by mistake."

The brunette smiles at me apologetically. She appears to be sober and has clearly assumed the babysitter role, trying to get the blonde to back off a little. "How old are you?" she asks me.

"Nineteen."

They look at each other and giggle.

"How old do you think we are?" she asks.

I'm not falling for that one. I know they're older than I am, but I'm not providing them with an estimate. I could be honest and tell them what I think, which would only offend them by being a little too accurate, or I can be cautiously sweet and guess low, in which case they'll just think I'm stupid.

"I'm not answering that question," I tell her.

"Why not?"

"I don't wanna get myself in trouble."

The blonde is uninterested in the conversation and has decided to evaluate my physique. Lifting my shirt, she runs her hand over my stomach and I quickly flex my muscles because she doesn't know muscles aren't always contracted and my naturally tight stomach will impress her.

She lifts up my sleeve and looks at the tattoo on my arm. "How many tattoos do you have?"

"Three."

She peels away parts of my shirt until she finds all of them. "Where do you live?" she asks me.

"Mountain View."

"Mm," she frowns. "That's kinda far from Concord."

It's about an hour away on the freeway. This is far. But I'm not going to discourage what I think is about to happen because of logistical complications. "Not that far," I shrug.

"Well, we're going home," the blonde smiles at me. "You coming?"

I glance at K. He's clearly not invited. "Uh…"

"I'm not taking you all the way back to Mountain View, though," she says, "so you'll have to figure out a way to get home."

"Uh…"

The blonde grabs my arm and starts tugging me down the sidewalk. "Come on, let's go."

I'm standing on Eleventh Street in the middle of the night with two girls I've known for approximately five minutes. Going with them would mean missing a possible opportunity to meet Henry Rollins and leaving my best friend to drive home by himself knowing I'm somewhere getting laid with no effort or emotional entanglements. I have ten dollars in my wallet and no way to get home. Conclusion: Bad idea.

"OK."

· · ·

I'm stuffed uncomfortably in the back seat of a very small car listening to the girls repeatedly play the same limp song by a certain limp band with an extremely limp front man on the stereo while I rapidly approach the point at which I put my fist through the dash—pretending it's the limp singer's face—to make it stop. Fortunately, music taste has no relevance to the current situation.

Finally reaching Concord, we drive directly to a Safeway for alcohol. I wander through the brilliantly lit aisles with the girls while they try to decide what they want, quietly contemplating my latest exercise of poor judgment. With the new company of a six-pack, we head back to the blonde's apartment and I manage to crawl out of the half-scale-car-model's imitation of a back seat and stagger upstairs behind the girls. While the brunette unloads the beers into the refrigerator, I carefully inspect the photos on the door, finally admitting to myself I would have preferred she drag me home instead of the blonde. But when you're me, you take what you can get.

The brunette notices me looking and points to a picture of a little girl. "That's my baby girl."

Shit, she has a kid?

"How old is she?" I ask her.

"Five."

The blonde flips on the television and I sit down next to her with the brunette on my other side. The Dating Game is on. I glance at the two girls. I appear to be the only one who thinks it's fucking hilarious. The blonde turns and lays her legs across my lap.

The brunette holds up her beer. "You sure you don't want anything?"

"I don't drink anymore," I tell her.

The blonde laughs. "You're sober and you came with us?"

I shrug. I don't need alcohol to be stupid.

"So did you shave your head because you wanna be like Henry Rollins?" the brunette asks me.

"Henry Rollins's head isn't shaved," I remind her.

"Well, it used to be," she says.

"Yeah, in 1981 along with every other head in LA."

The blonde is still uninterested in conversation. "Let's play naked twister," she says.

Negative. No naked twister. Possibly the absolute worst activity imaginable for someone as insecure as I am. I look down at the twister mat folded up on the floor. Either she had this planned or she does this way too often.

"I'm too tired," the brunette says.

"Yeah," I agree quickly. We win.

The blonde's spirit isn't broken. "Stand up and take your shirt off," she tells me. "I wanna see."

"What?"

"You heard me, get up."

I'm a little hurt. What about the real me? Doesn't she want to know about my successes and failures, my fears and my dreams? I stand up and pull my shirt off. She didn't bring me home to talk about my feelings.

"Turn around."

I follow instructions and turn my back to them, feeling their hands running over the swells of muscle I'm presently wishing were much larger than they are.

"Pretty good," the blonde says.

They pull me back down onto the couch and I consciously avoid sitting in a position that might create rolls in my stomach because rolls in one's stomach are not attractive and have the potential to discourage casual sex with strangers. We go back to watching empty late-night programming, but the blonde is restless. And I think she wants a little more than the initial agreement suggested. Her hands are all over me, but her bare foot is getting intimate with the brunette's chest.

This is the typical male fantasy: two girls at the same time. I consider the situation. It doesn't give me that much of a hard-on. It seems like it would be more awkward and complicated than anything else, and I really don't have an overwhelming need to double the possibility of humiliation. I check out the brunette's reaction to the blonde's foot. She's clearly not a team player.

"So what do you think about piercings?" the brunette asks me, shifting out of the blonde's reach. "I just pierced my belly button."

"I don't know," I shrug. "I used to have a lot of earrings."

"Really?"

"Yeah, you can still feel the scar tissue," I tell her, rubbing my earlobe. For the sake of scientific confirmation, the brunette moves in slowly and begins sucking on my ear. Leaning my head back and closing my eyes, I slowly absorb the unfamiliar combination of nervousness and relief. My already limited confidence with the opposite sex has dwindled to immeasurable levels since Staci's removal of any remaining scraps. But this is helping. The brunette slips off the couch and onto her knees in front of me. I feel her hand moving from my thigh to my zipper and I'm suddenly ventilated.

She stops abruptly and glances at the blonde. "Look at this," she laughs, indicating the recently opened hole in my pants. "I can't believe I'm doing this."

Making her jealously obvious, the blonde stands and wanders down the hallway into the dark. The brunette watches her go, then looks up at me and bites her lip like she's struggling to decide what to do. I am one with the universe. The universe wants us to have sex. The universe needs us to have sex. I will trust the universe to guide her decision making process.

"This couch is too small," she says softly. "Let's get on the floor."

I look at the wad of white vinyl stuffed tightly into the corner by our feet. "I think we killed the twister mat."

"Yeah..." The brunette pulls closer to me and rests her head on my shoulder. "You smell good," she says.

"Really?"

"Why, do you not usually smell good?"

"No, but I was sweating a lot at the show."

I look at my pants crumpled on the floor by the couch and I'm suddenly struck by the absurdity of the situation. I'm lying naked on the floor of a stranger's apartment in a city I've never been to with a woman whose name I still don't know. I thought I was going to have sex with her friend, who apparently wanted to have sex with both of us. I met them in San Francisco while talking to an aging transsexual in black vinyl who wrote weird things to me in a copy of her book and offered to introduce me to Henry Rollins. The absurdity slowly fades and I begin thinking of the trouble I probably got myself into: the more base lack of a way to get home to the sobering realization that I just barebacked a girl I don't know at all twice. I probably have AIDS and she's probably pregnant.

"You're the first guy I've been with since I left my husband," the brunette tells me quietly.

"What happened?"

"I caught him in bed with some toothless cakehole."

Note to self: Use the term *toothless cakehole* at least once before dying.

"So what're you gonna do?" I ask her.

"I'm divorcing him."

"Good." I can't stand women who put up with men's weak bullshit. He cheats on you? Leave him. There are men out there who won't. He hits you? Leave him. There are men out there who won't. The longer you stay and the more you try to justify it to yourself, the harder it's going to be to leave and the harder it's going to be to escape the emotional damage that piece of shit caused you with his lies and his abuse. The more women allow men to get away with their juvenile, misogynistic behavior, the more men are going to believe they're doing nothing wrong, and the more I'm going to be associated with subhuman jerk-offs just because of our common gender.

The brunette runs her hand down my chest and back up my neck. "So how old do you think I am?"

I thought I got out of this question.

"I don't know," I shrug. "Looking at you I'd say early twenties, but you have a five-year-old daughter and a husband, so I'd say maybe twenty-seven or twenty-eight."

She laughs a little. "I'm thirty-two," she says. "And I have two other daughters. One's eleven, one's thirteen."

I think I just achieved with a single act every sexual goal I'm interested in achieving. I'm nineteen and she's thirty-two. She's married. She has three kids, one of whom is twice as close to my age as she is. I had sex with her an hour after meeting her, and I still don't even know her name.

I'm a fucking rock star.

But I still probably have AIDS and a child on the way.

I look out the sliding glass doors. The sky is growing light through the trees. I still have to figure out how I'm going to get back to Mountain View.

"Let's sleep a couple hours," the brunette says, "and I'll take you home."

CHAPTER EIGHT

I dump the last milk crate on the floor of my new apartment and look around. None of the windows actually close or lock, I can see sunlight beaming in all around the door—which must be pushed forcefully with one's shoulder to allow the deadbolt to be thrown—one of the bedroom doors won't close, the carpet is torn and covered with unidentifiable stains I'm afraid to touch, the blinds are broken, and the bathrooms are irreparably gross. But it's cheap and I'm intense.

It takes me about twenty minutes to unpack because I moved about twenty minutes worth of possessions to Chico. I throw my two-inch-thick shredded-cardboard-filled futon mattress on the floor, set my thirteen-inch television—finally purchased exclusively for watching the news and News Radio—on a milk crate against a wall in the living room, and rebuild my desk with two fewer milk crates to create a coffee table, which seems somewhat odd considering the lack of accompanying seating. Under the window, I place the real desk that doesn't sway with heavy breathing I finally decided was a reasonable investment.

I'm unfortunately making the transition from hippie college to a conventional community college, meaning I actually have exams, grades, and classes before 11:00 A.M. Instead of applying immediately for the fire academy as planned, I've decided to first complete an associate's degree because of the rapidly increasing competition in the fire service that will soon require even volunteers who do nothing more than clean up real firefighters' messes to have masters' degrees. That process, I find, involves sitting through the most unendurably heinous classes imaginable at times of the morning I should not be awake.

The phone rings. I stare it for a little while and decide to answer it because my answering machine is broken and it might keep ringing for a long time if I don't.

"Yeah."

"Is this Greg?"

"Yeah."

"This is Katy. Remember me?"

No, I forgot about the married thirty-two-year-old mother with whom I had completely irresponsible casual sex three weeks ago.

"Yeah, I remember you."

"Well what're you doing next weekend?" she asks me.

Sitting in my dark piece of shit apartment being depressed and entertaining wild delusions of writing grandeur resulting in sex with beautiful women.

"Nothing, why?"

"I wanna come see you," she says.

"Are you kidding?"

"Why, do you not want me to?"

"No, I do."

She laughs. "So how do I get there?"

□   □   □

I answer the knock on my piece of shit door and Katy smiles at me from the dark outside.

"Hey cutie," she says.

I'm a cutie.

"Hey back."

I step aside to let her in and she kisses me quickly, dropping her purse on the floor next to my stunning plywood coffee table. In a brief lapse of my excessive minimalism a few days ago, I actually bought a metal-framed futon couch to make the coffee table seem a little less ridiculous, although I made sure to find the shittiest one available to maintain an appropriate level of intensity. My new furnishings will undoubtedly impress my guest and ensure sexual intercourse later in the evening. Katy sits down and calls her oldest daughter to let her know she's arrived without incident.

"I like your place," she says after she hangs up the phone.

"Why?"

"It fits you."

I look around thoughtfully. "Broken and ugly and empty?"

"Shut up," she laughs.

Katy opens a bottle of wine and pours herself a glass. I amuse myself with the surreal juxtaposition of red wine and plywood coffee tables and decline a glass of my own.

"My oldest daughter doesn't like you," Katy tells me.

"I've never met her."

"She just doesn't like the idea of me seeing a nineteen-year-old," she explains.

"Yeah, but my maturity level exceeds that of most middle-aged men," I shrug.

"I actually told her that," she laughs.

"Oh. I was just kidding."

Katy smiles. "You're more mature than her dad is, but I don't think that's the problem. She said you were young enough for her to date."

"She's thirteen!"

After agreeing that no amount of creative rationalization will actually make the situation normal and that it may unfortunately be uncomfortable for her children, then quickly dismissing any such discomfort as immaterial, we space out on the plush couch in front of the television until Katy's hand starts wandering into my pants, followed soon by her face. Finally she grabs the waist of my unzipped jeans and pulls me back into my unfurnished room.

Katy is precisely what I've always envisioned a thirty-something divorced woman to be. Her life consists of her profession—which has allowed her to do faux paint finishes in the home of Dilbert's creator, who apparently doesn't resemble in the slightest the stand-in Scott Adams from one of the greatest episodes of the ever-wonderful television program News Radio—

her children—who are unfortunately equipped with fathers who tend to pay less than adequate child support—and me, her nineteen-year-old escape from life's continual grind. She's through with the various formalities of the traditional male-female relationship and wants only to enjoy the limited time we spend together. This of course means an abundance of sex.

I begin driving to Concord every weekend to stay with her. Like cocaine once did, Katy manages to make my weekends progressively longer, causing me to miss an increasing number of classes. Everyone knows sex is more important than college: the whole idea of a college education is to impress intelligent women and encourage them to have sex with you.

My lingering illusion of a casual relationship slowly begins dissolving as I find myself making Katy's five-year-old breakfast, driving her thirteen-year-old and her friends to the mall, and being elected to deal with nervous teenage solicitors at the door. I am becoming a father.

"It is a possibility," Katy says over dinner one night.

"I guess," I shrug, not at all agreeing that marriage is a possibility.

My attraction to Katy fades rapidly as reality seeps in and I find myself rubbing my burning eyes while the television flickers quietly across the room, Katy's arm around my stomach, her head nestled in under my chin. I don't want to be here. Maybe I'm just worn out. I've never had so much sex before. We wake up and have good-morning sex. We get in the shower and have shower sex. She comes home from work and we have I'm-back-from-work sex. We eat dinner and have after-dinner sex. We hang out and have lack-of-a-better-activity sex. We get tired and have I'm-falling-asleep-so-let's-get-one-more-in-tonight sex. And now I'm just numb. I'm disgusted. I'm disgusting. I can't do this anymore.

Katy rolls away from me. "If I were over here, would you even touch me?"


Katy sniffs and I stare out the windshield silently. Since my attempt to explain to her last night that I couldn't see her anymore, we've maintained a continuous conversation regarding the situation, pausing occasionally to have we-may-be-breaking-up-so-let's-get-in-a-little-more-sex-before-we-do sex. My truck remains partially disassembled in a garage thirty minutes south of Chico awaiting a replacement for the head gasket I blew on my last trip to Katy's, which means I'm driving Katy's car back to Chico.

Unfortunately she's in it.

"I don't understand," Katy says.

"I don't know," I shrug. "I just can't."

"Don't you like being with me?" she asks.

"Yeah, I do, I just... There's just too much going on, I can't do it."

"Is it my kids?"

"No, it's... Well, yeah, kind of," I struggle. "I don't know. It's your life and it's my life and there's just too much. I don't know, it's everything."

"Why do you keep saying, 'I don't know?'" Katy asks me. "What aren't you telling me?"

"Nothing."

"Why're you holding back, just tell me."

"I'm not holding anything back," I tell her. Except for the fact that if I fuck you one more time I think I'm going to freak out.

"What do you need?" she asks me. "Why can't we just work things out?"

"I don't know, Katy, fuck. I don't know. I just can't do it."

She shakes her head. "What'd I do?"

"You didn't do anything."

The conversation maintains its exhausting circularity for the remainder of what becomes the longest drive of my misguided youth. Finally reaching the First Ave exit, we drive in silence to the apartment and Katy sullenly follows me upstairs.

"I'll miss you," she says softly over the kitchen counter.

"I'll miss you too," I tell her more sympathetically than honestly.

Leaning in and kissing me one last time, Katy turns slowly and walks out the door. From the balcony, I watch her car slip out of the parking lot and step back inside, contemplating the quiet room. Something's wrong.

Shit. I actually do miss her.

I look at the clock. Almost midnight. Tonight is New Year's Eve 2000, an empty box on the calendar that, thanks to the shameless exaggerations and fabrications of the financially gluttonous corporate media empire, has the television-receiving segment of the world trembling and theorizing and preparing for judgment day, whether God's or the government's. Despite the dramatic warnings of global chaos, I've chosen to neither pray nor stockpile assault rifles. I'm thoroughly comfortable with my current spiritual status and understand that if the government decides to declare martial law in order to gain control of my home like too many gun show-attending delusionally paranoid television dependents believe they will, a few AKs in my closet will not prove to be an adequate defense. Tonight my plans include sitting on the couch and watching television.

But I think. In the slight chance this is in fact the end of the world, I should probably find an appropriate exit. I don't want to go out like this: sitting alone on a piece of shit couch in a piece of shit apartment watching a piece of shit television. It needs to be a little more intense than that.

I walk back into the bathroom and look at the narrow mirrored cabinet doors above the sink. Prying at the cheap metal, I pull out one of the doors and carry it back to the couch with me. With limited time and materials, looking into my own eyes as I die seems to be the most intense solution to my problem. It's been January First in New York for three hours, and in other parts of the world for even longer, but everyone knows God is from LA. I hear the countdown begin on the television and bury my gaze deeper into my reflection. This is it.

Nothing happens.

I drop the mirror and change the channel.

With the over-hyped demarcation of the new millennium fading rapidly into forgotten history, the days begin blurring into unrecognizable smears. Studying for my EMT certification occupies most of my excessive waking hours. I've quickly realized that what distinguishes me from most of my fellow students is my apparently silly belief that it's actually somewhat important to completely understand emergency medicine when considered professionally capable of administering emergency medicine. In my boredom, I mistakenly encouraged a relationship with the single female student who shared both this anomalous belief and my table in the classroom. She wasn't stunningly gorgeous, but she wasn't horribly ugly either, and my attraction to individual women is apparently magnified abnormally by a lack of options. Finally after a few weeks of unproductively touching each other like eighth-graders in the grass, I couldn't stand her sitting around on my couch watching TV every night while I tried to work and told her it was over.

I officially applied for the county sheriff's search and rescue unit upon the completion of my required three months of training to prove my dedication and commitment. After my stunning interview, in which I assured my oral board I'm capable of remaining calm and collected in emergencies and the presence of dead bodies, they accepted me—pending a successful background check.

"It's thorough," the lieutenant warned me. "They'll be talking to people you didn't even know you knew."

He handed me the enormous stack of paperwork and I knew I was out. There was a ten-page section on drug use alone. *Have you ever sold illicit substances? Have you ever held any illicit substances as a favor for someone? Have you ever used any illicit substances? When was the last time you used any of the following illicit substances?* I knew it might mean disqualification, but I was inspired to be honest. Possibly by the knowledge I could be subjected to a polygraph test to confirm my answers.

☐ ☐ ☐

Instead of waiting for a phone call from the sheriff's office about my paperwork—in which I slightly underestimated the number of times I've used marijuana, hash, LSD, mushrooms, ecstasy and cocaine as five to ten each—I applied and tested with a local ambulance company whose hiring policies don't involve background investigations. I was hired immediately.

I'm now in the office enjoying the air-conditioning and waiting to fill out the necessary paperwork. Turning to the opening door, I slide my hands into my pockets to conceal the erection I'm expecting soon. The same beautiful Mexican girl I noticed in the hallway before my interview takes the chair across from me and smiles.

"Did you just get hired?" I ask her. Conversation is the first step to building an intimate relationship involving sexual intercourse.

"Yeah," she says. "You?"

I nod and extend my hand. "My name's Greg."

"Lacy," she grins, shaking my hand gently.

The operations manager waves us back into the conference room and explains the series of forms we're to fill out. I pay slight attention while concentrating instead on what I imagine Lacy would look like without clothing. Finally the manager leaves the room and I help Lacy with a few of the forms even though I don't know what I'm doing any more than she does. We're just lame and need a seemingly legitimate excuse to move closer to each other.

The manager appears again to collect our paperwork.

"So where do we have to get our physicals?" I ask her.

"At the clinic down the street," she points. "Just take our form and the DMV form with you."

I look at Lacy. "You wanna just go down there right now?"

"Sure."

I follow her outside, consciously preventing my eyes from wandering too frequently to her ass. Squinting in the bright sunlight, I stop beside her. "You wanna drive or walk?"

"We can walk."

I walk as casually as I can, attempting to keep my metabolic functions near baseline to minimize any increase in body temperature and associated sweating. I must stay fresh and smelling clean.

"You look like a Marine," Lacy says.

I laugh. "Shoulda seen me when I was younger. Had hair down to my shoulders."

She watches me. "I can't picture that."

"Yeah. It was a long time ago."

I follow her into the clinic and we step up to the counter to collect more paperwork in dire need of being filled out.

"The last group they hired," I tell Lacy, sitting down next to her. "Out of eight people, six failed the drug test."

Lacy laughs as a nurse opens a side door and waves her back. She stands up and smiles at me. "Good luck."

Following my own drug test and physical—the DMV portion of which seems troublingly easy to pass, particularly considering that my blood pressure has been elevated by my intensity to the absolute acceptable limit and would have likely exceeded that limit if the nurse had retaken it to verify the results as is generally considered good practice—I wait patiently in the exam room for the absent doctor. Returning, she closes the door behind herself and drops my charts on the counter.

"Have you ever been told that you have any kind of cardiac arrhythmia?" she asks me.

"No." Cocaine damage.

"OK, well I want to do a twelve-lead EKG and see what we find."

I shrug and pull off my shirt.

The EKG woman steps in and hooks up the leads, and I lie patiently while she collects her data and tries not to stare at my naked upper body. She disappears again and I pull the leads off.

The doctor brings in the printout. "Your T-waves are a little high, but that could be normal if everything else is," she tells me. "I want to do a chest X-ray to make sure your heart isn't enlarged."

I shrug again and follow her into the X-ray room.

The X-ray tech smiles at me while she sets up her gear. She must think I'm cute with my shirt off too. When she's done taking her pictures, I wait again in the little room for the doctor's analysis. With no better way to occupy my time, I steal the Prozac pen from off the counter. I've always wanted a Prozac pen.

The doctor finally reappears. "It doesn't seem to be enlarged, so I'm going to set up an appointment for you with a cardiologist to get an echocardiogram and see what we can find."

I shrug and put my shirt back on.

The doctor pats her pockets and looks around the room. "Where'd I put my pen?"

◻   ◻   ◻

Straightening my uniform shirt, I step into the dispatch office and pull a schedule from a box on the wall. I worked my first training shift yesterday on the ambulance company's transport vans—essentially Medicare-covered taxis for wheelchair-bound patients or those otherwise requiring some kind of minimal medical supervision during their trip from the nursing home to the doctor's office. It's not the most desirable job, and I could make twice as much money folding shirts in the mall, but I'm stuck chauffeuring bitter, frustrated invalids around town until I complete my ambulance training and a position on an ambulance shift opens. I lean against a cabinet behind the dispatchers and check the clock.

"Who's training you today?" one of the dispatchers asks me.

I glance at the schedule again. "Bodie."

She laughs. "He'll be here in about ten minutes."

Bodie has just managed to make a poor first impression without even being present. If you're ten minutes late consistently enough for your coworkers to know you'll be ten minutes late, set your alarm clock ten minutes earlier. It's pretty basic math.

Finally some guy stumbles into the room still buttoning his shirt, his hair matted unevenly from the pillow he obviously rolled off of five minutes ago. I guess this is Bodie.

"Hey," Bodie says to the dispatchers. He takes a schedule and reads it over quickly, then looks at me. "You Greg?"

"Yeah."

"Well all right," he says. "Let's go."

Bodie picks up a radio and keys and I follow him to the back parking lot. He unlocks our van and grabs a binder from between the front seats.

"Did you go over all this shit?"

"Yeah."

He drops the binder and tosses me the keys. "You're driving."

Following a "test of my driving abilities" in the McDonald's drive-through, we begin our scheduled work. I don't know whether Bodie underestimates my intelligence or overestimates the difficulty of this job and his present role in the emergency medical profession—which in fact is no role at all—but I find myself continually clenching my jaw to refrain from reminding him that the sequence of rolling a loaded wheelchair onto a hydraulic lift, clipping a safety strap, pressing a button to raise a platform, rolling a loaded wheelchair into the back of a van, clipping more safety straps, pressing the second of two available buttons to store a hydraulic lift, and closing two doors of a van is not what I would consider exceedingly difficult and does not require repeated instruction.

"You know to bend you knees when you lift, right?"

"Yes," I assure him.

Bodie proves quickly to be less than the ideal mentor. While in the passenger seat of what is essentially a billboard for his employer, he decides honking the horn and leaning across me to yell out my window at a passing pedestrian he knows "from the fire academy, dude" is a good idea. Fortunately, I'm not very impressionable.

After I'm reminded again how to unload a "patient" at one of our most frequented nursing homes, we walk around to the back of the building and Bodie lights a cigarette.

"Smoking isn't exactly smiled upon at this company," he tells me through the smoke. "I think I'm the only one besides the night dispatcher who smokes."

I nod.

"You don't care, do you?"

"No."

He takes another drag and looks around. "So have you met that girl who works in billing?"

There are probably a dozen women who work in billing. And I know exactly which one we're talking about. "Lisa," I nod.

"Yeah," he says. "What do you think?"

"About what."

"Her."

I shrug. I was actually considering the consequences of asking her out last week. Fortunately before I did the ever-knowledgeable dispatch staff informed me she's only seventeen years old.

"One of these days we should all hang out," Bodie says.

I grin. "You know she's only seventeen, right?"

After working nearly every day for the past few weeks, I've learned little more than the inappropriateness of fifty-percent polyester uniforms in a town that apparently shares a thermostat with Hell, and that despite everything Bodie's done to dissuade me, I actually like the guy. His behavior isn't intentionally ill planned: he just grew up too close to his family to fully comprehend his place in reality. A night spent on the porch of his apartment watching him smoke revealed just about every detail of his personal life—particularly that he has no reservations about disclosing every detail of his personal life to a guy he's known for less than seventy-two hours.

Stepping into the relief of the air-conditioned building, I turn off my radio and put it back on the shelf. "You can down-staff me," I tell the dispatchers, unbuttoning my shirt and dropping myself in a chair.

"That's your Yukon out there, right?" one of them asks me.

"Yeah."

"Are you still making payments on it?"

"It's paid," I tell her.

"How'd you pull that off?"

"Selling drugs and stripping."

She stares at me. "Are you serious?"

"No, I don't sell drugs," I smile.

She stares at me again and slowly resumes brain function. "I don't think I could strip. I'd be too embarrassed."

I shrug. "You get over it."

Tones come over the radio and she turns reluctantly to dispatch the call. She wants to see me naked. Adequately refrigerated, I smile at her and walk out to the back parking lot. The door swings open behind me and I turn as Lacy steps out and waves at me.

"Hey, I hardly see you around here," she says. "You going home?"

"Yeah."

"What're you doing this weekend?"

"Going down to the Bay Area tomorrow."

"I've never really been there before," she says.

"You should come with me."

Lacy looks at me and smiles. "You serious?"

"Yeah I'm serious."

She smiles again and grabs the pen from my cargo pocket. "You have any paper?"

I hand her a notepad from my car and she writes carefully against my chest. I take the pad back and look: first and last names, home phone, and pager. I guess she actually wants me to call her.

"Oh shit, wait," she frowns. "I have to work tomorrow night."

"Here?"

"No, I have another job."

I'm not going to ask. She's probably a stripper.

"All right," I shrug, "well how about I call you when I get back and we do something."

She smiles. "How about you call me tonight?"

Deciding it's time I begin repairing my crippled social skills—not primarily of course because I'm interested in developing healthy and rewarding friendships, but instead to aid in my relations with women—I've been forcing myself to actually interact with people outside of work as normally functioning individuals apparently do. Bodie has become the insistent voice motivating me to occasionally leave the apartment for reasons other than attending work or purchasing food. His persistence is flattering, although bordering on obnoxious. But he is an undeniable source of entertainment.

"Dude, she's seventeen!" I yell at him.

"Yeah."

"You're twenty-one!"

Bodie looks at me and laughs. "Yeah. This is such a bad idea."

"Then why're you doing it?"

"Because she's hot!"

I shake my head and park in front of seventeen-year-old Lisa's house. Bodie has decided to ignore my better judgment and proceed with his pursuit of her despite my sincere discouragement, which has included sharing with him the sentencing practices for statutory rape.

Bodie looks at me as we get out and laughs. "Dude, why're you letting me do this?"

"I take no responsibility for this scandal," I tell him calmly.

"Dude, you gotta make sure I don't do anything stupid!"

"Keep your fucking pants on!"

Making our way slowly up the long driveway, Bodie and I stop at the front door and attempt to contain our laughter. I'm not sure exactly why we're laughing. I know I wouldn't be laughing if a judge were sentencing me to six years in state prison where the applicable definition of rape would quickly shift from legal to anal.

"Dude," Bodie says. "This is ridiculous."

"Are her parents home?"

"I don't think so." Bodie raises his fist to knock and freezes. "Why're you letting me do this?"

"Fuck you."

Bodie finally knocks and I turn away to stifle my returning laughter. Seventeen-year-old Lisa opens the door cautiously.

"Hey," she smiles.

"Hey," Bodie says.

I nod vaguely in greeting and look past Lisa into the house. Two of her underage friends are watching us from the safety of the couch. Maybe they'll let Bodie and me share a cell.

"You guys ready?" Bodie asks.

I turn before Lisa's friends even make it to the door and retreat quietly to the car. I don't think I really want to be involved in this. We drive back across town with the girls aligned neatly in the back seat like stuffed animals, Bodie and me up front making obscene comments and gestures out the windows at undeserving pedestrians. I feel someone tugging on my sleeve and turn slightly as seventeen-year-old Lisa pulls it up and leans forward to look at the tattoo on my arm. I ignore her in an effort to redirect her attention to Bodie. I'm not going to prison because some grey-haired puritan doesn't think a seventeen-year-old girl can make responsible decisions.

I park in front of Bodie's apartment—actually his absent girlfriend's apartment. She and Bodie are apparently in the process of breaking up in long-distance installments over the phone. Now I'm bringing an underage girl he wants to have sex with to her apartment. This will be a nice way for me to make a first impression.

◻   ◻   ◻

Lacy sits up on the couch and holds her face in her hands, rubbing her eyes. I turn and look through the kitchen window at the sky growing light above the trees. The dark skin on Lacy's lower back distracts me from my growing sleep deficit and I concentrate instead on my growing erection. Reaching over, I slide my hand down her back and over her smooth skin. She looks back over her shoulder at me, her cheeks swelling with a smile.

"It's late," I say. "I should probably let you go to sleep."

"Probably," she smiles.

I sit up next to her and rub my own burning eyes. I didn't expect Lacy to be here tonight. Despite the abundance of contact information she provided me, I dismissed her as just a nice girl trying to let me down gently. But she's here. And now the sun is coming up and I don't want her to leave because then she won't be here anymore. Lacy stands slowly and I follow her outside onto the landing above the stairs. She stops and leans against the iron railing.

"Thanks for having me over," she says.

"Thanks for coming over."

Lacy smiles and her cheeks swell and her dark eyes glisten in the dim light.

"I probably shouldn't do this," I say quietly, leaning in and kissing her.

"Maybe not," she whispers. "But I'm glad you did." Her hand curls around my neck and pulls my lips back to hers. Leaning away softly, Lacy looks up at me. "Can I stay with you tonight?"

□   □   □

I roll onto my side and stare at the clock. Almost 3:00 A.M. I still can't sleep. Lacy's at a party I declined to attend and I don't even know what to do with myself without her anymore. She's utterly consumed me, slipping her face into my dreams and her voice into my mind. There's a youthful glow of freedom in her deep brown eyes that pulls me in until I can't see anything but her dark skin and her disarming smile. We spend every hour we have together. She doesn't seem troubled by my complete lack of interest in normal social interaction and is consistently the one who encourages the taking out of teriyaki bowls and the watching of the Simpsons as a substitute for more traditional dating activities. I have a feeling this is closely related to Lacy's extensive inventory of euphemisms regarding intimacy and relationships. Apparently until her recent move, she was living with her boyfriend of six years—which puts her at the age of fourteen at the relationship's inception—who regularly hit her and assured her no one else would ever love her. I imagine this is the root of her inability to call what we do anything other than *hanging out*.

Before she left tonight, she reached into her purse and pulled out a little pink card for me. I took it from her and read her writing on the back:

*I know you'll like this.*

I flipped the card over.

I was right. She's a stripper.

She was wrong. I do not like this.

"I dance," she said.

Call it whatever you want, but you're getting paid to remove your clothing, not to dance. Either she failed to notice my complete lack of excitement or she ignored it, but she kissed me and left and now I'm here without her.

The phone breaks the silence and I reach for it.

"Hey, it's me," Lacy says quietly. "Were you asleep?"

"No, what's going on?"

"I'm still at the party, but I don't wanna be here," she says. "I wanna be there."

"Are you drunk?"

"No, I only had a couple beers."

"You want me to pick you up?"

"No, don't get outta bed. I'll drive."

"You sure?"

"Yeah, I'm fine," she says. "I'll see you soon."

Fifteen minutes later I hear the door open and watch Lacy's approaching shadow in the hallway. She drops her purse on the floor and climbs onto the bed, kicking her shoes off and straddling me.

"I missed you," she says, kissing me.

Lacy pulls away from my lips and gently drags her fingers over my face, stopping abruptly. "Baby, I'm getting scared," she whispers.

I look at her eyes in the dark. "Of what?"

"I'm afraid I'm falling too hard for you," she says quietly. "I feel like I'm starting to depend on you and it scares me."

"Don't be scared," I tell her, running my fingers through her hair comfortingly instead of offering her any convincing reason to not be scared.

Lacy smiles and kisses me again, leaning back and pulling her shirt off. She slides her hands down my chest and over my stomach, slipping the tips of her fingers gingerly under the waistband of my boxers. Rolling off of me, she pulls me on top of her and I kiss her neck, moving slowly down her chest with my lips, tasting her soft brown skin.

I stop and lower my head. "Are you drunk?" I ask quietly.

"No."

I look into her eyes.

"I promise," she whispers. "I want this."

◻   ◻   ◻

Lacy is attempting to domesticate me, a hopelessly low-rent minimalist with cardboard boxes and milk crates for furniture, with blank white walls and mismatched towels and sheets, with only the crudest and most necessary tools for survival. Before now, anyone who attempted to change my lifestyle and reduce my intensity would have been regarded as unacceptable and not deserving of my company. But this is Lacy.

"Baby, you need new towels," she tells me.

"I guess."

"You do."

I look at Lacy's smile and give in.

I follow her through the store aisles looking at the assorted domestic accessories. Look at this shit. I've been getting by just fine without it. I don't even know what that thing is, even though I'm sure that with enough spare time I could imagine an endless number of creatively incorrect uses for it.

"What color do you want?"

I look at Lacy. She's holding a soap dispenser in each hand. "Do they have invisible?" I ask her.

She rolls her eyes at me and holds out a dark green ceramic soap dispenser and toothbrush holder. "Get this set and then you can get green towels to match."

"How about stainless steel," I suggest, picking up the industrial set. "I could get grey towels to match."

Lacy cringes. "You can get a grey hand towel for the other bathroom."

"OK," I shrug. I really don't care. It's my bathroom. No one is even going to see it except Lacy, and she's the only one I care about pleasing because she's the only beautiful girl who's having sex with me. We wander back to the towel aisle and find the matching green towels. I stare at Lacy as she pushes the shopping cart, her long hair flowing behind her. She's beautiful. And she's redecorating my bathroom. Maybe it's the surrounding expanses of terry cloth and cute bathroom accessories, the brilliant white floors and fluorescent lighting, the smell of scented body cleansers and aerosol potpourri that's inspiring this revelation, this thoroughly unnatural nesting instinct, this romantically blurred vision of domestic bliss, but I can't ignore it. She stops in the bedding aisle and I step up behind her and wrap my arms around her stomach, kissing her neck, breathing the scent of her soft brown hair.

Lacy smiles and turns to kiss me quickly. "You need new sheets, too."

□   □   □

Exhausted by Bodie's tendency to share with me every detail of his inability to actually break up with his still-absent girlfriend despite the obvious failure of the relationship and his attraction to seventeen-year-old Lisa—with whom he, and unfortunately I, have continued to spend an inordinate amount of time—I've abandoned subtlety and begun instructing him explicitly to end it.

"Dude, we broke up," Bodie finally tells me over the phone. "I gotta find a place to live fast."

"Yeah."

"But I have no money."

"You're fucked," I agree.

Bodie starts into an incoherent monologue about his dire situation and utter lack of housing options. I wait patiently for the question I know he's going to ask.

"Dude, I hate to ask," he says, "but how would you feel about having a roommate?"

See?

I've never had a roommate other than Geoffrey, and he was never even home long enough for anything more than a few gin & tonics. I do have a two-bedroom place obviously intended to accommodate two residents, but do I really want to share it? A roommate would force me to reduce my intensity to a level that would allow regular social interaction. I'm not sure I'm ready to take that step yet. And what if I want to walk around naked or try new emotionally uncomfortable yoga positions in my living room? What if I want to have sex with Lacy on the kitchen floor just to see what it sounds like against the linoleum?

Lacy. From the beginning she's been exceedingly clear our relationship does not exist in the eyes of our employer and coworkers.

"It's unprofessional," she explained.

"And moonlighting as a stripper when you work for an ambulance company isn't?"

"I know," she said. "But still. I don't want people to be talking about us."

I shrugged. "Bodie already knows something's going on."

"All he knows is that we've been hanging out, unless you told him more."

"I haven't told him anything," I lie. It's impossible to avoid telling Bodie anything.

If Bodie moves in, Lacy is going to kill me. But she'll understand.

Bodie's got nowhere else to go.


Lacy glares down at me. "You did what?"

I don't know why we're in the bathroom, but I'm sitting on the edge of the bathtub looking up at Lacy. The green towels look nice with the green soap dispenser and toothbrush holder.

"He's got nowhere else to go," I tell her.

She shrugs. "I guess I'm just not coming over here anymore."

"What?"

"I don't want people at work knowing," Lacy says. "You know that."

"You're just not coming over here anymore."

"I have an apartment, you have a car."

"What is it with this covert sex operation?" I ask her. "It's starting to seem a little shady."

"*Shady*? Since when do you say *shady*?"

"Since things started getting shady."

"You've been talking to Bodie," she says. "He's the one telling you it's shady."

"No, it's shady."

"Why?"

"Lacy, you stay here almost every night," I explain. "We have sex, you do your laundry here, your razor and shaving gel are in my shower, you have bras in my closet, you even redecorated my bathroom— But I can't be your boyfriend. We're just *hanging out*."

"So what?"

"So what's going on?"

"Nothing's going on." Lacy looks away uncomfortably and turns back to me. "You know how I feel about the whole boyfriend thing."

"I know," I tell her, "but what am I supposed to think?"

"Don't you trust me?"

"I try."

"You try?"

"Sometimes you make it real hard, Lacy."

She shakes her head and looks out the small window over my head. I look down at the floor. The bathmat matches the towels.

Lacy sniffs and looks down at me again. "I'm leaving."

. . .

Bodie throws his mattress onto the floor and looks around his new room. I drop the box from my hands and furtively mourn my impending departure from peak intensity.

"Dude," Bodie says, "I think I'm gonna just leave my mattress right here in the middle of the room."

"OK."

"*Maxim* says girls like access to the bed on three sides," he explains even though I didn't ask.

"What?"

"You know, *Maxim*, that magazine," he says. "There was an article on how to make your bedroom more appealing to girls."

"That is fucking retarded. I can't believe guys pay for that shit."

"It has a lot of hot girls in it," he shrugs.

"So does legitimate pornography."

Bodie thinks about that one and slides his mattress up against the wall.

We walk downstairs and grab the rest of his gear from our cars. Back inside, we sit on the couch and I glance around the formerly empty apartment. Maybe this was a bad idea. I don't want a roommate. I don't know if I'm ready to deal with someone else like this.

"Dude, you sure you're OK with this?" Bodie asks me.

"Yeah."

He nods. "So what's going on with Lacy?"

Bodie is the interpersonal Ronald Reagan. He wants to discuss everything in great depth. This is an awkward combination with my utter lack of interest in interpersonal communication and severe social retardation.

"I don't know," I shrug. "She called me at 2:00 this morning crying and saying she didn't know what to do. I just told her I couldn't believe she was willing to drop it so easily after everything."

"So what're you gonna do?"

I shake my head. "Nothing, it's over. I'm done with it."

□   □   □

I'm done with it. I'm available. I'm a strapping young lad who looks devastatingly handsome in a uniform, who deftly utilizes his stunning charm and wit to indicate to those women in his general vicinity he is not only available, but thoroughly irresistible, and has virtually no moral reservations related to sex and the free and casual participation therein.

I don't need Lacy. All I need is this close-cropped hair, this honest, innocent, clean-shaven face, this duty belt, these polished boots that finally push me over six-feet tall, and the glimpse of the tattoo on my arm made available fleetingly from under my sleeve as I move gracefully, inciting an undeniable feeling in aforementioned women of romantic mystery grounded in the contrast the ink provides against both my skin and my seemingly proper and virtuous professional lifestyle.

I also need to check ID.

In my post-Lacy haste, I found myself presented with an opportunity, and I, like most people, am an opportunist. On one of my regular visits to the hippie store on my way home from work to retrieve necessary organic consumable supplies, I encountered only one working cashier, presently occupied with another customer, leaving me forced to wait like any other common non-strapping-uniform-clad-romantically-mysterious customer. But from behind me came the beautiful song my ears ached for, the sonorous, invisible voice that said:

"I can take you over here."

Consumed by the beauty, I followed my serenader to an adjacent register and admired her graceful cashier prowess as she efficiently sorted through the contents of my basket—the exact items and quantities that fill my basket every week, a little necessary simplicity in an unnecessarily complicated life.

"How are you?" she sang with a smile.

"Good," I answered, creating the positive tone necessary for further social engagement. "You?"

"Good," she smiled.

I basked in the radiant beauty of my current situation while the other cashier appeared and placed my perishables with great care and calculation into a paper bag.

"You always steal my customers," the bagger said to my savior.

"Only the cute ones," my savior replied with a glance and a smile in my direction.

And here my opportunity presented itself with open arms, with its own welcoming song, with undeniable perfection. I considered my options while waiting patiently for the time when once again my savior and I would be alone.

Seizing my chance, I extended my hand. "My name's Greg, by the way."

*By the way* was an entirely unnecessary addition considering there was no prior unrelated conversation, yet that simple phrase somehow transforms an awkward introduction into a casual demonstration of confidence.

"Lisa," she smiled, taking my hand into hers.

I was unsure how to feel about her sharing a name with my roommate's seventeen-year-old girlfriend, but dismissed it as immaterial and relieved the confusion by adding a *Two* to my Lisa's name. But verbal confusion was to be the least of my problems.

"How old are you?" Lisa Two asked me tonight, her head in my lap.

"Twenty."

"That's it?" she said. "I thought you were older."

"Why, how old are you?"

Lisa Two shifted on the couch and ran her hand slowly up my thigh. "Seventeen."

□   □   □

I sit down on the couch in crew quarters and start working on my last patient report. Two sheriff's deputies had to escort us on this one because the address had been flagged for previous criminal violence. My partner recognized the patient as a drug addict who routinely abuses our insurance-covered taxi service to bring him to the hospital for painkiller prescriptions. After several tense minutes of convoluted reasoning and laughter suppression, we finally got him into the back of the ambulance, where I tried to conduct my assessment while he repeatedly complained about my voice being too loud because he'd recently undergone spinal surgery and his ears hurt.

Being an EMT on an ALS ambulance means you're responsible for all the bullshit calls and dealing with all the patients who don't actually have emergent medical problems requiring a paramedic. It means you end up in the back of the ambulance trying to give your radio report to the hospital like this:

ME: Whatever Hospital, Medic 3, Code-2 BLS traffic.

MICN: Medic 3, this is MICN Whoever at 1733. Go ahead.

ME: Whatever Hospital, Medic 3, EMT Everett, Paramedic Whoever, currently en route to your facility Code-2, ETA of about four minutes. On board is a seventy-three-year-old female, chief complaint of right knee pain. Patient states she fell while trying to get up from the couch and landed on her right knee. Patient denies hitting her head or losing consciousness. Apparently this happens fairly frequently to her.

PATIENT: No it doesn't.

ME: Break. Doris, you told me it's happened several times, a few very recently.

PATIENT: Yeah, but it's not frequent.

ME: OK, well I need to let the hospital know it's happened before.

PATIENT: It doesn't happen frequently.

ME: OK, Doris.

PATIENT: It doesn't.

ME: OK, Doris. Medic 3 continuing: Patient is alert and oriented times four, skin is pink, warm and dry, head is atraumatic, pupils are PERL, neck is atraumatic, trachea midline with no JVD, chest is atraumatic with equal bilateral rise and fall, lung sounds clear and equal, abdomen is soft and non-tender, pelvis is stable with no signs of incontinence, patient moves all extremities well with equal grips and push-pulls. Right knee is atraumatic with no visible swelling or deformity. Pulse is eighty-eight, BP one-thirty-two over eighty-four, respirations sixteen. Patient is resting comfortably, and our ETA is now about one minute. Any questions or orders?

MICN: No questions or orders. We'll see you in a minute.

ME: Copy no questions or orders. Medic 3 clear on Med 7.

PATIENT: It doesn't happen frequently.

ME: OK, Doris.

I finish the report—reluctantly omitting my personal opinion of the patient—and answer the phone.

"Hey," Bodie says. "You gotta come home."

"I'm doing reports."

"Dude, you need to come home."

"Why."

"There's a girl you gotta meet," he tells me. "Just come downstairs when you get home, we're down here."

I managed to escape the seventeen-year-old Lisa cult without incident—aside from breaking a young girl's heart by denying her the pleasure of sexual intercourse with me—so I'm in dire need of another bad situation to get involved in. I'm sure Bodie has one waiting for me. I file my reports and drive home, walking straight into the apartment below us.

Bodie looks up from the couch. "Greg, this is Amy," he says, pointing to the girl across from me. "Amy, this is Greg."

"Hi," she smiles.

"Hey." I sit down and surreptitiously evaluate my bad situation while Bodie and I discuss my shift and the crazy guy with the bullets on his windowsill whose ears hurt because of his spinal surgery. Blonde, pretty face, nice body. All right. Let's create some more emotional damage.

□   □   □

I knew I could count on Bodie. It turns out Amy is mentally unsound and in need of professional treatment [This of course is a point of contention. But I like to imagine I'm the stable one]. Unfortunately she's unusually skilled and unreserved in bed—the primary setting of our three-week relationship—making my escape from her a little more difficult. But I'm relying on a method that's never failed me: ignoring her until she hates me and leaves on her own.

"I need to talk to you," Crazy Amy says.

Looking up from whatever manuscript I'm working on, I wait for her to talk. She just stares down at me. I guess this is a real talk. I get up and take her over to the couch.

"Maybe this isn't a good time," she says.

"Amy, you said you needed to talk to me. This is a good time."

She glances back into my room and back at me.

"OK, we can go back there," I say.

Crazy Amy sits on my bed and I close the door behind myself.

"What's going on?" she asks me.

I lie down next to her and look up at the ceiling. "I don't know."

"You just ignore me now," she says. "I feel like I'm in your way."

Must be that woman's intuition.

"I know you have a lot to do and you're always working, but something's different between us."

Yeah, I don't want you around anymore because your sexual prowess is no longer overcompensating for your delusional psychosis.

"Are you pushing me away because you're afraid of hurting me?"

Crazy Amy has read almost everything I've ever written and quickly picked up on the fear-of-commitment-because-I'm-afraid-of-hurting-the-girl theme. Unfortunately it doesn't apply to Crazy Amy. I just don't like her that much anymore.

"I don't know," I shrug.

"Why won't you talk to me?"

"I don't know what to say."

"Why don't you just tell me the truth?"

"The truth is that I don't know what to say."

Crazy Amy shakes her head. "I didn't wanna come up here because I don't know what I want. I don't wanna break up with you. I thought maybe I should sleep on it."

"No, don't sleep on it, let's take care of it now."

"Well then you have to talk to me," she says. "Do you not want me around?"

"No, well, no, I don't know. I just have a lot of shit to do."

The front door opens and I hear familiar voices. Lacy. She's been showing up unannounced the last couple weeks without explanation. This might get ugly. I try to ignore Lacy and pretend I'm listening to Crazy Amy while our conversation rapidly disintegrates into an argument.

"Look," I say finally. "Maybe you should sleep on it, cause we're not getting anywhere."

Crazy Amy jumps to her feet and explodes. "We're not getting anywhere cause you're not talking to me!"

She runs out and slams my door behind her, then slams the open front door for further dramatic effect. She probably saw it on MTV or something. I drop back onto my bed and run my hands over my face. That's not at all what I wanted. But at least she's gone. My door opens and Lacy bursts in, jumping onto the bed and hugging me.

"Oh, Baby, are you OK?" she asks sweetly.

I hug her back and smell that smooth brown hair. I'm fine.

□　　□　　□

Lacy must have a schedule of upcoming bad times for her presence in my life. "Hey," she smiles when I answer the unexpected knock on my door.

"Uh, Crazy Amy is on her way over right now," I tell her. "Probably wants to call me names or something."

Lacy invites herself in before I finish and sits on the couch. "She needs to get over it."

I sit next to her and look down at her hand. "That's quite a ring you got there."

She wiggles her finger and checks out the diamond. "It's an engagement ring."

"Are you engaged?"

Lacy grins and leans against my shoulder. "No, I just like it."

"Look," I tell her, "when Crazy Amy gets here, just let me talk to her, OK?"

Lacy smiles reassuringly and shakes her head at my apparently unwarranted distrust of her.

A few minutes later, Crazy Amy knocks on the open door and pokes her head in. Her face drops when she sees Lacy. I stand up and walk outside with her before she starts screaming.

Crazy Amy glares at me. "You didn't tell me she was here."

"She wasn't," I explain. "She has a bad habit of showing up unannounced."

"Well look, I just wanted to talk to you," Crazy Amy says. "I know I stormed outta here the other night, but I wanna make sure we can still be friends."

Yeah, I'll come visit you in the psych ward all the time.

"Yeah, sure."

Crazy Amy's face slowly softens into a smile. "Can I have a hug?"

I step forward and hug her, bracing myself for the blade she's going to plunge into the back of my neck. Instead of stabbing me, she kisses my cheek. Her lips are probably poisoned or something.

"Call me, OK?" she says.

"Yeah."

I'm still a liar.

Crazy Amy smiles and heads out to her car. Despite my typical failures, it seems we've ended the episode relatively well. I walk back to my apartment and I'm almost run over by Lacy as she explodes from the door.

"Amy!" she yells across the parking lot. "Can I talk to you real quick?"

I stop her. "Lacy, what're you doing."

"Don't worry, Baby," she grins. "I just wanna talk to her."

"Lacy," I say again slowly. "What are you going to do."

"Nothing, just go back inside."

My curiosity slowly overpowers my concern for Crazy Amy's well-being and I let Lacy slip past me. She runs down the stairs and out into the parking lot while I walk back into my room to observe from my window. From above, I see Lacy catch up to Crazy Amy and I strain to hear the conversation.

"So you're that girl Greg had a little fling with," Lacy says.

Crazy Amy's face hardens. "I guess..."

"Well look," Lacy continues, "Greg and I had our problems, and for a while I didn't know what I wanted. But now I know all I want is him."

Crazy Amy waits.

"And I'm wearing this again." Lacy holds up her left hand and wiggles her ring finger—which now holds the engagement ring.

I step back from the window. I can't believe she just did that. I can't believe I'm standing up here watching her do it. I can't believe what an asshole I am. Still stunned, I walk back out into the living room and sit stiffly on the couch. Lacy strolls in with her innocently beautiful smile and sits down next to me.

I shake my head incredulously. "I can't believe you just did that."

"She won't bother you anymore," Lacy shrugs. Swinging her leg over me, she straddles my lap and curls her hands around the back of my neck. "What would you say if I told you I wanted to sleep with you again?"

□   □   □

Despite its nearly irresistible physiological appeal, I rejected Lacy's proposal on principle—the principle of trying to keep unnecessary drama to a minimum at a time when Crazy Amy has been baking me cookies—which I of course make Bodie taste first to check for poison or sharp non-edible components—and having her roommate call me to come take care of her when she's drunk, which I politely decline to do, citing conflicting obligations that don't actually exist such as needing to pick up a friend from the airport at 3:00 A.M. or eating broken glass.

I've spent the last couple months distracting myself from girls— apparently the only ones I attract anymore are crazy, married, ugly, or probably infected with things penicillin won't clear up—with work and my discussions with Bodie about wanting to pull a RIC maneuver over our balcony. This is a firefighting technique so dangerous that it's no longer even taught in fire academies, intended for use in only in the most dire of situations, when a firefighter must exit a window and get down a ladder as fast as possible to avoid certain death, and involves essentially a cartwheel over the ladder [balcony railing].

"Dude, it won't work."

"Yeah it will."

"The balcony sticks out too far below the railing."

"So what."

"So you'll hit it and break your arms."

"No I won't."

"Yes you will."

"No I won't."

Eventually we were both convinced of the maneuver's impossibility in the given configuration, but impossibility is no reason not to try, particularly at a moment when I'm exhausted and delirious from working every day this month but racing with nebulous sexual energy because I haven't had sex since Crazy Amy stomped out of my apartment and Bodie is pointing a video camera at me.

Yelling something unintelligible, I run outside onto the balcony, and ignoring all logic and reason, because logic and reason suddenly don't make that much sense, I grab the railing and flip myself over it.


I look around slowly. Bright white floor tile, X-ray boards, bio-hazard cans... This is like an emergency room.

"Dude, where's your insurance card?" Bodie asks me.

This is an emergency room.

I'm not used to seeing it from on a bed in the hallway. I'm usually pushing me. I squeeze my eyes shut and wince, trying to remember how I managed to have my head run over by an unusually large vehicle. I glance down at my arm and follow the IV line up with my eyes. The 1000 mL bag is empty. I've been here awhile.

"Huh?"

"Your. Insurance. Card," Bodie repeats slowly. "Where is it."

I shrug.

A nurse walks over to me. "We're just getting your paperwork together and you'll be ready to go," she says.

I sit up and the IV tugs at my arm. I pull it out slowly and look at the garden-hose-sized catheter that's now curved sharply from me bending my elbow around it.

"Do you even remember what happened?" Bodie laughs.

I have a series of vague and brief recollections of realizing my hand was slipping from the balcony railing, looking up at one of our paramedics while my head was taped to a backboard, an invisible voice asking me to transfer from the gurney to the CT table, which I did with a strange fuzzy tunnel-vision, and the rest is completely blank until a couple minutes ago.

"Not really."

"That's OK," Bodie says, holding up the video camera. "I got it on tape."

I watch the playback and see myself lying unconscious on the cement below the balcony, my head turned sharply to one side, obstructing my airway enough to make my labored breathing disturbingly loud. I touch my aching jaw and feel an abrasion, then touch the tender side of my head above my temple. Slowly I imagine what happened off screen: When my hand slipped off the railing, I hit my jaw and then my head on the cement balcony that was supposed to break my arms and knocked myself out before I even hit the ground. My jaw won't close all the way, my head is throbbing with the worst headache I've ever experienced, I've misplaced the last few hours of my life, I'm completely disoriented, and I can't even construct full-length coherent thoughts.

I should start a publishing company.

CHAPTER NINE

It's probably the recent head injury, but I've been overcome with entrepreneurial inspiration. Delusion, more accurately, considering independent publishing is probably the highest-risk least-lucrative business imaginable. But I'm going to do it anyway. Why? Because fuck everyone.

I've obtained all the licenses and permits and permissions and legal paperwork. I've emptied my personal bank accounts and filled new official business accounts so I can empty them with official business expenses and be officially broke. I've terminated my recently signed literary agent's contract because my agent was a worthless piece of shit and couldn't place my work anywhere—possibly because I'm exceedingly impatient and never gave him a chance to, but more likely because I'm not a talented writer. All I have to exploit is my youth. I have to get this shit in print before I get old and ordinary. Grundle Ink Publications is now a legitimate company, not just a partially-developed fantasy with a stupid name only appearing on the copyright pages of a few hand-bound copies of a retarded book no one reads.

Also certainly related to my recent head trauma is my sleeping with another Lisa (dubbed Lisa Three to avoid confusion), who not only happens to be the close friend of Crazy Amy who conspired with Bodie to set me up with her, but my downstairs neighbor's very recent ex-girlfriend. I'm beginning to think I'm less attracted to the girls themselves than the bad situations they're a part of. At least Lisa Three is eighteen and legally capable of engaging in sexual intercourse with me. But forget all that. Right now I have to take my anatomy lecture final.

I step into the lecture hall and take my customary seat right next to the back door for easy escape in case of earthquake or fire or the overwhelming urge to walk outside and scream profanities for no other reason than that I like the words *fuck* and *shit* and they sound even better at high volume. I feel a gentle tap on my shoulder and turn. The girl who sits against the wall behind me holds out a little folded piece of paper.

"What's this?" I ask her.

She just smiles.

Whatever. I take the note and turn back around to read the light pencil:

*This is my last chance to tell you how much I've enjoyed looking at you each class. Most likely I'll never see you again. Better late than never.*

I read it again carefully to make sure it's not just the drug damage in my brain conspiring with my unrelenting need for female affection to trick me into setting myself up for humiliation. It still says what I thought it said.

I struggle to ignore the thought of this slim, tanned, dark-haired girl naked and moaning uncontrollably in orgasmic ecstasy and concentrate on the exam, but I seem to be more concerned with naked moaning and orgasmic ecstasy than osteogenesis and Haversion canals.

I finish filling in bubbles and writing in spaces and tear off a corner of the exam to write down Grundle Ink's website address for the girl. This is my attempt to placate both my conscience and my curiosity. By giving her my phone number, in effect I'm saying, Yes, I want to have sex with you and I'm not even going to try to avoid this bad situation. But by giving her only the website address of the company I own—which coincidentally contains my email address and business phone number—I'm saying, I might want to have sex with you, but I'm a morally upright young man who refuses to encourage any deviant sexual behavior that could result in unnecessary emotional trauma.

Dropping my exam off on the instructor's desk, I walk back up the stairs to where the girl is sitting, watching me with a shy but somehow confident smile. I hand her the scrap of paper and duck out the door.


Lisa Three hands the girl's note back to me. "She just gave that to you?"

"Yeah." I set the note on the milk crate next to my bed for safekeeping. This is the kind of thing you show your grandkids.

"You've never talked to her?"

"Not a word."

Lisa Three breathes deeply and nods. I don't know why she's looking at me like that. She should be happy to know she's currently sleeping with the most desirable guy in the world. Or at least in my anatomy lecture section.

What I conveniently forgot to tell Lisa Three is that when I got home last night after the test, I had four emails from the girl explaining the situation: She's twenty-seven with two kids and getting married in a few months. It seems she just needs one last guy before she takes those vows. Reluctantly, I declined her persistent series of offers. It's not that I'm not flattered by her stellar choice, it's that I'm a little concerned with the potential consequences, including anything from her developing some kind of emotional attachment that inspires her to call off the wedding, to me getting beaten to death with a hammer by an angry fiancée, to me suffering from performance anxiety due to the immense pressure being placed on my fragile psyche, knowing I'll be the last guy with whom she ever enjoys casual pre-marital sex—that pressure compounded by her statement that she doesn't just want to get fucked, she wants it to be unforgettable—and humiliating myself so intensely by being unable to achieve a sufficient erection that I'm never able to share an intimate moment with another woman, choked by my pervasive fear of failure.

I also have a problem sleeping with her because of Lisa Three, although our relationship is far from defined, and I'm far from convinced I even want to be involved with her. Lisa Three makes me uncomfortable. After breaking up with her boyfriend—who unfortunately lives directly below me—she started hanging out upstairs. A few days of casual interaction later, we somehow ended up in my bed with her on top of me. She stopped kissing me abruptly and looked at the wall above my head.

"What."

"I don't know," she shrugged.

"You don't know?"

She shrugged again. "It's a concept."

"A concept?"

"Yeah."

"Like the theory of relativity?"

"No."

"Oh. Which concept?"

Lisa Three just smiled shyly and shrugged again. Our interpersonal communication skills are not extraordinarily well developed. She leaned down and started kissing me again, then sat back to pull her shirt off. I unhooked her bra and tossed it across the room, and she huddled back down against me, unnecessarily self-conscious of her bare chest.

"That's the concept," she said.

What, taking off your bra?

"How many people have you done this with?" she asked me quietly, kissing my neck.

Oh, sex.

"A few..." I said uncomfortably.

She nodded slowly, absorbing my intentionally vague response. "You're only number two," she said.

Uh-oh.

Her inexperience became immediately apparent, demonstrated by an obvious lack of understanding of angles of entry, range of motion, and other anatomical and biomechanical concepts. But worse than this was her complete ignorance of inappropriate verbal communication.

"Say it," she said suddenly, looking up at me.

Say it? Say what?

Holy shit, is she asking me to say I love her?

Oh. Fuck.

Oh fuck, oh fuck, oh—

Maintain the erection!

—fuck, oh fuck.

Wait, no, she's Crazy Amy's friend, the last girl in her position (currently the standard missionary—good for beginners). They must have girl-talked. What did I say to Crazy Amy?

"You feel so good," I whispered in her ear.

Lisa Three moaned quietly in delight and pulled me against her.

I guess tonight is New Year's Eve or something. Bodie and Lisa One dragged me out to some bullshit high school party because Lisa One is in bullshit high school and Bodie will do anything to please her, including volunteering my presence at such bullshit events.

"I'm not going," I told them when I found out.

"Come on," they said.

"I got work to do."

"So take a break."

"I don't want to."

"Come on, it'll be fun," Lisa One said.

"Watching other people get drunk is not as fun as you seem to think."

"Come on..."

Finally I just gave in. Now we're standing in the backyard of some kid's house, apparently the son of a local politician I'm sure would be thrilled at the site of his home being overrun by drunk underage kids stumbling between kegs and ruining his furniture along with his chances for re-election. I pull his campaign sign from the lawn and throw it on the roof because I'm an asshole and I think it's funny.

Bodie and I have distanced ourselves from the crowd and are having our own party by the pool because he's tired of talking to them and I'm tired of entertaining them by putting cigarettes out on my tongue. We find an anonymous kid slumped in a chair next to us, looking like he's struggling desperately to maintain consciousness.

"Hey," we say.

The kid's head rolls on his shoulders.

"Hey fucker."

He tries to look up.

"Hey, are you gonna puke?"

"Cause it looks like you're gonna puke."

"Puke, fucker."

"Here's a bucket. Puke in it."

"You look like you're gonna puke your guts out, fucker, bring it up."

Bodie and I begin making vomiting sounds in his face until one of his sympathetic friends drags him away from our harassment.

Pussies.

I light a cigarette and look over at the house, at all the gorgeous young girls who won't ever have sex with me because their impressionable young minds have been deformed by growing up watching MTV. I smoked a cigarette a couple weeks ago for the first time in years because Bodie had the video camera again and I'd already flipped over the balcony, so I figured smoking was the next most shockingly entertaining thing for me to do, it being well-known and understood that I no longer do things like smoke cigarettes. And now that my cigarette abstinence has been broken, I have no reservations about smoking in a situation like this. I'm exceedingly uncomfortable around these people and their drinking and drugs and I need something like a cigarette to occupy my hands and mouth and make me look cool because I'm twenty years old and at a high school party and this is not cool. Extinguishing cigarettes on my tongue has also proven to be a convenient substitute for conversation.

"Who wants to kiss me!"

Lisa Three finally left me. It sounds cool when I say it like that. Like a blues song. Except unlike singers of the blues, I don't care that she left me because I'm still the same socially retarded dickhead who finds creatively cowardly ways to encourage break-ups without actually confronting the issues and being honest like a mature adult.

Lisa One walks over with one of her cute underage friends who won't have sex with me and nods at the nearby keg. "Is that one empty?"

"Affirmative."

The girl who won't have sex with me holds out a camera to Bodie. "Could you hold this while we go dance?"

Bodie takes the camera and shoots me a look. I wink. Never leave people like us unattended with your camera.

"Thanks," the girls say, walking back to the house.

Bodie rolls the empty keg over to a row of hedges and proceeds to urinate on it, then snaps a photo of his exposed gear with the girl's camera.

Happy New Year!

□     □     □

Every afternoon—even Sundays sometimes, because I don't always know what day it is, so even though I understand mail is not delivered on Sundays, I expect it to be waiting there for me in its little metal closet, smiling in orderly fashion, aligned and perfect, except on days when I receive an excessive amount of mail, in which case it'll be bent and folded and torn from the large mail-delivering woman who smells like patchouli oil stuffing it in there carelessly, clearly not understanding the beauty and wonder of mail and the receiving thereof—I walk down the stairs in front of our apartment—which are too small to take one at a time and too big to take two at a time without that strained, thrusting stride that makes even the most mature and physically developed of adults appear to be little children struggling up the steps of some playground structure that most likely includes a slide and some kind of pole—and through the narrow cement courtyard—always wearing shoes, because unlike other residents of this building, I know what's on that cement: things like melted polyester from the shirt Bodie lit on fire and dropped off the balcony, orange vomit from the anonymous guy downstairs who ate tomatoes and then got a little too drunk and ate tomatoes backwards, and urine deposited remotely from our balcony on nights when Bodie was drunk or otherwise inclined to stop talking mid-sentence and unzip his jeans to urinate over the railing, another surface I tend to avoid touching unnecessarily—and into the small tunnel that houses the building's mailboxes, sliding my key into the lock of our mailbox—which has never had a number but I determined was ours through the process of elimination—and reveal the waiting joy. But today I'm behind schedule, sitting idly on a milk crate on our balcony while Bodie smokes.

Bodie decided a few weeks ago it would be a good idea to set me up with his ex-girlfriend Summer, the same girlfriend I unintentionally disrespected by assisting Bodie's deviant behavior with seventeen-year-old Lisa One.

"Dude," I said, "you don't think that'd be weird?"

"No, man. She's my friend, you're my friend. I think it'd be cool."

Eventually his persistence and my attraction to Summer actually overrode my better judgment, which I'm beginning to realize tends to offer little resistance to overriding. I was in desperate need of a new bad situation. Summer and I seem to be getting over the initial weirdness of the circumstances, although we regressed a little a few nights ago when we were making out on the couch with Bodie passed out on the floor close enough for me to kick him in the head.

"Did you get the mail?" Bodie asks me.

"Uh-uh."

"I'll get it."

"Put your shoes on."

Bodie slips on his sandals—the same surfer thongs that grace his feet every day of the year, regardless of the temperature or the precipitation or the depth of the puddles he must ford, regardless of people's comments about the temperature and precipitation and puddle depth being inappropriate for the wearing of sandals—and gets the mail.

He hands me my stack and sits on the milk crate next to me. I shuffle through my mail, dropping those pieces of no immediate consequence, and freeze at the last letter.

Fuck.

Oh fuck.

"Oh fuck," I say.

Bodie flicks his cigarette over the railing and glances at me. "What."

I stare at the letter in my hand, at the handwriting I recognized immediately, at the way she wrote my address—wait, that's not my address, I live on First Ave, not First Street, and she didn't put the apartment number on it, how the fuck did this even get here—and at the return address in LA I don't know.

"What," Bodie says again.

I keep staring. "It's a letter from Kala."

"Kala?"

"Fucking Kala."

"As in *The* Kala?" Bodie knows about Kala.

"The Kala," I nod. "She's in LA."

Bodie watches me. "So are you gonna open it or what?"

I keep staring at the letter. It's been almost three years since I've seen this girl, since I've even heard about her. Almost three years I've spent thinking about not thinking about her because she was the last thread, the one who represented the entire life I walked away from to be this intense, and to maintain my intensity, I've had to deny myself all contact with her.

"I don't know if I want to," I say finally.

"Why not?"

"I wanna burn it and forget I ever saw it."

"What?"

"I don't want this," I tell Bodie. "I don't even wanna acknowledge she's still alive."

"Dude," Bodie says, "you gotta at least read it."

"No I—"

"What if she's changed?"

"I—"

"What if she did what you did?"

"She—"

"She's in LA, right?"

"Yeah, but—"

"She left the Bay Area."

"So—"

"Maybe she wanted a new start like you did."

"She—"

"You gotta read it," Bodie says. "At least read it. You don't have to do anything else. You can burn it after you read it if you want."

I look one more time at Kala's handwriting and drop the envelope at my feet. "Yeah."


Summer sits uncomfortably on the couch next to me. I lean forward with my arms on my knees and try to explain.

"I got a letter from Kala," I tell her.

Summer knows who Kala is. She understands what I'm trying to tell her even though the words are stumbling from my lips. She understands I'm trying to tell her I can't be with her anymore because I'm afraid I still have feelings for Kala and that's not fair to her.

"What're you gonna do?" Summer asks.

"I don't know. I thought about just throwing away the letter, but I can't."

We talk about it for a while and I apologize to her.

"It's OK," Summer says, kissing me on the cheek. "I understand."

I like Summer. She kisses me on the cheek and understands.

When she leaves, I return to my corner in the kitchen and my desk and my computer and try to work. I've finished the page layouts for two books and I'm trying to get the cover designs finished so I can send the books out to the printer so my publishing company will have actually published something so I don't have to deal with those conversations with people who don't understand.

"So what kind of publishing is it?"

"Books."

"Oh, what kind of books?"

"Uh…"

It's a little awkward. I walk away feeling like a sterile junior high school health class discussion of masturbation.

I'm beginning to realize what a poor choice for a company name Grundle Ink Publications was. The *publications* part is fine, but the rest just doesn't work, particularly over the telephone, the unfamiliar words made even more incomprehensible by my complete lack of enunciation skills.

"Grundle Ink."

"What?"

"Grundle. G-R-U-N-D-L-E."

"Oh. OK. Grundle Incorporated."

"No. Not incorporated. Ink. I-N-K. Like the stuff in a pen."

"Oh. OK."

"On the card, it says I-N-C. I need—"

"What does Grundle mean?"

I hang up the phone and think of all the other names I could have come up with: Morning Three Publications, Channel Three Publishing, Fuck You and Your Whole Family Press. So many names that don't include Grundle or Ink. But instead of dwelling on something I can't change without extreme inconvenience, or dwelling on any kind of business plan, or any kind of anything even vaguely related to business or planning, because I find business and planning tedious and uninteresting and somehow believe I can avoid them entirely, I spend my days—which begin in the afternoon and end a little while before dawn—tucked into the kitchen corner sitting in front of my computer writing, perfecting page layouts and cover designs—which I don't really know how to do, but do anyway because I can't afford to hire a graphic artist—continually building and altering and repairing the company's website—which I also don't really know how to do but do anyway for the same reasons I do everything else: a lack of funds and a undeniable need for total control—or sometimes just reading and editing manuscripts, trying to find some inspiration within the pages, some compelling reason to keep myself awake until 4:00 A.M. working for a company that's doing little more than rapidly draining my bank accounts.

Bodie and Lisa One come home from doing whatever emotionally-healthy girlfriends and boyfriends do with each other, and Bodie goes back to take a shower. Lisa One leans against the kitchen counter and watches me.

"You work too much," she says.

"What?"

"You're always in here at your desk. I never see you anywhere else."

"I have shit to do," I tell her.

"Don't you ever get bored?"

"Not really."

"What time did you go to bed last night?"

"5:30 this morning."

"Greg..." she scolds. "You need to get out sometimes."

"I went out on New Year's."

"That was like three months ago," she laughs.

"So what."

"So you need to get out more. You need to have fun."

"I do have fun."

"What do you do for fun?"

"Work."

"What do you do besides work?"

"Work."

"Greg..."

"What, I don't wanna do anything else," I tell her honestly. "I don't drink, I don't get fucked up, and I don't like people that much when I'm not drunk or fucked up, so what am I supposed to do?"

Lisa One shrugs. "I don't drink and I still go out and have fun."

Lisa One is Christian. I mean really Christian. Like Christian to the point of scaring the shit out of me. But the upside to seventeen-year-old Lisa One's religious dedication is her virginity and her commitment to maintain it until marriage, which is currently keeping my roommate and friend out of prison.

"Yeah," I say, "but I don't have fun like that."

"So how do you have fun?"

"Free-basing in strangers' bathrooms and barbecuing young Christians in public parks."

"Greg!"

"You asked."

Lisa One shakes her head at me, but still laughs. Free-basing in strangers' bathrooms and barbecuing young Christians in public parks is pretty fucking funny.

□   □   □

Bodie steps into the kitchen and opens the refrigerator door without looking inside. "So are you gonna start coming out to the bars with me?"

I turn twenty-one in a few days. My plans include going to the DMV to request a driver's license without that intrusive red stripe that immediately indicates underagedness and not going to the bars.

"No."

"Why?"

"What do most people go to bars to do?" I ask him.

"Drink."

"Right. What does that mean, then, that most people at bars are going to be?"

"Drunk."

"Right. What don't I like?"

"Drunk people."

"Right."

"Yeah, but how am I gonna meet new girls?" Bodie complains. He broke up with Lisa One three days before her eighteenth birthday.

"I don't know."

"Dude, just come out," he says. "You could meet a cool girl."

"The chances of me meeting a girl I think is cool at a bar are slim," I tell him, silently realizing there might actually be other people in the universe whose friends coerce them into attending bars, and that some of the other people to whom this happens may be women, and furthermore that some of these women may actually be quite cool, yet also lack the particular sensibility to avoid involvement with someone like me.

"Dude, I haven't had sex in so long!" Bodie laughs desperately.

"Not my fault you had a seventeen-year-old Christian virgin for a girlfriend."

Bodie looks disappointed. I ignore him and go back to my work. I sent both of the books to the printer and I'm now working on a book of K's writing we started putting together a couple years ago. I'm hoping it will relieve some of my discomfort in being the only writer I've published and the resulting feeling of wankness. But K insisted we include a section of my letters, so my relief will be incomplete.

After a year of lame excuses, Paul finally sent me the completed manuscript for his ingenious book. Bodie asked to read it because, like me, he was intrigued by the concept. He made it through two of Paul's pages and gave up. What I failed to realize when I signed on for the project is that concepts only get you so far when you're working with Paul.

He called me the other night. I told him to call me back and gave him the Grundle Ink phone number.

"So I have to call the business line?" he asked when I picked up the other phone.

"Yes."

Paul was silent while he absorbed that one. "Well, I read through the contract you sent me," he said finally. "I just have a few questions."

"What."

Paul rattled off anticipated questions about percentages and terms and rights and I supplied him with my premeditated responses. In the end, I agreed to changing the term of the contract to the first printing instead of one year and a few other minor concessions he somehow believed were to his advantage but were actually to mine. I failed to explain that to him.

I mailed him a new contract with his requested changes and made a few changes of my own—namely decreasing his royalty percentage because I no longer feel sorry for him and decided to be reasonable. I have no obligation to him and I'm becoming increasingly less interested in the book now that the content has eclipsed the concept. I think I'm actually hoping he'll reject the changes so I can tell him to get fucked and spend my money on something worthwhile.

"So are you gonna go to sleep tonight?" Bodie asks me.

"Fuck no," I tell him. "Sleep is for lightweights."

"Then you must weigh about twenty pounds," Bodie says, "cause I haven't seen you get outta bed before 1:00 in a long time."

Needing more time to prevent Grundle Ink from failing prematurely, I stepped down from my recent promotion at the ambulance company and requested a per diem position. I now supply my supervisor with an availability calendar, generally giving him one to three days a month to schedule me. This is my way of quitting without actually quitting. It seems my approach to women and jobs are disturbingly similar. Regardless, I'm now unhindered by scheduling fascists and free to maintain my non-sleep-conformist status, meaning my entire day is regularly staggered about six hours later than the typical Pacific Time resident's.

"Hey," Bodie says. "Let's go steal a newspaper stand."

□ □ □

The days are all the same again. They run together and slip away and lose me in their vague incompleteness. My days on the ambulance are gone— the twenty-four-hour shifts, the blood and the vomit and the urine and the feces, the being awakened at 4:00 A.M. for chronic back pain, the never going to sleep at all because we're running calls continuously for twenty-four hours, the straining to lift an enormous woman from a reclining chair and onto a flat, trying to hold her head higher than her feet so she won't suffocate in the fluid in her lungs, struggling to carry this shifting weight that grabs at things through a hallway only wide enough for three firefighters and me to squeeze through with one hand each on the stretcher, out onto the landing, where we're unable to turn the flat in the tight space to carry her down the stairs and have to break apart the wooden railing and lower her over the edge onto the gurney without dropping her six feet onto the dirt while my partner verbally reprimands her for not yet moving downstairs.

The days have become the day. The day that begins in the afternoon and drifts languidly into the early morning hours when the rest of the world sleeps and dreams and recovers and I sit alone in a dark corner of my kitchen in the frozen glow of a computer screen, drowning in the endless blurring words and the clatter of keys under my shaking fingers. I cannot sleep. There's no time for sleep, no time for rest. There's work to be done, work that must be done now, not later, because later is a time for those who wait for change, and waiting for change is waiting for nothing because change must be orchestrated by sleepless minds in dark apartment kitchens that can't wait any longer for the evolution, the revolution, the stunningly subversive leap into the future of this crumbling youth culture that I will, with my poorly named publishing company and its poorly written books, resurrect and fill with power and purpose and determination, burning away this suffocating smog of social complacency that chokes us all and leaves us lost and crawling.

I answer the phone because it's the fastest way to make it stop ringing. "Grundle Ink Publications."

"Greg?"

I know this voice. "Yeah…"

"It's Deanna."

Deanna. Deanna? Cheerleader Deanna. Is there a way to kill someone through a phone line? I pull the phone a little farther from my ear in case anything sharp or poisonous comes out of it.

"Deanna…" I repeat cautiously.

"So how're you doing?"

We talk for over an hour. She tells me everything she's been doing in the last three years, tells me about leaving her boyfriend, about finding out she had an ovarian cyst, about having a mild heart attack last year, about how her AA meetings were across the street from her favorite bar. My story suddenly sounds like a coloring book. I ask her in a joking tone if she still hates me, even though I'm completely serious, because she should still hate me. She says she's done a lot of growing up in the last few years and couldn't hate me anymore for something she never understood. I put the phone back to my ear.

"So when're you coming up to Chico?" I ask her.

"I don't know," she says. "Soon."

"You better."

She's quiet. "Why don't you come down here and see me?"

"Right now?"

"Sure."

I look at the clock. It's past eight. I'm unshowered, unshaven, and a three-and-a-half-hour drive away. "I'll see you in four hours."


It's late and I'm driving to the Bay Area. I'm driving very fast because I drive very fast. I must stay pumped and ignore the fear of getting another speeding ticket for driving very fast because I can't go to traffic school again for a while, so I put in a Minor Threat CD and yell along with Ian MacKaye because he only yells one note throughout the entire album and my singing/yelling range happens to be limited to the three notes in this note's immediate vicinity, so my ability to sing along makes me feel like an accomplished vocalist instead of just a guy who writes stupid books driving very fast down Highway 99 wearing no shirt or shoes because he must remain fresh and clean-smelling should an intimate situation arise in which unappealing body odors may hinder success.

And then I'm in front of Deanna's house, still smelling crisp and recently bathed. The place looks exactly like I remember it. I think about all the nights I stormed out of my house after fighting with my mother and stayed with Deanna until 6:00 in the morning, sneaking out before her father woke up and driving to the bike shop to sleep uncomfortably in my 4Runner until K showed up and pounded on my window and told me to get my skinny ass to work. I take a breath and knock.

The door opens and Deanna looks out at me. Her hair is long again, darker. But I know those big blue eyes and those lips.

Her smile spreads. "Hi…"

I step in and hug her and I'm eighteen again, sneaking out of her house, my skin dry and stiff from the hot tub except for my upper back where Deanna massaged lotion into my tattoo, my eyes burning with exhaustion because we've been doing things on her bed all night that don't involve sleeping, watching the shelves on the wall above us because we knew they would fall on us eventually. I follow her into the living room and give her copies of my books like I promised I would.

"I'm a little afraid to read these," she says. "I'm not sure I wanna see what you thought of me."

"Uh, yeah," I say uncomfortably. "Just remember it was a long time ago."

We sit close to each other, but I'm afraid to touch her. We talk about everything, about nothing. We discuss her road trips and the cardboard signs she and her friends made to express to passing motorists their various feelings about them and their hairstyles. She finally admits she wasn't just drunk that night she broke her ankle and explains she was afraid I'd hate her if I knew she was using crank, which we now find completely amusing considering the cocaine abuse I was hiding from her at the same time. We argue about whether the voice of an old man on this particular episode of Scooby Doo was done by Don Knotts because this is very important, then wait anxiously for the credits so we can prove our superior voice recognition skills to each other.

Deanna takes me back through the house and into her parents' bedroom. They've moved to Virginia and Deanna is living here until the house sells. After she has a cigarette outside, we lie on the bed—her parents' bed, which is just weird, because parents' beds are weird and should not be lain in with people you may be having sex with—and she shows me pictures from the last three years— Three years. It feels like so much longer. It feels like yesterday.

"Yeah, I remember you," Deanna says after one of my smart-ass remarks. I shrug. "What else am I good for but being a smart-ass?"

She smiles and lies back next to me. "Obviously nothing else."

OK. This is one of those female subtlety code things. What she actually just said was: *You're clearly not any good for sex since we're not having any right now.* I want to have sex with her. I really want to have sex with her. But I can't get myself to take that first step. Maybe my interpretation of her code was wrong. I don't know where my boundaries lie anymore. I don't know if I'm allowed to have sex with her.

And besides, it's her parents' bed.

□   □   □

It all looks great from my desk. It seems like a good idea. From my desk, this is a good idea. Ideas are good at desks, visible only to their architects and protected from external perspective. But I'm almost afraid to see it become real. Sometimes I sit back and it overwhelms me. Sometimes I have to stop and ask myself what I'm doing.

"What're you doing?"

"What?"

"This publishing thing, the books, what're you doing?"

"I don't know."

"You think you're gonna change the world, don't you."

"No. Well, yeah."

"And you think some books are gonna do that."

"Not the books themselves. What they represent."

"And what's that."

"Progress, change, inspiration, creative expression, the using of pain to fuel change, because pain is what gives us the power to change."

"You're really losing it, aren't you."

"You don't see it?"

"All I see is a guy who sits at a computer in his apartment kitchen in a college town ghetto working until 4:00 A.M. for a publishing company that doesn't make any money."

"I'm not in it to make money."

"Then what're you in it for?"

"Progress."

"I don't understand."

"Revolution."

"You need to explain this one."

"Somehow I ended up in Chico, this small, isolated conservative town with all these imported college students. I look around and I see all this youth, all this energy, this passion, this virility. But it's all getting channeled into drinking."

"So what."

"So it's depressing. It's a waste of that passion, of that youth."

"You have a problem with drinking?"

"Not really."

"It sounds like you think no one should drink, no one should have any fun. Just because you're dry now you think everyone else should be."

"No, I—"

"Look, not everyone's as perfect as you."

"I never said—"

"You think you're so enlightened, so superior because you've reformed yourself and you don't stoop to such pedestrian methods of social interaction."

"All I—"

"People just want to have fun. Are you saying no one should have any fun?"

"No, I just—"

"Cause that's what it sounds like you're saying."

"Well it's not."

"So what're you saying?"

"I've been trying to tell you, but you keep—"

"Try to explain without pointing fingers, God."

"I don't think I'm God."

"Whatever."

"I just think this town has so much potential going to waste. It's such a concentrated population of young people with so much energy. But instead of finding creative ways to use that energy, it gets directed into self-destruction. I'm not saying drinking is wrong. I'm not saying using drugs is wrong. And I'm not saying no one should ever do either. I'm just saying we need to find better ways to survive ourselves."

"So they shouldn't get drunk."

"No, that's not what I'm saying."

"Then why don't you drink at all?"

"Because I resort to extreme measures."

"You can't control yourself."

"It's either all or nothing for me."

"Maybe you have a problem. A psychological predisposition to addiction or something."

"Yeah maybe, whatever. Look, this is what I'm trying to say: You're young and full of energy, you're not yet jaded and exhausted from life's brutality. This is the time to do it."

"Do what?"

"Everything."

"That sounds like a lot to ask."

"I just mean everyone has dreams. Everyone wants something. This is the time to reach for your dreams."

"This is starting to sound like an after school special."

"I can't help it."

"Maybe your dream is to be a motivational speaker."

"No, I can't speak. I have this fucked up voice that sometimes fades in and out and then my mouth gets all dry and I get really self-conscious about my lips sticking to my teeth because it would probably look funny, I have this thing about my mouth, you know, that's why I don't smile very much, I don't like my smile, and sometimes I get nervous in front of people and you can hear it in my voice, it gets weak and it wavers and sounds like I'm about to cry or something."

"We're getting off subject."

"What were we talking about."

"Youthful energy, revolution, Chico."

"Right. I'm tired. I'm fucking exhausted and dragging my feet through every day. I'm tired of seeing the same blank faces drooling the same hollow words. I'm tired of screaming and only hearing my own voice echo back. You're twenty-one, eighteen, twenty-five, whatever, shouldn't you be fucking exploding with passion? Shouldn't you be knocking everything and everyone out of your way to grab what you want? Shouldn't you be punching your fists to the sky in defiance? Shouldn't you be yelling *Fuck You!* at anyone who ever tried to hold you back, anyone who ever spit on your dreams, anyone who ever said No? Fuck them! This is your chance. This is the time. There is no later. There's only right now. You have to use right now because it's gone before you know it. We've let the power slip from our fingers. We've let them steal from us for so long they don't even have to steal anymore. We give it away. I want to walk down the street and see fury in your eyes and hear passion in your voices. I want to know you refuse to take it anymore, you refuse to be stepped over, pushed aside, shelved and catalogued and forgotten. I want to believe it's not over. I want to believe it's just begun."

"Wow. That was inspiring."

"Thanks."

"So whatever happened with that girl Deanna?"

"What the hell does that have to do with anything?"

"Nothing, I'm just curious. You never finished the story. You have a bad habit of leaving things unresolved."

"I know. I'm a shitty writer. I don't care enough to correct it."

"So Deanna."

"Right. She came up to Chico a few weekends and we had a lot of sex. You know she was the first girl I'd slept with in a hundred forty days?"

"A hundred forty days?"

"I checked the calendar."

"You need a hobby."

"We came up with the term *All-day Asia*."

"All-day Asia?"

"Yeah. Remember that song *Turning Japanese?*"

"Kind of. From the eighties."

"Right. You know what it's about?"

"It's from the eighties. I didn't think it was about anything."

"It's about jacking off, as in the squinty-eyed face you make when you come so you resemble one of Asian descent."

"I'm a little uncomfortable with what you just said."

"What?"

"It doesn't seem too politically correct."

"If you don't understand why what I just said should in no way be offensive to anyone, you need to kill yourself."

"OK."

"May I continue?"

"Please."

"OK, I need to back up. Deanna likes the word *fabulous*. When Deanna would say *fabulous*, she would do this crazy motion with her hands, this exaggerated dance move thing, right?"

"Yeah that's weird, but OK."

"Anyway, some guy saw her do it one day and told her that in sign language, the movement she was doing meant *All-day Asia*."

"That doesn't make any sense."

"Of course it doesn't make any sense, that's why it's funny. So instead of saying *fabulous*, she started saying *All-day Asia*."

"I'm not seeing the connection with the song."

"When she would come up to Chico, we'd have sex all the time. When we were finally done this one night, I told her I couldn't get that song out of my head. She laughed and said she turned Japanese four or five times that night."

"It sounds like you're just sharing this anecdote to show off."

"No, I'm explaining *All-day Asia*."

"OK."

"So then she said she wished she could turn Japanese eight or nine times a day. And I said, 'Yeah, All-day Asia.'"

"Oh, I get it. *All-day Asia* means you're coming all day long."

"Right."

"That's stupid."

"It seemed funny at the time."

"So then what happened?"

"Then she left. She moved to Virginia."

"And then you did it again, didn't you."

"Did what."

"Had sex with some girl just because you could."

"I thought we weren't going to bring that one up."

"We weren't. But I did anyway."

"I was just there. She approached me."

"And who was she?"

"One of my apartment building's resident managers."

"That sounds complicated. What happened?"

"The old manager left and three girls moved in to take his place. One of the girls came up while I was out on the balcony and introduced herself and she hung out all night."

"And you had sex."

"No, we didn't. I knew it was a bad idea and I kept my distance. I tried to make myself as undesirable as possible. I kept telling her stories of my casual sexual exploits with other girls and sounding as gross and heartless as possible. But it didn't work. She kept hanging out all the time, and she kept pushing me more and more."

"Peer pressure."

"Right. I stopped her on two different nights when she was undressing me."

"Wow."

"I know. But then I couldn't stand it anymore and I broke down."

"You had sex with her."

"Right. It sucked."

"You have to stay strong."

"Yeah. I need to work on that."

"So then what?"

"Then the other two girls kicked her out for drinking too much or something and she moved away. Haven't seen her since."

"You're an asshole."

"Why am I an asshole?"

"All this casual, meaningless sex. You have no soul."

"It's not meaningless. And I've got lots of soul for a whiteboy."

"You say that a lot. Have you ever considered the possibility that you're entirely full of shit?"

"More than a few times. But what's your point."

"You talk a lot about feelings and emotions and all that new-ager shit, but you don't demonstrate much concern for anyone but yourself."

"What do you mean?"

"You have sex with these girls and then just throw them away when you're done."

"That's not how it is."

"That's how it looks."

"I know, and I feel bad about it. But I can't help it."

"Of course you can help it. No one's holding a knife to your throat."

"That's not what I mean. I'm not good with girls."

"Sure you are. You haven't waited more than five days to sleep with a girl since high school."

"That's not good. That sucks."

"Why, isn't that what you want?"

"No. I want something real. I want to fall in love."

"That sounds really lame. You should audition for one of those MTV shows, that one where all those whiney, irresponsible jack-offs live in a weird house and just sit around on ugly couches making drama out of the slightest inconven—"

"I don't know how else to put it. That's what I've always wanted."

"But see, this is what I'm talking about. You say that, but I don't see much love. I see a lot of self-gratifying sex and self-aggrandizing writing about said sex, probably just to impress more girls and convince them to fuck you."

"Self-aggrandizing? I've spent the majority of this book making fun of myself."

"Says you."

"Fine, what do you say?"

"That ya silly ass don't want a revolution; ya silly ass want a fan club of vaginas."

"I resent that."

"Of course you do. That's your racket. You play the shy, innocent, selfless guy who just gets trampled on by the rest of the world. It's transparent."

"Fuck you."

"No, fuck you."

"Look, what would it take to convince you?"

"Of what? That you're not full of shit?"

"I guess."

"Writing a real book not featuring you and all your sexual exploits."

"Yeah, but I've already explained that I'm a shitty writer. I avoid writing real books because that's the best way to conceal my embarrassing lack of talent."

"OK, fine, then stop talking shit about love and social revolution."

"I'm not talking shit, though."

"So what you really want is to find a girl you can fall in love with."

"Right."

"So you fuck these girls for a couple weeks, then withdraw until they leave you. That doesn't make sense."

"They're just the ones I end up with. I can't meet girls. I end up with the ones who seek me out, and the ones who seek me out tend to be sexually aggressive because they have to compensate for my insecurity. I go into these accelerated dysfunctional relationships with the hope that she'll be The One, and even though part of me knows she's not, I need her to be. Sex is just what happens while I'm arguing with myself about my contrived emotions."

"That's sad. So what happened with Kala? You never said much about her either."

"There's not much to say. Kala was a momentary lapse of reason I didn't feel like taking the time to discuss in depth. Making that situation interesting isn't worth the required effort. I refer you to my previous claims of talent deficiency."

"So you set up this big, important part of the story, then just leave it hanging?"

"Yes. I don't care."

"But didn't you originally write the whole thing?"

"Yeah. I cut it out because it was boring and really didn't matter. She's the same girl I walked away from. She just thinks she's different and wants me to believe she is so she can have a symbol of change—me—around to help convince herself she's changed."

"She was using you to make herself feel better."

"Yes."

"So basically, you found closure in the realization that you never loved her, that she was really nothing more than another opportunity for sex."

"You make that sound really bad, but yes."

"And now you can finally let go of that part of your life and move the fuck on, drop this ridiculous 'no one understands my pain' routine based on your abrupt departure from her and all your friends."

"Yeah, pretty much. And now I don't have any good excuses for my lack of social skills."

"So what you're saying is that your publishing company is going to inspire a social revolution among the country's youth and change their lives."

"Right."

"You're delusional."

"Probably."

"Your books just sit in a rented storage unit and you just sit at your computer. How is that going to change the world?"

"It's hard to sell books to people who don't read."

"Yeah, I can see the problem. You need promotion."

"Yeah, but I'm not good at promotion."

"You're embarrassed to promote the company, aren't you."

"So far it's only published my own books because I can't afford to pay anyone else for theirs. You know how humiliating it is to try to sell yourself like that?"

"People do it all the time."

"Yeah, but I'm not a good writer."

"Maybe you should quit."

"A little late for that now."

"Fine. So how are you gonna get this thing off the ground?"

"I don't know. I'm doing the standard press kit and news release racket, but that's bullshit. I want to do something different to promote the company because the company is different."

"Like what?"

"Like hand out Grundle Ink sweatshirts to all the homeless people in Chico."

"You have a term for that, don't you."

"Responsible Capitalism."

"That's very clever."

"Thanks. But I think stickers are going to be the best local promotion. People like stickers because they stick to things. And if they're stuck to things in public view, they become advertising."

"So you hand out stickers. That's not very original."

"I know. I've thought about selling books door-to-door."

"Like punker Jehovah's Witnesses."

"Right, but we wouldn't suck."

"Why do you think people would buy books from you at their doors?"

"Because we can personalize our sales pitches. We can offer different incentives to buy to different customers."

"Like what?"

"With the college students, we'll give them some stickers and vomit beer on their lawns. With the underage punks, we'll offer to purchase alcohol and cigarettes for them. For the middle-aged women, I'll offer to take my clothes off."

"What about people who just aren't interested?"

"We'll carry a tape deck with us and promise not to play a Puff Daddy song if they buy some books."

"And this will work."

"Probably not. But we're gonna run a television commercial in September and October. It starts in a few weeks."

"It's August now? Wasn't it May when we started this?"

"It's a long conversation."

"You just needed a clever way to get past several boring months and explain everything that was happening because you're a mediocre writer and couldn't do it properly."

"Right. I thought we'd established that already. Several times."

"OK, so a television commercial?"

"Yeah, I know it's lame, TV is bullshit, corporate America, all that. But we're trying to sell books to people who don't read. People who don't read watch TV."

"You keep saying *we*, like this is a real company."

"It is a real company."

"Yeah, but who is *we*?"

"Me. I say *we* because it makes the company sound legitimate and makes me feel like less of a wanker."

"So this is your promotion plan."

"Right. I don't think the ad's gonna work."

"That's pretty self-defeating."

"Yeah, I have low self-esteem."

"Why do you think that is?"

"Poor body image. I think I'm weak and unmuscular and generally unattractive to the opposite sex, and that insecurity manifests itself in various unrelated areas of my life."

"That's sad. Maybe you should talk to someone about that."

"Like who."

"I don't know, a therapist or something."

"You are my therapist."

"I'm not even a real person."

"So what. Neither am I."

"Right. So you don't think your promotion is gonna work."

"I'm getting a little worried. I need to pull something out or I'm gonna get fucked."

"It sounds like you're afraid to fail."

"Scared to death. All I've ever done in my life is left things unfinished. I take things to the limit of my natural ability and quit."

"So you're afraid of reaching a point when you don't wanna do this anymore."

"I guess. I think I'm also worried about having to give up because I'm homeless from never recovering any of my expenses."

"And your current lack of success is humiliating."

"Extremely. I get depressed sometimes and think I'll never pull it off. I lose all my motivation and I can't get anything done."

"So what do you do?"

"Order food at drive-throughs and then leave when they ask me to pull up."

"You are an asshole."

"But I'm funny."

"So you finally quit the ambulance job."

"You change subjects a lot."

"I have an agenda."

"It just wasn't what I wanted to be doing anymore. And I think I may have been in it for the wrong reasons. I liked the work itself, but I also liked the respect I got. I liked the way people looked at me in that uniform. To me that's unacceptable. You can't be in it for the glory."

"What's the worst thing you ever saw?"

"A big fat naked lady covered in her own shit."

"That's gross."

"And that was the first call I ever went on."

"Made you question your career choice, didn't it."

"Yeah. There's a lot of shit and nakedness in that business."

"You don't see that part of it on TV."

"No, they just show you the glamorous blood and guts. In the real world, you have to wash the shit and puke off your equipment outside the emergency room."

"Sounds like a wonderful job."

"It is if you love it."

"But you didn't."

"Not like I needed to. The publishing company took priority."

"So you're gonna hand out stickers and clothe the homeless to convince people to read your books to inspire the revolution."

"Right."

"And you're sure you're not talking shit? I don't think you want a revolution. I think you want recognition and fame."

"I don't want fame."

"Yes you do."

"No I don't."

"Do to."

"Do not."

"Do—"

"OK stop."

"Sorry."

"Look, if recognition and fame were really what I wanted, why the fuck would I write books? How many celebrity writers are there?"

"About none."

"Right. I've thought about fame and recognition and all that, but I realized it's not what I actually want. Recognition was just an intermediate step."

"See, now we're getting somewhere. What do you really want?"

"I think you know."

"Why don't you just tell me?"

"It's embarrassing."

"You just wanted it to meet girls."

"Right."

"Isn't that what I've been saying?"

"No, I'm not just trying to meet more girls to fuck."

"You're trying to find The Girl."

"Yeah. I think."

"That makes no sense. You never leave your apartment because you're always working on the revolution, which means you never give yourself the chance meet any girls, the whole reason you're working."

"Yeah, it's fucked."

"You need to be committed."

"But I believe in the revolution. It's not just a ploy to meet girls. But the revolution will not be complete until I'm happy, and I won't be happy without Her."

"So you really do want to change the world."

"Right. I just want to meet girls in the process."

CHAPTER TEN

The school year begins once again, Bodie returns from the summer camp job anonymous drunk girls tell me is cute over the phone at 2:00 A.M., and we're finally graced with new neighbors downstairs. Our new neighbors are girls. Our new neighbors are cute eighteen- and nineteen-year-old girls.

We like our new neighbors.

But because of my embarrassingly deficient social skills, instead of introducing myself and perhaps interacting with these neighbors like a normally functioning member of the human community, I remain grafted to the milk crate under my ass on the balcony, continually rolling and smoking cigarettes as slowly as possible in an effort to be present at any time these neighbors may leave or return to their apartment, allowing them to approach me and relieve me of any social responsibility.

My cleverness eventually pays off when Taylor and Heather decide to have a little too much to drink, and in her exaggeratedly outgoing disposition, Heather runs up the stairs to meet me.

"Hi!" she says.

"Hey," I say, casual and uninterested.

Heather yells over the balcony at Taylor to come meet her new neighbor, and Taylor walks cautiously up the stairs, stopping a safe distance to my side. I guess she doesn't like me.

"So do you miss your old neighbors?" Heather asks me.

I flick my butt over the railing and shake my head. "They were knobs," I tell her, briefly explaining the many ways Bodie and I demonstrated our love for them, including regularly urinating on their cars.

"Wait," Taylor says, moving a little closer. "Are you Greg?"

"Yeah…"

"You're the one Lisa was sleeping with?"

"Yeah…"

"Her ex-boyfriend is a friend of mine," she says. "We went to high school together."

After the girls disappear, I smoke a few more cigarettes and reorganize my priorities. Taylor knows of my past sexual activity and its apparent casual and uncompassionate nature, and this limits the possibility of success in developing the intimate relationship with her I've been imagining. But I'm not going to abandon all efforts at developing a new intimate relationship. She has a roommate.


I'm running out of time. Every day I have one less day. No one understands. What do I have to distinguish myself? I write books. So what. Even half-retarded daytime talk show hosts write books. I own a publishing company. So what. There are already more independent publishers than the market can accommodate and they all sell more books than I do. I'm not a talented writer and I'm not a successful publisher. I'm a mediocre writer who impulsively invested money after a head injury into the most high-risk, non-profitable business imaginable. All that distinguishes me is my age. That's it. Without my age, I have nothing. I can't make myself any younger, so I have to push myself as hard as I can.

"You need to relax," they say.

"I can't," I tell them.

"You're only twenty-one," they say.

"No, I'm *already* twenty-one," I tell them.

I'm losing time. I'm getting older. I'm awake at 3:00 A.M. working because I cannot let myself sleep. I'm unable to sleep because sleep occupies time that must be used to compose and orchestrate the revolution. I'm stronger than exhaustion. I'm unstoppable. I'm working because there's work to be done. I'm working because I'm the one who must inspire the revolution. I'm answering the phone because it's ringing.

□   □   □

Heather and I talk. We sit in the courtyard of the apartment building and she cuts lines from spilled tobacco on the cement while we discuss candidly our respective emotional baggage and the various ways in which it prevents us from developing our relationships to their fullest. She comes upstairs and falls asleep on the couch watching stupid movies, comes and knocks on my door at 3:00 A.M. when she's afraid of being alone downstairs because she knows there's a guy in Chico who likes breaking into young women's homes and beating them to death with blunt carpentry tools and I'm always awake and available at unusual hours to provide her with a temporary sense of security.

Heather is only nineteen but seems to have a relatively clear perception of reality unlike most of her local peers. She's continually shifting with restless energy, always ready with a smile and the trite little twinkle in her eyes, always wondering if I want something to drink, how about something to eat, are you sure, are you really sure, it's no problem, I can get you something. She proves to be a nice distraction from the frequently absent and otherwise non-interactive Taylor.

In response to her recent introduction to the freedoms of independent living, Taylor seems to have simply amplified her high school lifestyle, seldom leaving the constant string of parties to come home. On the rare occasions she decides to drink at the apartment, she's surrounded by a collection of loud-mouthed snowboard-riding late-teenage guys whose teeth are in constant need of knocking out. Despite her seeming ease with social interaction, the farthest Taylor has ventured into my apartment is the end of the couch closest to the door, and she remained there nervously only for the amount of time it took her to convince Heather they needed to leave.

"Taylor's afraid of you," Heather explains when my curiosity finally overpowers my efforts to appear unconcerned. "She thinks you're a drug dealer."

I only weakly attempt to dispel this impression of me. Somewhere in my underdeveloped unconscious mind remains the notion that appearing to be an intimidating drug dealer is somehow irresistible to women.

I also still believe women will be impressed by my ostensible business accomplishments, so I ask Heather to model some Grundle Ink apparel for the website and have her sign a contract because contracts are very official and impressive to women. As compensation, I provide Heather with copies of all my books, which further impress her and stimulate her sexual attraction to me.

"I can't believe I'm actually reading," she tells me through her cigarette smoke. "I never read. Those books are addictive."

The openness of my books inspires Heather to share the most personal details of her life with me, and eventually our intimate conversations of past relationships and emotional trauma progress naturally to discussions concerning the redefining of our own relationship in a more emotionally and physically affectionate manner, presumably including sexual intercourse. But Heather arrests the progression before any significant steps are taken.

"I freak out when I get too close to guys now," she tells me. "I just don't think I can get involved in a relationship."

Fortunately, Heather's avoidance of intimacy with me coincides with Taylor's return to the apartment building. Taylor has apparently tired of the high school lifestyle and has abruptly distanced herself from the scene. Her rapid change inspires my curiosity again, and the focus of my occasional neighborly visits shifts quickly from Heather to her.

Taylor finally realizes that even if I happen to sell drugs [apparently the girls confirmed this theory with the presence of the credit card terminal in my kitchen, believing I somehow conducted my drug transactions with credit cards], I don't present an immediate threat to her personal safety.

"You wanna come with me to get decorations for Heather's birthday?" Taylor asks me late one night.

"Sure," I tell her, taking advantage of the opportunity to prove to her my general harmlessness and desirability.

We wander around the empty aisles of Wal-Mart for far longer than necessary while Taylor struggles indecisively with birthday decoration plans. Taylor has a youthful quality about her that until now has never really appealed to me. She shakes her fist at Bodie when he's obnoxious, manages to make the phrase, "Fucking shit, dude," undeniably cute, and spends a somehow amusingly excessive amount of time playing solitaire on my laptop while watching MTV. Finally we return home with some balloons and paper streamers to surprise Heather when she wakes up in the morning.

"I want one of your books," Taylor tells me, taping a piece of crepe paper to the wall.

"OK."

Her fear continues to fade as we spend more time together and my staggering writing talent and brilliance stirs her undeniable attraction to me. Soon I'm routinely on her couch with her head in my lap, running my fingers through her hair, pretending not to be violently disgusted by movies like *Notting Hill* and *Bridget Jones's Diary*. But it begins to seem Taylor doesn't find me as irresistible as she should.

"I'm just nervous," she explains the day after I kiss her goodnight for the first time. "I wanna take things slowly."

"I don't know what we're waiting for," I tell her in one of our many late-night discussions on the balcony couch, "but I'll wait."

□   □   □

I sit on the pleather couch on the balcony and light my cigarette. I'm smoking because Taylor doesn't like me smoking and this is my mature adult response to our current situation.

"Look," I told her when she came home from work earlier, "whatever we started, it's over. I'm wasting my time with this."

"Why do you think you're wasting your time?" she asked me.

"Because you're not interested. I don't wanna extend myself to someone who doesn't want me to."

Taylor gazed up at me with tearing eyes. "You're not wasting your time," she said, telling me everything she's told me before. "Let's just let things happen."

But things don't just happen. People make them happen. And if she wanted something to happen, it would be happening. All she wants is a lap dog. I've seen it before and I don't need it again. They're like junkies without junk. Always needing, always starving, always searching. They'll steal from you, they'll tear you apart, they'll do whatever it takes to get what they need. And they'll never stop smiling. They'll show you exactly what you need to see. Just enough to trust them so they can break in and rape you. But they don't take by force. They make you want. They make you need like they need. But what you need is something they'll never give you.

They'll tie you up and leave you hanging so they can pull you back in when you try to run. No matter what you tell yourself, their words mean more. You give them everything you have for nothing more than a glimpse, a brush of their hair against your skin, a blink of their beautiful eyes. You let them walk on you to keep their feet from the dirt. Nothing is too much and nothing is ever enough. One day you wake up and they're gone with everything. All they've left behind are dirty needles and a smiling memory you can't hate.

So I'm smoking. I'm chain-smoking non-filtered Lucky Strikes while I roll more cigarettes to further emphasize my dissatisfaction because I know if I smoke enough cigarettes Taylor will finally understand my pain and frustration and fall in love with me.

I tap the ash from my cigarette and look at the balcony railing where I first kissed stripper Lacy. Driving home past her apartment today, one of the less-developed parts of my brain directed me to drop in on her and explore the possibility of casual sex to both distract me from my frustration with Taylor and somehow inspire within her enough jealousy to motivate a change of heart. Fortunately, after a few minutes of reminiscent conversation with Lacy, I realized my mistake and quickly fled the scene with my pants still on.

Heather brought up her ex-boyfriend while we were enjoying a cigarette together earlier today, and ignoring my recent lessons with Lacy, I decided that by relating to her with a similar discourse on my ex-girlfriend, I could increase the possibility of the intimate relationship we've previously failed to develop, which now interests me not only because of the standard benefits of intimate relationships with attractive women, but also because it's another opportunity to achieve retribution for Taylor's emotional abuse.

"I saw my ex-girlfriend today," I told her.

"Where?"

"Her apartment."

"Did you sleep with her?" Heather asked me eagerly.

"No."

"Are you going to?"

"Hell no."

I flick my butt over the railing and put another cigarette in my mouth. Taylor is downstairs with Heather and Bodie watching TV and being incredibly beautiful because she is incredibly beautiful and I assume this does not change while she watches TV. But I don't want to see any of them right now.

I grab my keys and drive to the post office to get the mail. I don't get very much mail in the box even though Grundle Ink Publications is a completely legitimate and very real publishing company that publishes books that will eventually inspire the revolution. Tonight I get bills and another office supply catalog I didn't request, but I flip through it anyway, because unfortunately the revolution does require office supplies.

I sit in the parking lot and think. I don't want to go home. I don't want to see Taylor. I know how incapable I am of resisting her charm and maintaining my decision to break free from her. It's past midnight and I have nowhere to go. So I drive.

Turning up the stereo, I drive down the Esplanade until it merges with the highway and make a reckless U-turn. I turn the stereo up louder and drive through downtown to a liquor store on Twentieth Street—one of the liquor stores from which Bodie and I tried to steal a newspaper dispenser because he insisted we needed a table for the end of the couch to replace the cardboard box I felt was adequate and a newspaper stand seemed like the perfect solution at 3:00 in the morning, but after a couple hours of searching we realized all the good dispensers were chained to things that didn't move, so we just gave up and went to Denny's, where we sat at the bar and Bodie asked me to hit him and I refused because I don't consider hitting people to be appropriate restaurant behavior, but he continued asking me, then antagonizing me, so I backfisted him across the forehead, which made a surprisingly loud noise that drew the attention and subsequent wrath of the gacked-out waitress who had earlier told us to behave ourselves when I started throwing sugar packets at Bodie as he walked outside to have a cigarette—and grab a few newspapers.

Driving down Twentieth Street, I stop in an empty parking lot to read my newspapers by streetlight. And then it hits me. My stunning genius. I didn't even know I was doing this, but I am. Heather knows I saw Lacy today. Heather will tell Bodie. Bodie knows Lacy has been my fallback girl in the past.

They don't know where I am right now.

They'll both assume I'm having sex with Lacy.

And Taylor will find out.

And when Taylor finds out, she'll be upset, she'll hate me, and she'll no longer give me the opportunity to slip back into her abusive little game.

I check the clock and calculate the approximate amount of time necessary for a casual sexual encounter with no unnecessary emotion to determine the earliest time I should come home to ensure the credibility of my untold story. Going back to my newspapers, I wait patiently, reveling in my own genius, and at the same time thinking about what a worthless piece of shit a certain newsprint magazine is.

I should start a magazine just to criticize this one. But a magazine dedicated to the ridicule of another magazine is nearly as lame as the magazine deserving of this ridicule, and so this would not be an acceptable cause in which to invest my resources, which are in fact limited and not regularly replenished by selling drugs and stripping. I must create a publication to represent in a more easily accessible and consumable form the revolution I'm currently inspiring with my publishing company that doesn't sell any books. Contemporary American youths have been led astray by pop-culture consumer media and are intimidated by books. They seem heavy and cumbersome and are generally associated with learning and school and other unappealing things, while magazines are light and easy to digest, fun to flip through in no particular order, easily distributed: unassuming yet powerful.

But a magazine would require a large number of contributors willing and capable of consistently producing sufficient content with no financial compensation, because the revolution must remain genuine and unadulterated, uncorrupted by money and its inherent impurities, and because I don't want to pay anyone with money I'm not making from a free publication that will have an absolute bare minimum of advertising.

This is the next step toward the revolution.

But right now I need to go home and see what Taylor does.

I drive casually, wary of arriving too early and decreasing the chance of Taylor believing I have in fact been engaged in meaningless sexual intercourse with my stripper ex-girlfriend. Pulling into the parking lot and driving over all the broken glass, I see Taylor and Bodie and Heather outside in the courtyard with some of our other neighbors. This is perfect. They'll all see me returning home and an in-depth discussion concerning my whereabouts and my motives for being in said whereabouts will ensue— the only logical conclusions being Lacy's place and casual sex.

I slip out of my car with the same unlit cigarette still dangling from my lips and adjust my hat—the hat I never wore while I worked for the ambulance company that provided me with it but am now able to wear because I've grown out my Marine haircut and let my sideburns—the only facial hair I can actually grow—grow all the way down to my jaw, and for some reason this prevents the hat from appearing too large for my head and making me look like a twelve-year-old.

Taylor watches me. I watch her back.

"Where were you?" Bodie asks me.

I head up the stairs and shrug. "I don't know."

I sit down at my desk and get back to work on the revolution while they sit down there and talk about me and my sexual indiscretions. I feel someone walking upstairs [the entire building shakes when anyone walks on the stairs or along the balcony because this entire block of Chico is a sprawling failure of engineering, appearing as a large blank region on PG&E's service maps and therefore leaving us without electricity days longer than the surrounding city following a power outage] and Bodie steps in.

"Where were you?" he asks me again.

I shrug.

"Did you go see Lacy?"

I shrug again.

"You did, you were with Lacy!" he laughs. "You were fucking Lacy, weren't you!"

I just keep shrugging. I'm not lying to him. I'm just not telling him the truth.

Bodie shakes his head at me in disappointment. He's not extraordinarily fond of Lacy. "Dude..."

"What?"

"I can't believe you fucked Lacy again."

Bodie leaves and I lean back in my chair to wait. The building shakes again and Taylor appears in the doorway.

"Where were you?" she asks, walking back into the kitchen.

"I don't remember."

Taylor glares at me and shakes her head. "You're horrible."

□　□　□

I am horrible. I know it. I'm horrible and stupid and bad and deserve to develop some kind of obscure disorder that requires expensive medication and painful treatment. And Taylor is beautiful and sweet and wonderful—except when she yells and hits and throws things at me, which is all of course in good fun because yelling and hitting and throwing things can be good fun in the proper context—and I should have never made her believe I slept with Lacy.

I'm horrible and a horrible person smokes non-filtered cigarettes alone on a black pleather couch given to him by his roommate's ex-girlfriend and thinks endlessly about the sweet and beautiful girl living below him who should have never been tricked into believing the source of affection upstairs directed his affection to anyone but her.

I smoke my cigarettes and watch the sun fall over the apartment buildings on Second Ave and think about Taylor, about how it feels to hold her in my lap and smell her hair, about the feeling of her full lips against mine, about her glowing smile and the sound of her laughter, about how it feels when she wraps her arms around my back and pulls me closer, her cheek pressed to my chest. But I have to forget about her. I have to light another cigarette and forget all of it.

The building shakes and Taylor appears on the stairs. She approaches cautiously and sits next to me on the couch as I blow my smoke to the side.

"Hi," she says quietly.

"Hi."

We sit in silence while I smoke the cigarette down to my fingers and flick the butt into the parking lot.

"What's wrong?" Taylor asks me.

I shrug.

"Why don't you talk to me anymore?"

"I don't know."

Taylor is quiet. I glance at her and light another cigarette, spinning the lighter slowly on my leg.

"I don't understand how you can lose interest in me so quick," she says finally.

"I didn't."

"What do you mean?"

"I didn't lose interest in you," I explain. "I stopped letting myself be interested because it was a waste of time."

"It wasn't a waste of time at all," she says softly.

I look at her clear blue eyes glowing in the dim light. She's beautiful. "It wasn't a waste of time," she tells me again.

And we talk. We talk for a long time. We talk about her, we talk about me, we talk about us, and I believe her this time, and I don't smoke any more cigarettes because I'm not as horrible as I used to be. Taylor leans over and wraps her arms around my waist, burying her head in my chest. I run my fingers through her hair and kiss the top of her head and hold her, and slowly all the horribleness in me fades away.

□　　□　　□

They tell me they're interested in what I'm doing. They tell me how meaningful and powerful my writing is, how beautifully tragic and uniquely universal my feelings and experiences are, how much they can relate to me. They tell me how much respect they have for me and how much they admire what I'm doing, how important it is for people like me to stand up and steal a piece of the media and allow stifled voices to speak.

If they're so interested, why can't I sell any books?

They won't give me any money, but they want jobs. I get an email from a girl with a graphic design degree wanting to know if we have any need for a graphic artist or photographer. I call and explain that I'm the graphic artist even though my graphic art skill, like my writing talent, is limited and mostly faked and utilized only because of financial limitation, and that if I did find something for her to do, she wouldn't be compensated with anything beyond a little potential exposure, that exposure being only slightly greater than the potential for it considering I can't sell any books. She still wants to do it.

We meet a few days later. Kendra is dressed in all black, with knee-high socks and large leather footwear, stylish black-framed glasses, and an adequate supply of silver jewelry.

She is my soldier.

She will fight for the revolution.

I tell her to be careful not to sit on the broken part of the couch and Bodie and I proceed to ask her questions to determine her suitability for this prestigious position while we review work from her portfolio. I'm impressed. I've never seen a portfolio before, but hers seems impressive.

Satisfied with her qualifications, and comfortable with her attitude and willingness to put up with Bodie and me, I tell her about the magazine and how thoroughly imperative it is to the survival of local youth culture. She likes the idea and says she'd be willing to do the layouts. While we discuss various details, Summer shows up and apologizes for interrupting our official business meeting because she knows this is a real and official company.

The business phone rings and Bodie answers it in his official business manner. It's the freight company. K's book *Gone* will be arriving at our warehouse and we must receive the shipment because our warehouse is actually a rented storage unit with no full-time shipment-receiving staff.

Kendra accompanies us to the warehouse so she may see and understand the operation and its purity, its lack of ostentation and excess. I, the owner of the company, the tormented genius behind the revolution, am not unwilling to unload heavy cartons of books from the back of a large truck and carry them to a waiting skid in our warehouse.

I am a soldier like her.

We will fight together.

We recognize the truck driver and he recognizes us. We are not easily forgotten. Like the last time he delivered to us, I tear open a carton and give him the first book because the revolution will include unshaven day-haulers in flannel shirts.

"Yeah," he says, "I read that other book you gave me." Then he says something else I don't really understand—what I think is a compliment—to the effect that it wasn't your typical read.

"That's what we want," I tell him, hoping what he said was in fact a compliment and not a derogatory remark about my hair.

Today is Bodie's twenty-third birthday, and we're treating him accordingly. After I make him carry heavy things in the heat for me, Summer and I proceed to make fun of him. For Summer and me, making fun of Bodie is a team effort. We find our creativity and originality are magnified intensely when in each other's company.

For some unknown reason, Bodie and I have developed a pattern in our insults of each other and find the other's non-existent homosexual behavior to be a primary source of material. Like this:

"My calculator isn't working."

"Is it because you're gay?"

Or this:

"Dude, I'm starving."

"Yeah, you really work up an appetite having sex with boys."

Or this one when we come home:

"Hey look, you're still gay."

Or Bodie's favorite song—

"Ho-mo sapien, ho-ho-mo sapien..."

—accompanied by a dance involving an abundance of presumably homosexual hip thrusts.

We don't have a problem with homosexuality, its practice, or its practitioners. We just think calling each other gay is funny because we're stupid and we think stupid things are funny.

"I've got a gnarly headache."

"Maybe you shouldn't eat so much dick."

But today is Bodie's birthday and I must adjust my approach to reflect this.

"Dude, I'm so fucking tired," he says from the back seat.

"Happy birthday, maybe you should quit taking it in the ass."

Summer and I continue to make fun of him all the way back to the apartment, leading each comment with a *Happy birthday* because it's his birthday and we love him. We love all our little revolutionaries.

Even if they take it in the ass.

It comes in through the Grundle Ink newsletter subscription email thing, that thing people fill out on our website to receive the monthly newsletter I send out to inform everyone of the company's lack of developments. It's an incoherent rap about people in Chico being capable of reading between the lines, something about Jello Biafra and wanting to educate television zombies. Finally he gets around to the pitch: he wants to write for Grundle Ink.

His phrasing indicates he doesn't quite grasp the nature of Grundle Ink Publications, but I can't deny the revolution a potential soldier, so I call him anyway and tell him to meet me in front of a downtown bar to avoid disclosing the location of my residence to a guy who seems a little unstable and could conceivably believe murdering the owner of a local publishing company is an appropriate way of expressing his political views.

I smoke a cigarette and wait in front of the bar. A mildly punk guy with a skateboard walks slowly around the corner.

"Greg?"

"Yeah."

He doesn't have a book manuscript. But I like what he's saying, so I tell him about the magazine and my new soldier, Kendra. We discuss the content of the magazine and I explain it will contain whatever we want it to contain, that there will be no rules, no restrictions aside from my own discretion. We talk about distribution, advertising—or the lack thereof considering we'll be saying things with which most advertisers won't want to be associated—and the need for a large number of dedicated contributors willing to work for free.

I crush my last cigarette under my boot and shake his hand.

"This is gonna happen," he says. "We're gonna pull it off."

And I start to believe him. This is going to happen.

□    □    □

It's raining when I wake up. It's been raining all night. I crack the blinds and look down into the parking lot at the rain falling from the early morning sky and pounding violently against the dark grey pavement.

I'm going to go trail running.

I dress quickly. I don't know what the fuck I'm doing. I don't think I've run in five years. I don't mean I haven't run a long distance in five years, I mean I haven't even moved my legs at a frequency high enough to produce anything more than a walking stride in five years. I don't even know if I'm still physically capable of running.

But fuck it.

Bodie wakes up with the noise and wanders out of his room. I'm rummaging through what we refer to lovingly as the guest bathroom—the half bath we've transformed into a storage closet with a toilet no longer accessible for its intended use—trying to find the running shoes I own even though I don't run but purchased a few years ago knowing I would someday wake up six hours earlier than usual and decide to go trail running in the rain simply because the idea spontaneously materialized in my head and I'm not intelligent enough to listen to reason.

"What the fuck're you doing?" Bodie asks, staring at me incredulously. "Why're you awake?"

I find my shoes and stumble out of the bathroom.

"You're going running?"

"Yeah."

"What the fuck!" Bodie grabs his hair and staggers around the hallway in confused disbelief. I do not get up early and I do not run. "What the fuck is going on? My whole universe is crumbling!"

I laugh and tie my shoes.

"I don't— What— Early— Running—"

I leave Bodie freaking out in the hallway and drive to upper Bidwell Park—where there are no other vehicles because apparently no one else in the entire city is stupid enough to go running in the freezing rain—and park in front of the locked gate.

After walking down the dirt road for a few minutes, I slowly begin running. The impact of my feet against the dirt shakes unnaturally through my skeleton. I don't think it hurt like this the last time I ran. I feel my ankles collapsing under my weight, the bones in my knees slamming through the thinning cartilage. I should not run.

But I run anyway.

I run and the rain soaks through my shirt and paints it tightly to my chest. The rain streaks down my face and the mud splatters onto my legs and the dirty water sprays from under my pounding feet.

I run and I think of the manuscript that was sent to me by an eighteen-year-old girl in West Virginia. I remember the words, the staggering honesty and beautiful brutality, the way her mind fumbled through ideas and created stunning images with nothing but the trash tumbling down an empty street in the breeze. Hers will be the first real book I publish and she will be the answer to my promotional discomfort. She will be my soldier, my revolutionary.

I run and my body aches and my muscles burn and my face freezes in the rain and I think of the editor of a local entertainment magazine telling me she wanted an interview immediately and never contacting me again after I dropped off the books she requested, about hearing a few weeks later that the *Unforgotten* cover and a short write-up calling me a Chico twenty-something had appeared in the same magazine, how I drove to that liquor store and found the magazine and the cover of my book right there on the page, that fucking cover, that picture I didn't even mean to take, lying on an empty sidewalk at sunset, that book I wrote in the silent hours when the rest of the world slept and dreamed and held each other, that book I hated but couldn't stop writing, that book I used to tell my story, to tell their stories, to tell our story, because the stories are all the same, they're all the same endless story. The revolution is pulsing impatiently below the sidewalks, beating with the rhythm of our footsteps, waiting. It was always inside me, waiting to break out, burning and trembling and scraping inside me, yelling and screaming and tearing, telling me the truth I was afraid to hear. All the nights I crawled, all the empty nights I spilled my blood onto these endless pages, all the lonely, freezing nights I waited for something, waited for everything, waited for anything, all the nights I waited for you. You're all I've ever waited for. I do this all for you. I burn away the darkness alone and pull the sun back into the sky trying to find you. Nothing else means anything to me anymore. It's all words lost in the static, stepped over and forgotten, pushed aside for the next mouthful, the next wasted breath. It's all distractions and mistakes and uneven footsteps in the dark—

And when the sun is gone again with another day, fallen and lost behind the broken buildings on Second Ave, she climbs into bed with me and I pull her against my chest, her long hair spilling over her shoulders, cascading over the pillow, soft against my face. I breathe and smell her hair, taste the hot skin on her neck, slide my hand over her hip and across her smooth stomach, and she smiles in the dark and takes my hand, pulling my arm around her chest and holding my hand against her heart, and I feel it beating, I feel her heart beating in her chest, I feel my heart beating in my chest, and the warmth of her body swells around me and seeps into me and I close my eyes and fade away, fade away into this, this feeling, this endlessly ephemeral moment, and I know this is what I've been waiting for, what I've always needed, I know this is the emptiness I've spent all these nights trying to fill, and all I want is to stay here forever, to never leave her because I never want her to leave me, and I'm afraid of the sun ever rising again because I know she'll be gone and I'll be alone again with you—

And you want a resolution, some stupid fucking conclusion to something that's never ended, a tidy little exit to let you put this down and walk away and move on to the next bleeding string of whatever the fuck this is, except I don't have one, and I don't want to give you one, and I think you understand if you've come this far, and if you don't, it doesn't matter anyway because you never did before and I haven't lost a goddamned thing, and there's so much more I need to tell you, but the words will never be my own, never in the way I need them to be, because it's all been said and it's all been heard and I'm not even me anymore because me was never anything more than you and you were always everything, everywhere, stumbling through my head and making so much goddamned noise and keeping me awake at night, listening, trying so hard to hear myself over you because I didn't know there was nothing to hear, and what the fuck do you want from me, because I'll give it to you, I'll give you everything, because I finally understand— I finally fucking understand.

Made in the USA
Las Vegas, NV
28 December 2021